PENGUIN CLASSICS

THE WONDERFUL ADVENTURE
OF NILS HOLGERSSON

SELMA LAGERLÖF (1858–1940) was born and raised on a farm
in the Swedish province of Värmland. She was a teacher in a girls'
secondary school for ten years, one of a handful of professions
open to women at that time. In 1895, financial support from the
royal family and the Swedish Academy encouraged her to abandon teaching altogether and write full-time. She published sixteen
novels and seven volumes of short stories, including *The Saga of
Gösta Berling* (1891), *Lord Arne's Silver* (1903), *The Phantom
Carriage* (1921) and the memoir *Diary of Selma Ottilia Lovisa
Lagerlöf* (1932). In 1909 she became the first woman to win the
Nobel Prize, 'in appreciation of the lofty idealism, vivid imagination and spiritual perception that characterize her writings'. A
feminist and a beacon for the suffragette movement in Sweden,
Lagerlöf managed to buy back her family farm, Marbåcka, which
had been sold at auction in 1885, and, from 1910 onwards, she
was in charge of running the estate while also continuing to write.

Her best-known work, *The Wonderful Adventure of Nils
Holgersson* (1907), is a beloved children's book in Scandinavia and
has been translated into nearly fifty languages. Lagerlöf was first
commissioned to write it as a geography textbook for Swedish
schools, but she struggled with a more traditional structure until
she came up with the idea of creating a little boy who flies around
the country on the back of a gander. Throughout the book, she
drew on centuries of folklore and legends from the different Swedish provinces. Lagerlöf's work has been highly influential and she
has been praised by writers such as Kenzaburo Oe, Marguerite
Yourcenar and Gary Shteyngart.

SELMA LAGERLÖF

The Wonderful Adventure
of Nils Holgersson

Translated from the Swedish by
PAUL NORLÉN

Illustrations by
BERTIL LYBECK

PENGUIN BOOKS

PENGUIN CLASSICS

UK | USA | Canada | Ireland | Australia
India | New Zealand | South Africa

Penguin Books is part of the Penguin Random House group of companies
whose addresses can be found at global.penguinrandomhouse.com.

First published in Swedish as *Nils Holgerssons underbara resa genom Sverige* (1906–7)
This translation first published in Penguin Classics 2016
This edition published in Penguin Classics 2017
006

Translation copyright © Paul Norlén, 2016
All rights reserved

Cover design and illustration: Coralie Bickford-Smith

Set in 10.25/12.25 pt Adobe Sabon
Typeset by Jouve (UK), Milton Keynes
Printed and bound in Great Britain by Clays Ltd, Elcograf S.p.A.

ISBN: 978–0–241–20609–6

Contents

ONE
The Boy

The Gnome

There once was a boy. He was about fourteen years old, tall and lanky and flaxen-haired. He wasn't good for much; most of all he liked sleeping and eating, and after that he liked stirring up mischief.

Now it was a Sunday morning and the boy's parents were getting ready to go to church. The boy himself was sitting in shirtsleeves on the edge of the table, thinking how lucky it was that both Father and Mother were leaving, so that he would be left to himself for a couple of hours. 'Now I can take Father's shotgun down and shoot it without having to ask anyone's permission,' he said to himself.

But it was almost as if his father must have guessed the boy's thoughts, because just as he stood on the threshold ready to go, he stopped and turned towards him. 'Because you don't want to go to church with Mother and me,' he said, 'I think that you can at least read the sermon at home. Will you promise to do that?'

'Yes,' said the boy. 'I suppose I can do that.' And to himself he said, of course, that he wouldn't read any more than he felt like.

The boy thought that he had never seen his mother so nimble. In a flash she was over by the wall shelf, took down Luther's book of sermons and set it on the table over by the window, open to the sermon for the day. She also opened the book of Bible readings and set it next to the collection of sermons. Finally she dragged the big armchair up to the table, the one that was bought at auction at the parsonage in Vemmenhög the year before, and which otherwise no one but Father got to sit in.

The boy thought that Mother was going to far too much trouble with this preparation, because he did not intend to read more than a page or two. But now for the second time it was as if Father could see right through him. He went up to the boy and said in a stern voice, 'Remember to read properly! Because when we come back I'm going to question you on every page, and if you've skipped anything, you'll suffer for it.'

'The sermon is fourteen and a half pages long,' Mother said, as if to top it off. 'You'll have to start reading right away if you're going to get through it.'

With that they finally left, and when the boy stood in the door and watched them, he thought that he had been caught in a trap. 'Now they're probably congratulating themselves for having been so clever that I'm stuck with that sermon the whole time they're gone,' he thought.

But Father and Mother were certainly not congratulating themselves about anything; in fact, they were rather distressed. They were poor farm folk and their place was not much bigger than a garden patch. When they first moved there it could not feed more than one pig and a couple of hens, but they were unusually industrious and capable people and now they had both cows and geese. Things had gone quite well for them and they could have walked content and happy to church that lovely morning if they did not have their son to think about. Father complained that he was sluggish and lazy: he did not want to learn anything in school and he was so useless that you could barely get him to tend geese. And Mother did not deny that this was true, but she was most distressed that he was wild and mean, cruel to animals and unkind to people. 'May God break his malice and give him a different disposition,' Mother said. 'Otherwise he will be a misfortune both for himself and for us.'

The boy stood a long time and wondered whether or not he should read the sermon. But then he told himself that this time it was best to be obedient. He sat down in the parsonage armchair and started to read. But when he had been rattling off words half out loud for a while, it was as if that mumbling was making him drowsy and he noticed that he was nodding off.

Outside it was the most beautiful spring day. It was only the twentieth of March, but the boy lived in Västra Vemmenhög parish far down in south Skåne, and there spring was already well under way. It was not green yet, but it was fresh and budding. There was water in all the ditches and at their edges the coltsfoot was in bloom. All the scrubby brush growing on the stone wall had become brown and shiny. The beech forest far away seemed to swell and become denser with every moment. The sky was high and clear blue. The cottage door was ajar, so that the warbling of the larks was heard in the room. The hens and geese were in the yard, and sometimes the cows, who felt the spring air all the way into the stall, started mooing.

The boy read and nodded and struggled against sleep. 'No, I don't want to fall asleep,' he thought. 'Because then it will take me all morning to get through this.'

But no matter what, he fell asleep.

He did not know if he had slept a little or a long time, but he woke up when he heard a soft noise behind him.

On the windowsill itself right in front of the boy was a little mirror, and in it almost the whole room was visible. Just as the boy now raised his head, he happened to look in the mirror, and then he saw that the lid to his mother's chest had been opened.

It happened that his mother owned a big, heavy oak chest with iron fittings, which no one but her was allowed to open. There, Mother stored everything that she had inherited from her mother and about which she took particular care. There were a couple of old-time, farm-wife outfits of red cloth with short waist and pleated skirt and pearl-studded bib. There were starched, white, head-kerchiefs and heavy silver buckles and chains. People didn't want to wear such things nowadays, and many times Mother had thought about getting rid of the old objects, but then she didn't have the heart to do it.

Now the boy saw in the mirror quite clearly that the lid to the chest stood open. He could not understand how this had come about, because Mother had closed the chest before she left. Mother never would have left the chest open when he was home alone.

He suddenly felt scared. He was afraid that a thief had sneaked into the cottage. He did not dare move, but instead sat still and stared into the mirror.

While he sat like that, waiting for the thief to show himself, he started wondering what the black shadow was that fell across the edge of the chest. He looked and looked and did not want to believe his eyes. But what was there, which to start with was shadowy, became clearer and clearer, and soon he noticed that it was something real. It was none other than a gnome sitting astride the edge of the chest.

The boy had certainly heard of gnomes, but he had never imagined that they could be so small. The one sitting on the edge of the chest was no more than a hand's breadth tall. He had an old, wrinkled, beardless face and was dressed in black gabardine, knee breeches and a broad-brimmed, black hat. He was very dapper and fine with white lace around his neck and wrists, buckles on his shoes and garters tied in bows. He had taken an embroidered cap out of the chest and sat and looked at the old-fashioned work with such solemnity that he did not notice that the boy had wakened.

The boy was very surprised to see the gnome, but on the other hand he was not particularly afraid. It was impossible to be afraid of someone who was so little. And because the gnome sat there so preoccupied that he neither saw nor heard, the boy thought it would be funny to play a trick on him: knock him down into the chest and close the lid on him or something along those lines.

But the boy was still not so brave that he dared to touch the gnome with his hands, but instead he looked around the cottage for something he could nudge him with. He let his gaze wander from the sofa bed to the drop-leaf table and from the drop-leaf table to the stove. He looked at the saucepans and the coffeepot, which were on a shelf alongside the stove, at the water bucket by the door and at ladles and knives and forks and saucers and plates, which were visible through the half-open cupboard door. He looked up at Father's shotgun, which was hanging on the wall beside the portrait of the Danish royal family, and at the geraniums and fuchsias blooming in the window. Last of all his eyes fell on an old butterfly net that was hanging on the windowsill.

As soon as he caught sight of the butterfly net he grabbed it and ran up and swung it along the edge of the chest. And he surprised himself at the kind of luck he had. He was not quite sure how he had done it, but he had truly caught the gnome. The poor thing was at the bottom of the long net with his head downwards and could not get out.

At first the boy had no idea what he should do with his catch. He was just careful to swing the net back and forth, so that the gnome would not have a chance to climb up.

The gnome started talking and pleaded fervently to be released. He had done them good for many years, he said, and deserved better treatment. If the boy released him now, he would give him an old *speciedaler*, a silver spoon and a gold coin that was as big as the case on his father's silver watch.

The boy did not think this was much to offer, but since he had got the gnome in his power, he had started to be afraid of him. He realized that he was mixed up in something that was alien and awful and did not belong to his world, and he was simply happy to get rid of the nuisance.

For that reason he went along with the bargain and held the net still, so that the gnome could crawl out. But when the gnome was almost out of the net, the boy began to think that he should have demanded great wealth and every possible good thing. At least he should have made it a condition that the gnome would conjure the sermon into his head. 'I was so stupid to set him free!' he thought and started shaking the net, so that the gnome would fall down again.

But just as the boy did this, he got such a dreadful box on the ears that he thought his head would break into pieces. He fell first against one wall, then against the other, until finally he sank down on the floor and remained lying there, unconscious.

When he woke up again he was alone in the cottage. He did not see a trace of the gnome. The lid of the chest was closed and the butterfly net was hanging in its usual place by the window. If he had not felt how his right cheek was burning after the slap, he would have been tempted to believe that the whole thing had been a dream. 'In any event Father and Mother will probably say that it wasn't anything,' he thought. 'They probably won't make any allowance in the sermon on account of the gnome. I'd better sit down to read again.'

But now when he went towards the table, he noticed something peculiar. It could not be the case that the cottage had expanded. But why did he have to take so many more steps than he usually did to reach the table? And what had happened to the chair? It did not appear to be larger now than just before, but he had to first climb up on the crossbars between the chair legs and then clamber up to reach the seat. And it was the same way with the table. He could not see over the tabletop without getting up on the armrest.

'What in the world is this?' said the boy. 'I think the gnome has ruined the armchair and the table and the whole cottage.'

The collection of sermons was on the table, and apparently it was the same, but there must have been something crazy about it too, because he could not read a word without actually standing in the book itself.

He read a couple of lines, but then happened to look up. His gaze fell on the mirror and then he shouted right out loud, 'Look, there's another one!'

Because in the mirror he clearly saw a tiny, tiny imp, who was dressed in a knitted cap and leather breeches.

'He's dressed just like me!' the boy said, slapping his hands together in astonishment. But then he saw that the imp in the mirror did the same.

Then he started to pull on his hair and pinch himself on the arms and turn around, and instantaneously the one in the mirror imitated it.

The boy ran around the mirror a couple of times to see whether there was some little fellow hidden behind it. But he found no one there, and then he started to shiver with terror. For now he understood that the gnome had enchanted him, and that the imp, whose image he saw in the mirror, was himself.

The Wild Geese

The boy simply could not believe that he had been transformed into a gnome. 'It's probably just a dream and my imagination,' he thought. 'If I wait a few moments, I'm sure I'll be human again.'

He placed himself in front of the mirror and closed his eyes. He did not open them for several minutes, and then he expected that it would have passed. But it had not; he was still just as little. Otherwise he was just the way he had been before. The white flaxen hair and the freckles across his nose and the patches on his leather breeches and the darn on his sock, everything was the same, with the exception that it had been reduced in size.

No, it was no use to stand quietly and wait, he realized that. He would have to try something else. And the wisest thing he could do, he thought, was to search for the gnome and be reconciled with him.

He jumped down on the floor and started searching. He looked behind chairs and cupboards and under the sofa bed and in the baking oven. He even crawled down into a couple of rat holes, but he was unable to find the gnome.

While he was searching, he wept and pleaded and promised everything imaginable. Never again would he break his word to anyone, never again would he be mean, never again would he fall asleep over the sermon. If he only got to be human again, then there would be such a decent and nice and obedient boy of him. But no matter what he promised, it did not help in the least.

Suddenly he remembered that he had heard Mother say that the little people used to live in the cow stall, and he decided to go there at once and see if he could find the gnome. It was fortunate that the cottage door was ajar, because he would not have been able to reach the lock and open it, but now he got out with no difficulty.

When he came out on the landing, he looked around for his wooden shoes, because inside the cottage of course he had been in his stocking feet. He wondered how he would manage with the big, clumsy wooden shoes, but just then he saw a pair of small shoes on the threshold. When he noticed that the gnome had been so considerate that he had also transformed the wooden shoes, he became even more anxious. It seemed as if the idea was that this affliction would last a long time.

On the old oak board in front of the door, a grey sparrow was hopping. As soon as he caught sight of the boy he called, 'Tweet-tweet! Tweet-tweet! Look at Nils the goose-boy! Look at Thumbkin! Look at Nils Holgersson Thumbkin!'

At once the geese and hens all turned their gazes towards the boy, and there was a dreadful cackling. 'Cock-a-doodle-do!' the rooster crowed. 'It serves him right! Cock-a-doodle-do! He tugged on my comb!'

'Cluck, cluck, cluck! It serves him right!' called the hens, and they went on like that endlessly. The geese gathered in a tight cluster, stuck their heads together and asked, 'Who could have done that? Who could have done that?'

But the most remarkable thing about this was that the boy understood what they said. He was so surprised that he remained standing quietly on the step and listened. 'It must be because I've been turned into a gnome,' he said. 'That's probably why I understand birdsong.'

He thought it was insufferable that the hens would not stop saying that it served him right. He threw a rock at them and called, 'Be quiet, you rabble!'

But he hadn't thought that he was no longer anything the hens needed to be afraid of. The whole crowd of hens rushed towards him, gathered around him and shrieked, 'Cluck, cluck, cluck! It serves you right! Cluck, cluck, cluck! It serves you right!'

The boy tried to get away from them, but the hens ran after him and shrieked so that he was about to lose his hearing. He probably never would have escaped them if the cottage cat had not come along. As soon as the hens saw the cat, they fell silent and pretended not to think about anything other than scratching in the dirt for worms.

The boy ran up to the cat at once. 'Dear Pussy-cat,' he said, 'you know all the corners and crannies here on the farm, right? Please tell me where I can find the gnome.'

The cat did not answer at once. He sat down, set his tail neatly in a ring in front of his legs and stared at the boy. This was a big, black cat with a white patch on his chest. His fur was smooth and glistened in the sunshine. His claws were drawn in, and his eyes were an even grey with only a small, narrow slit in the middle. The cat looked very good-natured.

'Of course I know where the gnome lives,' he said in a silken voice. 'But that's not to say I want to tell you about it.'

'Dear Pussy-cat, you have to help me,' said the boy. 'Don't you see that he has enchanted me?'

The cat opened his eyes a little, so that the green malice started to shine forth. He purred and hummed with contentment, before he answered. 'Shall I perhaps help you, because you pulled my tail so often?' he said at last.

Then the boy became angry and completely forgot how little and powerless he now was. 'I can still pull your tail again, I can!' he said, running towards the cat.

The next moment the cat was so transformed that the boy could hardly believe it was the same animal. Every hair on his body stood on end. His back had arched, his legs were extended, his claws scraped the ground, his tail had become short and thick, his ears were pulled back, his mouth spat, his eyes stood wide open and shone with red fire.

The boy did not want to let himself be scared by a cat, but instead took a step forward. But then the cat made a leap, coming down right on the boy, knocked him over and placed himself over him with his front paws on his chest and his jaws open above his throat.

The boy felt how the claws pierced through his vest and shirt into his skin, and how the sharp canine teeth tickled his throat. He screamed for help for all he was worth.

But no one came and he thought, of course, that his last hour had arrived. Then he felt the cat draw in his claws and let go of his throat.

'There now,' he said, 'that's enough for now. I'll let you get away this time for the sake of my mistress. I only wanted you to know which of us has the power.'

With that the cat went his way and looked just as sleek and pious as shortly before, when he came in. The boy was so ashamed that he did not say a word, but instead only hurried to the cow stall to search for the gnome.

There were no more than three cows. But when the boy came in, there was such a mooing and a racket that you might well believe there were at least thirty.

'Moo, moo, moo!' May-Rose bellowed. 'It's good that there is justice in this world!'

'Moo, moo, moo!' all three chimed in. He could not hear what they said, they were bellowing so much at the same time.

The boy wanted to ask about the gnome, but he could not make himself heard, because the cows were in full uproar. They behaved the way they always did when he let a strange dog into their stall. They kicked with their hind legs, shook their neck chains, turned their heads out and took aim with their horns.

'Just you come here,' said May-Rose, 'then I'll give you a kick that you won't forget for a long time!'

'Come here,' said Sweet-Lily, 'then you'll get to dance on my horns!'

'Come here, then you'll get to feel how it tasted when you

threw the wooden shoes at me, like you did last summer!' Star
bellowed.

'Come here, then you'll get paid back for the wasp that you
let into my ear!' Sweet-Lily roared.

May-Rose was the oldest and wisest of them, and she was
the maddest of all. 'Come here,' she said, 'so that I can pay you
back for all the times you've pulled the milking stool out from
under your mother, and for all the obstacles you've set for her
when she's come carrying the milk pails, and for all the tears
she has stood here and shed over you!'

The boy wanted to tell them that he regretted having been
mean to them, and that he would never be anything other than
nice if they only told him where the gnome was. But the cows
were not listening. They were making so much noise that he
was afraid one of them would manage to tear herself loose,
and he thought it was best to slip away out of the cow stall.

When he came out again, he was completely dispirited. He
could understand that no one on the farm wanted to help him
find the gnome. And it would probably be of little avail if he
were to find him.

He crept up on the broad stone wall that went around the
croft and was overgrown with thorns and blackberry branches.
There he sat down to think about what would happen if he did
not become human again. When Father and Mother came
home now from church, they would wonder. Yes, they would
wonder all across the country, and people would come from
parishes all around, from Östra Vemmenhög and from Torp
and from Skurup, from all of Vemmenhög County they would
come to look at him. And perhaps Father and Mother would
take him along and display him at the market in Kivik.

Now, that was terrible to think about. He wanted most of
all that no human being would ever see him again.

It was awful how unhappy he was. No one in the whole
world was as unhappy as him. He was no longer human, but a
monster.

Little by little he started to understand what it meant to no
longer be human. He was separated from everything now: he
could not play with other boys, he could not take over the croft

from his parents, and he absolutely could not get any girl to marry him.

He sat and looked at his home. It was a small, whitewashed, half-timbered house and stood as if pressed down in the ground under the high, steep straw roof. The outbuildings were small too, and the patches of arable land were so narrow that a horse could barely turn around on them. But as small and poor as the place was, it was now much too good for him. He could not demand better lodging than a hole under the stable floor.

The weather was marvellous. There was rippling and budding and chirping all around him. But he felt so sad. He would never again be happy about anything.

He had never seen the sky so blue as today. And the migratory birds were arriving. They came from abroad and had travelled over the Baltic, steering right towards Smygehuk, and now they were on their way north. There were certainly many different types, but he did not recognize any but the wild geese, who came flying in two long rows that met at an angle.

Several flocks of wild geese had already gone past. They flew high up, but he still heard how they shrieked, 'Now it's off to the mountains! Now it's off to the mountains!'

When the wild geese saw the domestic geese on the farm-yard, they lowered themselves towards the ground and called, 'Come with! Come with! Now it's off to the mountains!'

The domestic geese could not keep from stretching their heads up and listening. But they answered quite reasonably, 'We have it good, as we have it! We have it good, as we have it!'

It was, as mentioned, an incredibly lovely day with air that must have been a true joy to fly in, so fresh and so light. And with every new flock of wild geese that flew past, the domestic geese became all the more restless. A couple of times they flapped their wings, as if they had a desire to follow along. But then an old goose mother always said, 'Don't be crazy now! They get both hungry and cold!'

There was a young gander, whom the call of the wild geese had given a real itch to travel. 'If one more flock comes, then I'm going with them,' he said.

Then came a new flock, shrieking like the others. Then the young gander answered, 'Wait! Wait! I'm coming!'

He spread his wings and raised himself in the air, but he was so unaccustomed to flying that he fell down to the ground again.

The wild geese must have heard his call anyway. They turned around and flew slowly back to see if he was going with them.

'Wait! Wait!' he called and made a new attempt.

The boy heard all this from where he was on the stone wall. 'It would be a great loss,' he thought, 'if the big gander were to go away. It would be a sorrow for Father and Mother, if he were gone when they come home from church.'

When he thought about this, he again completely forgot that he was little and powerless. He took a leap right down in the goose flock and threw his arms around the neck of the gander. 'Don't even think about flying away!' he shouted.

But just at that moment the gander had figured out what he had to do in order to raise himself from the ground. He could not stop to shake off the boy, but instead he had to follow along up into the air.

They were off towards the heights so quickly that the boy was dizzy. Before he could think that he ought to let go of the gander's neck, he was so high up that he would have been killed if he had fallen to the ground.

The only thing he could do to make it somewhat better was to try to get up on the gander's back. And he wriggled his way there too, although not without great effort. And it was no easy matter either to keep himself on the smooth back between the two swinging wings. He had to grip deeply into feathers and down with both hands so as not to fall to the ground.

The Chequered Piece of Cloth

The boy was so dizzy that for a long time he did not know how to react. The air whistled and hissed against him, the wings waved, and there was roaring in the feathers like a big storm.

Thirteen geese were flying around him. All of them flapped and cackled. His eyes could not focus, and there was whistling in his ears. He did not know if they were flying high or low, or where they were headed.

Finally he came to his senses enough to realize that he ought to find out where the geese were taking him. But this was not easy, because he did not know how he would get the courage to look down. He was quite certain he would get vertigo if he tried.

The wild geese were not travelling particularly high, because their new travelling companion could not breathe in the very thinnest air. For his sake they also flew a little slower than usual.

At last the boy forced himself to cast a glance towards the ground. Then he thought that below him a large cloth was spread out that was divided into an unbelievable number of small and large squares.

'Where in the world have I come to now?' he asked.

He saw nothing but square upon square. Some were tilted and some oblong, but everywhere there were corners and straight edges. Nothing was round and nothing was crooked.

'What kind of big, chequered piece of cloth is it that I'm looking down on?' the boy said to himself without waiting for anyone to answer.

But the wild geese who were flying around him called out at once, 'Fields and meadows! Fields and meadows!'

Then he understood that the big, chequered piece of cloth was the flat ground of Skåne over which he was travelling. And he started to comprehend why it looked so multi-coloured and square. The clear green squares he recognized first: those were the rye fields, which had been sown last autumn and stayed green under the snow. The yellow-grey squares were stubble fields where grain had grown last summer, the brownish ones were old clover pastures, and the black ones were empty grazing land or ploughed-up fallow fields. The squares that were brown with yellow edges were surely beech forests, for in those the big trees that grow in the middle of the forest stand bare in the winter, but the small beeches that grow at the edge of the forest retain their dry, yellowed leaves until spring. There were also dark squares with grey in the middle: these were the large, enclosed farms with the blackened straw roofs and stone-paved courtyards. And then there were squares that were green in the middle and encircled with brown: these were the gardens where the lawns had already started to turn green, although the bushes and trees that stood around them were still in bare, brown bark.

The boy could not keep from laughing when he saw how square everything was.

But when the wild geese heard him laughing, they called as if in rebuke, 'Fruitful and good land! Fruitful and good land!'

The boy had already become serious. 'How can you laugh, when you've been subjected to the most terrible thing that can happen to a person?' he thought.

He kept serious awhile, but soon he had to laugh again.

Because he had got used to the ride and the speed, so that he could think about something other than keeping himself on the gander's back, he started to notice how full the air was of flocks of birds that were flying north. And there was hollering and shouting from flock to flock. 'I see you've come over today!' some shrieked.

'Yes, so we have,' answered the geese. 'How do you think it's going with spring?'

'Not a leaf on the trees and cold water in the lakes,' came the reply.

When the geese flew ahead over a place where there were domestic poultry outside, they called, 'What's the farm called? What's the farm called?' Then the rooster stuck his head up and answered, 'The farm is called Lillgärde this year like last year, this year like last year!'

Most of the cottages were probably named after their owners, as is usually the case in Skåne, but instead of answering that this was Per Matsson's or Ola Bosson's, the roosters thought up names that they thought were suitable. Those who lived on poor crofts and smallholdings called, 'This farm is called Grainless!' And those who belonged to the very poorest shrieked, 'This farm's called Chew-a-little, Chew-a-little, Chew-a-little!'

The big, prosperous farms got fancy names from the roosters, such as Happy Acres, Egg Hill and Coinville.

But the roosters at the estates were too conceited to think of anything humorous. One of them crowed and called loudly, as if he wanted to be heard all the way up to the sun. 'This is Dybeck's estate! This year like last year! This year like last year!'

And a little farther away was one that called, 'This is Svaneholm! The whole world must know that!'

The boy noticed that the geese did not fly straight ahead. They drifted here and there over all of the southern plain, as if they were happy to be in Skåne again and wanted to visit every farm.

They came to a place where there were some large, massive buildings with tall chimneys and around these a number of smaller buildings. 'This is Jordberga sugar mill!' the roosters called. 'This is Jordberga sugar mill!'

The boy was startled, sitting there on the goose's back. He ought to have recognized that place. It was not far from his home, and he'd had a job here last year as a goose-tender. But it was probably the case that nothing was really the same when you saw it from above like that.

And think! And think! Åsa the Goose-girl and Little Mats, who were his friends last year! The boy would really like to have known if they were still here. What would they say if they thought that he was flying around high over their heads?

Then Jordberga was out of sight and they travelled away over Svedala and Skaber Lake and back over Börringe Priory and Häckeberga. The boy got to see more of Skåne in that one day than he had seen during all the years he had lived.

When the wild geese encountered domestic geese, they had the most fun. Then they flew up very slowly and called down, 'Now it's off to the mountains! Are you coming with? Are you coming with?'

But the domestic geese answered, 'It's still winter in the land. You're out too early. Go back! Go back!'

The wild geese came lower so that they could be heard better, and called, 'Come along, we'll teach you how to fly and swim!'

Then the domestic geese got annoyed and did not respond with a single cackle.

But the wild geese came down even lower so that they almost grazed the ground, and then they raised themselves, lightning quick, as if they had been terribly frightened. 'Oy, oy, oy!' they called. 'Those weren't geese! They were just sheep! They were just sheep!'

The ones on the ground were furious and shrieked, 'May you be shot, as many as you are, as many as you are!'

When the boy heard all this joking, he laughed. Then he remembered what a bad situation he was in, and then he cried. But in a little while he was laughing again.

Never before had he travelled around at such good speed, and he had always liked riding fast and wild. And, of course, he had never thought it could feel as fresh as it did up in the air, and that such a good smell of topsoil and resin rose from the earth. Nor had he thought what it might be like to travel so high above the ground. But it was like flying away from worries and sorrows and annoyances of every imaginable kind.

TWO

Akka from Kebnekaise

EVENING

The big tame gander, who had followed them up in the air, felt very proud about roaming back and forth over Söderslätt in the company of the wild geese and making fun of the domestic fowl. But no matter how happy he was, he could not help starting to get tired towards afternoon. He tried taking deeper breaths and flapping his wings faster, but no matter what he did, he was still several goose-lengths behind the others.

When the wild geese who were flying at the back saw that the domestic bird could not keep up, they started calling to the goose at the tip of the angle who led the parade: 'Akka from Kebnekaise! Akka from Kebnekaise!'

'What do you want from me?' the lead goose asked.

'The white one's behind! The white one's behind!'

'Tell him it's easier to fly fast than slow!' the lead goose called and kept on flapping like before.

The gander tried to follow the advice and pick up speed, but in doing so he became so exhausted that he sank all the way down towards the pruned willow trees that lined the fields and meadows.

'Akka, Akka, Akka from Kebnekaise!' called the ones who were flying at the back and saw what a hard time he was having.

'What do you want now?' the lead goose asked, sounding dreadfully cross.

'The white one is falling to the ground! The white one is falling to the ground.'

'Tell him it's easier to fly high than low!' the lead goose called. And she did not slow down in the slightest, but instead kept on flapping like before.

The gander tried to follow this advice too, but when he wanted to rise, he was so out of breath that his chest was about to burst.

'Akka, Akka!' the ones who were flying at the back called then.

'Can't you let me fly in peace?' the lead goose asked, sounding even more impatient than before.

'The white one is about to crash! The white one is about to crash!'

'Tell him that anyone who isn't able to keep up with the flock can turn around and go home!' the lead goose called. And it did not occur to her to reduce speed, but instead she kept on flapping like before.

'I see, so that's how it is,' the gander thought. He immediately understood that the wild geese never intended to take him with them up to Lapland. They had only lured him away from home in jest.

He felt really annoyed that his strength would fail him now, so that he would not be able to show those tramps that a domestic goose was also good for something. And the most annoying thing of all was that he had encountered Akka from Kebnekaise. For domestic goose that he was, he had heard about a lead goose whose name was Akka and who was more than a hundred years old. She had such great prestige that the best wild geese to be found would join up with her. But no one had such contempt for domestic geese as Akka and her flock, and he would have liked to show them that he was their equal.

He flew slowly after the others, while he debated with himself whether he should turn around or continue. Then suddenly that imp he was carrying on his back said, 'Dear Martin Gander, you do understand that it's impossible for you, who have never flown before, to go with the wild geese all the way up to Lapland. Shouldn't you turn around and go home before you destroy yourself?'

But the farmer's boy was the worst thing the gander knew, and no sooner did he realize that the poor thing believed he couldn't make the journey than he decided to hold out. 'If you say one more word about it, I'll throw you down into the first marl-pit we go over,' he said and at the same time got such energy from his aggravation that he started flying almost as well as any of the others.

He probably couldn't have continued that way for long, but it wasn't necessary either, because now the sun was setting quickly and just at sunset the geese set off straight downwards. And before the boy and the gander knew what was happening, they were standing on the shore of a lake called Vombsjön.

'I guess the idea here is that we should stay overnight,' the boy thought, jumping down from the gander's back.

He was standing on a narrow, sandy beach and before him was a rather large lake. It was horrid to look at, because it was almost completely covered by a crust of ice, which was blackened and uneven and full of cracks and holes, the way spring ice usually is. But the ice probably did not have much time left. It was already landless and had a broad belt of black, shiny water around it. Yet it was still there, spreading cold and the ghastliness of winter across the area.

On the other side of the lake there seemed to be open, light countryside, but where the geese had landed was a large plantation of pine. And it looked as if the pine forest had the power to bind winter to it. Everywhere else the ground was bare, but under the scrubby branches there was snow that had thawed and frozen, thawed and frozen, so that it was as hard as ice.

The boy thought he had come to a land of wilderness and

winter, and he felt so anxious that he wanted to scream out loud.

He was hungry. He hadn't eaten anything all day. But where would he get food? Nothing edible grows on the ground or on trees in the month of March.

Yes, where would he get food, and who would give him shelter, and who would make his bed, and who would warm him by their fire, and who would protect him from the wild animals?

For now the sun was gone, and now the cold came from the lake, and darkness sank down from the sky, and terror crept up in the tracks of twilight, and in the forest there started to be creaking and rustling.

Now there was no more good cheer, as the boy had felt while he was up in the air, and in his anxiety he looked around for his travel companions. He had no one else to turn to.

Then he could see that the gander was faring even worse than he was. He was still lying in the same place where he had landed and it looked as if he were about to die. His neck lay slack along the ground, his eyes were closed and his breathing came as only a faint hissing.

'Dear Martin Gander!' the boy said. 'Try to get a sip of water! It's not two steps to the lake.'

But the gander did not move at all.

The boy no doubt would have been harsh to all animals before, and to the gander too, but now he thought the gander was the only support he had, and he became dreadfully afraid of losing him. He started shoving and pushing him at once to get him down to the water. The gander was big and heavy, so it was a hard task for the boy, but at last he succeeded.

The gander came down into the lake head first. For a moment he lay quietly in the mud, but soon he stuck up his beak, shook the water out of his eyes and snorted. Then he swam proudly among the reeds and bulrushes.

The wild geese were in the lake before him. They had not looked around for the gander or the goose rider, but instead rushed down into the water at once. They had bathed and cleaned themselves, and now they were slurping up half-rotten pondweed and buckbean.

The white gander had the good fortune to catch sight of a small perch. He seized it quickly, swam up to the shore with it and set it in front of the boy. 'Here you go, as thanks for helping me down into the water,' he said.

It was the first time all day that the boy had heard a friendly word. He was so happy that he wanted to throw his arms around the gander's neck, but he could not bring himself to do it. And he was happy about the gift too. At first he thought it would probably be impossible to eat raw fish, but he wanted to try anyway.

He felt for whether he had brought the sheath knife with him, and, as it was, it was still hanging behind him on the trouser button, although it was so reduced in size it was no longer than a matchstick. Well, it would do in any event to scale and clean the fish, and it did not take long before the perch was eaten.

When the boy was full, he felt ashamed that he could eat something raw. 'It seems like I'm not human any more, but a gnome,' he thought.

The whole time that the boy was eating, the gander stood silently beside him, but when he had swallowed the last bite, he said in a low voice, 'It seems we've fallen into the hands of a stuck-up crew of geese who despise all domestic fowl.'

'Yes, I've noticed that,' said the boy.

'It would be very honourable for me if I could go with them all the way up to Lapland and show them that a domestic goose is good for something too.'

'Yes,' said the boy and smiled a little, because he did not believe the gander could pull this off, but he did not want to contradict him.

'But I don't think I can manage alone on such a trip,' the gander said. 'Instead I want to ask if you would come along and help me.'

The boy of course had not thought of anything other than turning around for home as soon as possible, and he was so surprised that he didn't know how to answer. 'I thought we were enemies, you and me,' he said. But the gander seemed to have forgotten this completely. He only remembered that just now the boy had saved his life.

'I suppose I should go home to Father and Mother,' said the boy.

'Yes, I'll probably bring you back to them towards autumn,' said the gander. 'I won't leave you until I can set you down on the threshold at home.'

The boy thought that it might be a good thing not to show himself to his parents for a while yet. He was not disinclined to the proposal, and he was about to say that he would go along with it when they heard a loud booming behind them. It was the wild geese who had come up out of the lake, all at once, and stood shaking off the water. Afterwards they arranged themselves in a long row with the lead goose in front and came up to them.

When the white gander now observed the wild geese, he did not feel at ease. He had expected that they would be more like domestic geese and that he would feel more kinship with them. They were much smaller than him and none of them was white, instead they were all grey with a brown moire pattern. And he was almost afraid of their eyes. They were yellow and shone as if there were a fire burning behind them. The gander had always been taught that it was most appropriate to walk slowly and waddle, but they did not walk, instead they almost ran. However, he became most anxious when he looked at their feet. They were big with worn, tattered soles. It was noticeable that the wild geese never questioned what they stepped on. They made no detours. They were very neat and well-cleaned otherwise, but on their feet you saw that they were poor, wilderness folk.

The gander did not have time to more than whisper to the boy, 'Now answer quickly for yourself, but don't say who you are!' before they were there.

When the wild geese had stopped in front of them, they curtsied with their necks many times, and the gander did too, even more times than them. As soon as they were done greeting, the lead goose said, 'Now we'd like to hear what sort of thing you are.'

'There's not much to say about me,' said the gander. 'I was born in Skanör last spring. Last autumn I was sold to Holger Nilsson in Västra Vemmenhög and I've been there ever since.'

'You don't seem to have any family to pride yourself on,' said the lead goose. 'So what is it that makes you so bold that you want to be mixed up with wild geese?'

'That could be because I want to show you wild geese that we domestic geese are also good for something,' said the gander.

'Yes, it would be good if you could show us that,' said the lead goose. 'We've already seen how knowledgeable you are about flying, but perhaps you're more skilled in other sports. It may be that you are strong in distance swimming.'

'No, I can't pride myself on that,' said the gander. He seemed to notice that the lead goose had already decided to send him home, and he did not care how he answered. 'I've never swum farther than straight across a marl-pit,' he continued.

'Then I expect you're a champion at running,' said the goose.

'I've never seen a domestic goose run and I've never done so either,' said the gander, making the matter worse.

The big white bird was now certain that the lead goose would say that in no way could she take him with them. He was very surprised when she said, 'You answer questions bravely, and anyone who has courage can be a good travel companion, even if he is unskilled to start with. What do you say about staying with us a couple of days, until we see what you are good for?'

'I'm very satisfied with that,' said the gander, completely happy.

Then the lead goose pointed with her beak and said, 'But who is it you have with you? I've never seen anyone like him before.'

'That's my friend,' said the gander. 'He's been a goose-herder all his life. I'm sure it will be useful to have him along on the journey.'

'Yes, that may be good for a domestic goose,' the wild one answered. 'What do you call him?'

'He has several names,' the gander said hesitantly, thinking on his feet, because he did not want to give away that the boy had a human name. 'Yes, his name is Thumbkin,' he said at last.

'Is he a gnome?' asked the lead goose.

'At what time do you wild geese usually settle down to sleep?' the gander said quickly, trying to avoid answering the last question. 'My eyes close on their own at this time of day.'

It was easy to see that the goose who was speaking with the gander was very old. All of her plumage was ice-grey with no dark streaks. Her head was larger, her legs were rougher and her feet more worn than anyone else's. Her feathers were stiff, her shoulders bony and her throat was thin. All this was the work of age. It was only her eyes that time had not got the better of. They shone more clearly, as if younger than any of the others.

She now turned very arrogantly towards the gander. 'You should know, gander, that I am Akka from Kebnekaise, and that the goose who flies closest to me on the right is Yksi from Vassijaure, and the one to the left is Kaksi from Nuolja! You should also know that the second goose to the right is Kolme from Sarjektjåkko, and that the second goose to the left is Neljä from Svappavaara, and that behind them fly Viisi from Oviksfjällen and Kuusi from Sjangeli! And know that these, like the six goslings who fly last, three to the right and three to the left, are all high-mountain geese of the best family! You should not take us for tramps, who strike up company with just anyone, and you should not think that we let anyone share our sleeping place who does not know what family he is from.'

When Akka, the lead goose, spoke in this way, the boy quickly stepped forwards. It distressed him that the gander, who answered so quickly for himself, gave such evasive answers where he was concerned. 'I don't want to keep who I am a secret,' he said. 'My name is Nils Holgersson and I'm the son of a farmer, and until this day I have been a human, but this morning—'

The boy got no farther. As soon as he said that he was a human, the lead goose recoiled three steps backwards and the others even more. And they all extended their necks and hissed angrily at him.

'I suspected as much, ever since I first saw you here on the shore,' said Akka. 'And now you must be off at once. We tolerate no humans among us.'

'It can't be possible,' the gander intervened, 'that you wild geese can be afraid of someone so little. Tomorrow he will probably head for home, but you must let him stay here with us overnight. None of us can be responsible for letting such a poor little thing manage on his own with weasels and foxes at night.'

The wild goose now came closer, but it showed clearly that she had a hard time controlling her fear. 'I was taught to be afraid of everything to do with humans, be they big or small,' she said. 'But if you, gander, will be responsible that he doesn't do us any harm, then he can stay with us tonight. But I don't believe our sleeping arrangements will please either you or him, because we intend to settle down to sleep on the landless ice out here.'

She probably thought that the gander would be doubtful when he heard this. But he did not let anything bother him. 'You are wise who understands to choose such a safe place to sleep,' he said.

'But you are responsible for him taking off tomorrow to his own home.'

'Then I too will have to leave you,' the gander said. 'I've promised not to abandon him.'

'You are free to fly wherever you want,' the lead goose said.

With that she raised her wings and flew out over the ice, and one after another of the wild geese followed her.

The boy was distressed that his Lapland journey was not going to happen, and he was also afraid of the cold night quarters. 'It's getting worse and worse, gander,' he said. 'First of all we're going to freeze to death out on the ice.'

But the gander was in good spirits. 'There's no danger,' he said. 'I'll only ask you to quickly gather together as much chaff and grass as you can carry.'

When the boy had his arms full of dry grass, the gander took hold of his neckband, lifted him and flew out on to the ice, where the wild geese were already sleeping with their beaks under their wings.

'Spread the grass out on the ice now, so that I have something to stand on and don't get frozen stuck! If you help me, then I'll help you!' said the gander.

The boy did that, and when he was done the gander grasped him again by the neckband and stuck him in under his wing. 'There, I think you'll be nice and warm,' he said, pressing with his wing.

The boy was so embedded in down that he could not answer, but lying there was warm and cosy and he was tired, and he fell asleep within a moment.

NIGHT

The truth is that ice is always faithless and nothing to rely on. In the middle of the night the landless crust of ice moved on Vombsjön, so that in one place it happened to bump up against the shore. It so happened the Smirre Fox, who at that time was living on the east side of the lake on the park-like grounds of Övedskloster, noticed this place when he was out on his nocturnal hunt. Smirre had already seen the wild geese that evening, but he had not dared hope to be able to get at any of them. Now he made his way out on to the ice.

When Smirre was very close to the wild geese, he happened to slip, so that his claws scraped against the ice. The geese awoke and flapped their wings to throw themselves up into the air. But Smirre was too quick for them. He lunged forwards, as if he had been thrown, seized a goose by the wing-bone and rushed back again towards land.

But this night the wild geese were not alone out on the ice; instead they had a human among them, little as he was. The boy woke up when the gander spread his wings. He had fallen down on the ice and remained sitting, half-asleep. He had not understood any of the commotion until he saw a little, short-legged dog running away across the ice with a goose in its mouth.

The boy hurried after at once to take the goose from that dog. He probably heard the gander calling after him, 'Watch out, Thumbkin! Watch out!' But the boy thought that he didn't need to be afraid of such a little dog, and stormed off.

The wild goose that Smirre Fox dragged with him heard the clatter when the boy's wooden shoes struck against the ice and she could hardly believe her ears. 'Does that little fellow intend to take me from the fox?' she wondered. As miserable a state as she was in, she started cackling merrily deep down in her throat, almost as if she were laughing.

'The first thing that will happen to him is that he will fall down into a crack in the ice,' she thought.

But as dark as the night was, the boy saw all the cracks and holes in the ice clearly, and took bold leaps across them. That was because he now had the good night vision of the gnomes and could see in the dark. He saw both lake and shore equally clearly, as if it had been daylight.

Smirre Fox left the ice where it bumped against land, and just as he was working his way up the slope of the shore, the boy called to him, 'Put down the goose, you scoundrel!' Smirre did not know who was calling, and did not take time to turn around, but instead just picked up speed.

The fox now made his way into a forest of large, magnificent beech trees, and the boy followed without a thought that he might be in any danger. On the other hand, he was thinking the whole time about how scornfully he had been received by the wild geese the night before, and he really wanted to show them that a human is still a bit superior to everything else in creation.

He called again and again to that dog to get him to set down his prey. 'What kind of dog are you, not to be ashamed of stealing a whole goose?' he said. 'Put her down at once, otherwise you'll see what a beating you get! Set her down, otherwise I'll tell the farmer how you behave!'

When Smirre Fox noticed that he had been taken for a dog afraid of a beating, he found this so comical that he was about to drop the goose. Smirre was a master thief, who was not content simply to hunt rats and voles in the fields, but also ventured up to farms to steal hens and geese. He knew that he was feared across the whole region. He had not heard anything so crazy since he was a little cub.

But the boy ran so fast that he thought the thick beeches were gliding backwards past him and he caught up with Smirre. Finally he was so close to him that he got hold of his tail. 'Now I'm taking the goose from you anyway!' he called and held on as best he could. But he did not have strength enough to stop Smirre. The fox pulled him along, so that the dry beech leaves whirled around him.

But now Smirre seemed to have realized how harmless his pursuer was. He stopped, set the goose down on the ground and placed his front feet on her so that she could not fly away. He was just about to bite off her throat, but prior to this he could not refrain from teasing the imp a little. 'Hurry off and complain to the farmer, because now I'm killing the goose!' he said.

If anyone was surprised when he saw what a sharp nose and heard what a hoarse and angry voice the dog that he had pursued had, it was probably the boy. But he was also so angry that the fox was making fun of him that he did not think about being afraid. He grasped the tail more firmly, braced himself against a beech root, and just as the fox held his jaws over the goose's throat, he tugged for all he was worth. Smirre was so surprised that he let himself be pulled backwards a couple of steps, and the wild goose was free. She flapped heavily upwards. One of her wings was injured, so she could barely use it, and added to that she could not see a thing in the dark forest, but instead was as helpless as if she were blind. For that reason she could not help the boy in any way, so instead she escaped through a gap in the forest canopy and flew down to the lake again.

But Smirre threw himself towards the boy. 'If I don't get one, then I'll just have the other,' he said, and in his voice you could hear how wicked he was. 'No, you shouldn't think that you will,' the boy said, quite exhilarated because he had rescued the goose. He was still holding firmly on to the fox tail and turned with it over to the other side, when the fox tried to capture him.

It became a dance in the forest that made the beech leaves whirl. Smirre twirled around and around, but his tail twirled too, and the boy held on firmly to it, so that the fox could not seize him.

The boy was so cheerful after this success, that to start with he just laughed and made fun of the fox, but Smirre was persistent, as old hunters often are, and the boy started to fear that he would be captured at last.

Then he caught sight of a small young beech, which had shot up in height as slender as a stick to soon reach the free air above the canopy, which the old beeches formed over it. He suddenly let go of the fox's tail and climbed up the beech. Smirre Fox was so eager that he continued to dance around after his tail a long time. 'Don't bother to dance any more!' said the boy.

But Smirre could not put up with the disgrace of not getting the better of such a little imp, and he lay down at the foot of the tree to wait him out.

The boy was not in a good way where he sat, riding on a weak branch. The young beech did not yet reach up to the high canopy. He could not get over to another tree, and he did not dare climb down to the ground.

He was so cold that he was about to get numb and let go of the branch, and he was terribly sleepy, but he did not dare fall asleep, fearing he would fall down.

It was unbelievable how ghastly it was sitting like that at night out in the forest. He had never known before what night really meant. It was as if the whole world had been petrified and would never come back to life again.

Then it started to get light and the boy was happy because everything became like itself again, although the cold felt even sharper than before during the night.

When the sun finally came up, it was not yellow but red. The boy thought it looked angry and he wondered what it was angry about. Perhaps it was because the night had made it so cold and gloomy on the Earth, while the sun had been away.

The sunbeams shot ahead in big bundles to see what the night had done, and it was evident how all things blushed, as if they had a bad conscience. The clouds in the sky, the silky-smooth beech trunks, the small, intertwined branches of the forest ceiling, the frost that covered the beech leaves on the ground, all flared up and turned red.

But more and more bundles of rays shot through space, and soon all the awfulness of the night had been driven away. The petrifaction was gone, and then a remarkable number of living things emerged. The black woodpecker with the red neck started hammering with its beak against a tree trunk. The squirrel scampered out of its nest with a nut, sat on a branch and started shelling it. The starling came flying with a bundle of roots, and the chaffinch sang in the treetops.

Then the boy understood that the sun had said to all these small things, 'Wake up now and come out of your nests! Now I'm here. Now you don't need to be afraid of anything.'

From the lake the call of the wild geese was heard as they prepared themselves for flight. Immediately after that all fourteen geese came flying over the forest. The boy tried to call to them, but they were flying so high up that his voice could not reach them. They probably thought that the fox had eaten him up long ago. They did not even bother to search for him.

The boy was on the verge of tears from anxiety, but the sun was now standing golden yellow and happy in the sky, filling the whole world with courage. 'It's not worth it, Nils Holgersson, for you to be anxious or worried about anything, as long as I'm around,' said the sun.

Goose Games

MONDAY, 21 MARCH

Everything remained unchanged in the forest for about as long as a goose needs to have her breakfast, but just as early morning was turning to forenoon, a solitary wild goose came flying under the dense forest canopy. She made her way hesitantly forwards between trunks and branches, flying very slowly. As soon as Smirre Fox saw her, he left his place under the young beech and sneaked towards her. The wild goose did not avoid the fox, but instead flew rather close to him. Smirre made a high leap after her, but missed and the goose continued down towards the lake.

It didn't take long before another wild goose came flying. She took the same route as the first and flew even lower and more slowly. She too went close by Smirre Fox and he made such a high leap after her that his ears grazed her feet, but she avoided him, unscathed, and continued as silent as a shadow on her way towards the lake.

A short time passed and again a wild goose came. She flew even lower and more slowly, seeming to have even more difficulty making her way between the beech trunks. Smirre made a tremendous leap and he was only a hair's-breadth away from catching her, but this goose too escaped.

Right after she disappeared came a fourth wild goose. Although she flew so slowly and poorly that Smirre believed he could catch her without any great difficulty, he was now afraid of failing and intended to let her fly past unmolested. But she took the same route as the others and just as she was right over Smirre, she sank so low that he was enticed into jumping after her. He reached so high that he touched her with his paw, but she quickly threw herself to the side and saved her life.

Before Smirre had stopped panting, three geese in a row were seen. They flew ahead in the same way as the others and Smirre made high leaps after them all, but he did not succeed in catching any of them.

Then came five geese, but these flew better than the previous ones, and although they also seemed to want to coax Smirre to jump, he resisted the temptation.

A really long time later came a solitary goose. It was the thirteenth. This one was so old that she was completely grey and did not have a dark streak on her body. She did not seem to really be able to use one wing and flew pitifully poorly and crooked, so that she was almost touching the ground. Smirre not only made a great leap after her, instead he pursued her, running and jumping all the way down to the lake, but he did not get any reward for his efforts this time either.

When the fourteenth one came, it looked very beautiful, because it was white, and glistened like a clearing in the dark forest as it waved its white wings. When Smirre saw it, he summoned all his strength and jumped halfway to the canopy, but the white goose went past completely unscathed, just like the others.

Now it was quiet for a while under the beeches. It appeared as if the entire flock of wild geese had gone past.

Suddenly Smirre remembered his captive and raised his eyes towards the young beech. As expected, the imp was gone.

But Smirre did not have much time to think about him, because now the first goose came back from the lake and flew slowly like before under the canopy. Despite all his bad luck Smirre was happy that she came back, and he rushed after her with a high jump. But he was in too much of a hurry and did not give himself time to calculate the leap, but instead ended up on one side of her.

After this goose came yet another and a third, a fourth, a fifth, until the cycle was ended with the old ice-grey and the large white one. They all flew slowly and low. Just as they hovered over Smirre Fox, they came down, as if they were inviting him to capture them. And Smirre pursued them and made jumps that were six feet high or more, but he was not able to catch a single one of them.

It was the most awful day that Smirre Fox had ever known. The wild geese flew ceaselessly over his head, coming and going, coming and going. Big, magnificent geese, fattened up on German fields and moors, hovered the whole day long through the forest so close to him that many times he touched them, and he could not quiet his hunger with a single one.

Winter was still barely over and Smirre remembered days and nights when he had to wander around unoccupied without any quarry to hunt, when the migratory birds were gone, when the rats hid under the frozen ground and the hens were enclosed. But hunger had not been as hard to endure all winter as the miscalculation of this day.

Smirre was not a young fox. Many a time he had had the dogs after him and heard bullets whistling around his ears. He had lain hidden deep in his lair, while the dachshunds crawled into the passageways and were close to finding him. But all the anxiety that Smirre had experienced during that stressful hunt was nothing compared to what he felt every time he failed to catch one of the wild geese.

In the morning, when the game began, Smirre Fox had been so fine-looking that the geese were amazed when they saw him. Smirre loved splendour, and his coat was shining red, his chest was white, his nose black and his tail as bushy as a plume. But when evening came that day, Smirre's coat was tangled, he was bathed in sweat, his eyes had no lustre, his tongue was hanging far out from his panting jaws, and foam was flowing from his mouth.

In the afternoon Smirre was so tired that he was getting dizzy. He saw nothing but flying geese before his eyes. He took leaps towards patches of sun that he saw on the ground, and towards a poor tortoiseshell butterfly that had come out of its cocoon too soon.

The wild geese were still tirelessly flying and flying. They continued to torment Smirre the whole day. It did not move them to sympathy that Smirre was worn out, worked up, crazy. They kept on implacably, although they understood that he hardly saw them, that he was making leaps after their shadows.

Only when Smirre Fox sank down on a pile of dry leaves, completely weak and lifeless, almost ready to give up the ghost, did they stop making fun of him.

'Now you know, Fox, what happens to anyone who dares to attack Akka from Kebnekaise,' they called into his ear, and with that they left him in peace.

THREE

Wild Bird Life

At The Farm

THURSDAY, 24 MARCH

At that same time an incident occurred in Skåne which was much discussed and even reported in the newspapers, but which many believed to be fictional, because they could find no way to explain it.

What happened was that a female squirrel had been caught in a hazel thicket growing on the shore of Vombsjön and carried to a nearby farm. All the people on the farm, both young and old, were delighted with the beautiful little animal with the big tail, the wise, curious eyes and the dainty little feet. They thought they would have all summer to enjoy watching its nimble movements, its handy way of shelling nuts and its merry games. They quickly fixed up an old squirrel cage, which consisted of a little house painted green and a squirrel-wheel made of steel wire. The squirrel would use the little house, which had a door and window, as kitchen and bedroom; for that reason they placed a bed of leaves there with a bowl of milk and some nuts. The wheel, on the other hand, she would have as a playhouse, where she could run and climb and swing around.

The humans thought they had arranged things very well for the squirrel and were surprised that she didn't look happy. Instead she sat in a corner of her room, sullen and sorrowful, and from time to time she let out a sharp cry of complaint. She did not touch the food and she did not once swing on the wheel. 'It's probably because she's scared,' the humans on the farm said. 'Tomorrow, when she feels at home, she's going to eat and play.'

However, it so happened that the women on the farm were getting ready for a banquet and the very day that the squirrel was caught, they were busy with baking. And either they had bad luck with the dough not wanting to rise or else they were dawdling, because they had to work long after it was dark.

There was naturally a lot of hustle and bustle in the kitchen and probably none of them took the time to wonder how the squirrel was. But there was an old woman in the house who was too advanced in age to help with the baking. She understood this, but even so she did not like being left out of everything. She felt sad and for that reason she did not go to bed, but instead sat by the window in the sitting room and looked out. In the kitchen they had propped open the door because of the heat, and through the open door a bright light streamed out on to the yard. It was an enclosed farm, with buildings connected around an interior yard, and it was so well lit up that the old woman could see cracks and holes in the plaster on the opposite wall. She also saw the squirrel cage, which was hanging right where the light fell the brightest, and she noticed how the squirrel was running all night from her room out into the wheel and from the wheel into her room without resting a moment. She thought there was a peculiar restlessness in the animal, but she assumed, of course, that the bright light was keeping it awake.

Between the cowshed and the horse stable at that farm there was a broad, covered entrance gate, which was also lit up. And as the night advanced, the old woman saw that out of the archway a little imp, no more than a hand's breadth tall but in wooden clogs and leather trousers like any labourer, came slowly and carefully sneaking into the farm. The old woman understood at once that it was the gnome, and she was not the least bit scared. She had always heard that he lived there on the farm, although she had never seen him before, and a gnome brought luck with him, wherever he appeared.

As soon as the gnome had entered the stone-paved yard, he ran right up to the squirrel cage, and as it was hanging so high that he could not reach it, he went to the tool shed for a switch, leaned it against the cage, and then swung up, the same way a sailor climbs up a rope. When he got to the cage he tugged at the door of the little green house, as if he wanted to open it, but the old woman sat quietly, because she knew that the children had put a padlock on the door, out of fear that the neighbour boys would try to steal the squirrel. The old woman saw that when the gnome could not open the door, the squirrel came out into the wheel. There she and the gnome had a long discussion. And when the gnome had heard all that the captured animal had to tell him, he rode the switch down to the ground and ran out through the farm gate.

The old woman did not think that she would see the gnome any more that night, but in any event she lingered by the window. After some time had passed, he came back. He was in such a hurry that she thought his feet hardly touched the ground, and he rushed up to the squirrel cage. The old woman saw him clearly with her far-sighted eyes, and she even saw that he was carrying something in his hands, but what it was she could not make out. What he had in his left hand, he set down on the pavement, but what he was holding in his right hand he brought with him up to the cage. Here he kicked the little window with his wooden shoe so that the pane broke, then he gave what he had in his hand to the squirrel. Then he rode down again, took what he had set on the ground and climbed up to the cage with this too. And right after that he rushed off again in such haste that the old woman could barely follow him with her eyes.

But now it was the old woman who no longer sat quietly in the room. She went out on the farmyard and placed herself in the shadow of the pump to await the gnome. And there was one other who had also noticed him and become curious. It was the farm cat. He came slowly sneaking and stopped by the wall, just a couple of steps outside the brightest streak of light.

Both of them stood and waited a long time in the cold March night, and the old woman was thinking about going in again, when she heard clattering against the stone pavement and saw that the little impish gnome came trudging in again. As before, he had a load in both hands, and what he was carrying peeped and struggled. And now a light came on for the old woman. She realized that the gnome had run over to the hazel grove and fetched the squirrel's babies, and that he was carrying them to her so they wouldn't starve to death.

The old woman stood quietly so as not to disturb, and the gnome didn't seem to notice her either. He was about to set the one baby down on the ground to be able to swing himself up to the cage with the other, when he caught sight of the farm cat's green eyes glistening right beside him. He stood there, quite puzzled, a baby squirrel in each hand.

He turned around, looking in all directions, and now became aware of the old woman. He did not reflect for long, but instead approached her and handed up one of the baby squirrels.

And the old woman did not want to show herself unworthy of the confidence, so she leaned down and took the baby squirrel and stood and held it, until the gnome had swung himself up to the cage with the other and came and retrieved the one he had entrusted to her.

The next morning, when the people on the farm gathered for breakfast, it was impossible for the old woman to keep from telling them about what she had seen the night before. Everyone laughed at her, of course, and said that she had only been dreaming. There were no squirrel babies this early in the year.

But she was sure of herself and asked them to look in the squirrel cage, which they did. And there on the bed of leaves were four small, half-naked and half-blind babies, which were at least a couple of days old.

When the farmer saw the babies, he said, 'Be that as it may, but it is certain that we here on the farm have conducted ourselves shamefully before both animals and humans.' And with that he picked the squirrel and all the babies out of the cage and set them in the old woman's apron. 'Go out to the hazel grove with them,' he said, 'and give them back their freedom!'

This incident was what was so much discussed and even got into the newspapers, but which most did not want to believe, because they could not explain how something like that could happen.

Vittskövle

SATURDAY, 26 MARCH

A few days later another such peculiar incident happened. A flock of wild geese came one morning and landed on a field over in eastern Skåne, not far from a large farm called Vittskövle. In the flock were thirteen geese of ordinary grey colour and a white gander, who was carrying a little imp on his back, dressed in yellow leather trousers, a green vest and a white knitted cap.

They were now quite close to the Baltic Sea, and on the field where the geese had landed the earth was mixed with sand, as it often is by sea coasts. It seemed as if in that area there must have been shifting sands before that needed to be secured, because in several places you could see that extensive pine forests had been planted.

When the wild geese had grazed awhile, some children came walking on the headland. The goose that was standing guard threw herself up in the air at once with resounding wing strokes, so that the whole flock would hear that danger was imminent. All the wild geese flew up, but the white one walked calmly on the ground. When he saw the others flee, he raised his head and called after them, 'You don't need to fly away from them. It's just some kids.'

The little imp who had been riding on his back was sitting on a tuft of grass at the forest edge and picking apart a pine cone to get at the seeds. The children were so close to him that he did not dare run across the field up to the white one. He hid quickly under a large, dry thistle leaf and at the same time let out a warning call.

But the white one had evidently made up his mind not to be frightened. He was still walking on the field and did not once look for where the children were headed.

They turned off the road, however, walked across the field and approached the gander. When he finally looked up, they were right next to him, and now he was so disturbed and confused that he forgot he could fly and hurried away from them, running. The children followed, chased him down into a ditch and caught him there. The oldest one stuck him under his arm and carried him away.

When the imp under the thistle leaf saw this, he ran up, as if he wanted to take the gander from the children. But then he remembered how little and powerless he was and instead threw himself down on the tuft of grass and hammered furiously on the ground with his fists.

The gander called for help with all his strength. 'Thumbkin! Come and help me! Thumbkin! Come and help me!' But at this the boy started to laugh in the midst of his anxiety. 'Sure, I'm just the right one to help anybody,' he said.

He got up and followed the gander anyway. 'I can't help him,' he said, 'but at least I want to see what they do with him.'

The children had a good lead, but the boy had no difficulty keeping them in sight, until he came to a hollow in the ground, where a spring creek rushed past. It was neither wide nor mighty, but in any event he had to run along the edge, before he found a place where he could jump over.

When he came out of the hollow, the children were gone. He could still see their tracks on a narrow path that led into the forest and he continued to follow them.

Soon he came to a crossroads and here the children must have separated, because there were tracks in two directions. Now the imp looked completely abandoned.

But just then he saw a little white feather on a tuft of heather. He realized that the gander had dropped it by the side of the road to show him in which direction he had been carried, and for that reason he continued his journey. He then followed the children through the whole forest. He did not see the gander, but wherever he might lose the way, a little white feather was lying there to guide him.

The imp continued faithfully to follow these feathers. They led him out of the forest, across a couple of fields, up on to a road and at last down the lane to an estate. At the end of the lane gables and towers of red brick could be seen, adorned with light edges and decorations. When the imp saw that this was an estate, he thought he understood what had become of the gander. 'The children must have brought the gander up to the estate and sold him there, so he is probably already slaughtered,' he said to himself. But he wanted to find out for sure and ran ahead with renewed eagerness. He met no one on the whole lane, which was good, because someone like him is usually anxious about being seen by humans.

The estate that he came to was a grand, old-fashioned building and consisted of four wings that surrounded a courtyard. On the east side was a deep archway, which led into the courtyard. So far the imp ran without hesitation, but when he got there, he stopped. He did not dare go farther, so here he remained standing and wondered what he should do next.

The imp was still standing with his finger on his nose, thinking, when he heard steps behind him. He turned around and saw a whole crowd of humans come walking up the lane. Quickly he slipped behind a water barrel that happened to be standing beside the archway and hid himself.

The arrivals were two dozen young men from a folk high school, who were out on a hike. They were followed by a teacher, and when they had made it to the archway, the teacher asked them to wait there for a moment, while he went in and asked if they could take a look at the old stronghold of Vittskövle.

The new arrivals were hot and tired, as if they had been on a long hike. One of them was so thirsty that he went over to the water barrel and leaned down to drink. He had a tinplate specimen case hanging around his neck, and he must have thought it was in the way, because he threw it down on the ground. With that the cover opened, so that you could see there were spring flowers in it.

The specimen case fell down right in front of the imp, and now he must have thought that this presented an excellent occasion to get into the stronghold and find out what had become of the gander. He quickly slipped down into the specimen case and hid, as best he could, under wildflowers and coltsfoot.

He was hardly hidden before the young man picked up the specimen case, hung it around his neck and snapped the lid shut.

The teacher now returned and said that they had received permission to come into the stronghold. To start with he led them in no farther than the courtyard. There he stopped and started talking with them about the old building.

He reminded them that the first people here in the country had to live in cliff grottos and holes in the earth, in animal-hide tents and lean-tos, and that a long time had passed before they discovered how to construct houses out of tree trunks. And then, how long they must have had to work and strive before they had progressed from a one-room log cabin to erecting a castle with a hundred rooms like Vittskövle!

It was three hundred and fifty years ago that the rich and powerful built such castles for themselves, he said. It was apparent that Vittskövle was erected at a time when war and robbers made it unsafe in Skåne. Around it there was a water-filled moat, and over this in times past was a bridge that could be hoisted up. Today there was still a watchtower over the archway; along the sides of the castle ran guard passages, and in the corners were solid towers with walls a metre thick. But even so, this castle was not erected in the very wildest time of war, because Jens Brahe, who built it, had also taken pains to make it a grand and richly decorated building. If they were to see the large, solid stone building at Glimminge, erected only a generation earlier, they would easily notice that Jens Holgersen Ulfstand, who was its builder, had not asked for anything other than to build big and solid and strong without giving a thought to making it beautiful or comfortable. If, on the other hand, they saw castles such as Marsvinsholm and Svenstorp and Övedskloster, which were built a century or two later than Vittskövle, then they would find that the times were more peaceful then. The lords who built these places had not equipped them with fortifications, but instead only endeavoured to have large, magnificent residences.

The teacher spoke slowly and exhaustively, and the imp, who was enclosed in the specimen case, was probably impatient. But he must have been lying very quietly, because the owner of the specimen case did not even notice he was carrying him.

Finally the whole company went into the castle, but if the imp had hoped that he would get an opportunity to slip out of the specimen case, he was deceived, because the student kept it on him and the imp had to follow along through all the rooms.

It was a slow tour. The teacher stopped at every moment to explain and instruct.

In one room was an old hearth and the teacher halted in front of it to talk about the various fireplaces that people had used throughout time. The first indoor hearth had been a stone slab in the middle of the floor with an opening for smoke up in the ceiling, which let in both rain and wind; the second had been a large, brick oven without a chimney, and it probably made the room warm, but also filled it with smoke and cooking odours. When Vittskövle was built, people had just advanced as far as the open hearth, which had a wide chimney for the smoke.

If that imp had ever been eager and impatient, that day he got some good practice in patience. Now it was already a good hour that he had been lying there motionless.

In the next room the teacher arrived at, he stopped in front of an old bed with a high canopy and plush curtains. And at once he started talking about beds and bedsteads of the past.

The teacher was in no hurry. But he didn't know either that there was a poor little thing enclosed in a specimen case, just waiting for him to stop. When he came to a room with gilt leather tapestries, he talked about how, ever since the earliest times, people had decorated their walls; when he came to an old family portrait, he talked about the varied fortunes of fashion; and in the banquet rooms he described ways of celebrating weddings and funerals in times past.

After that the teacher also talked a little about the many capable men and women who had inhabited the castle: about the old Brahes and the old Barnekows; about Kristian Barnekow, who had given the king his horse in the midst of flight; about Margareta Ascheberg, who had been married to Kjell Barnekow and as a widow ran the estate and the whole area for fifty-three years; about the financier Hagerman, who was the son of a crofter from Vittskövle and became so rich he bought the whole estate; and about the Stjernsvärds, who obtained better ploughs for the people in Skåne, so that they could abandon the old troublesome wooden ploughs, which three pairs of oxen could barely budge.

During all this the imp lay still. If he had ever been naughty and closed the cellar door on Mother or Father, now he got to learn how they had felt, because it took hours before the teacher stopped.

At last the teacher went out on to the courtyard again, and there he talked about the long labour of the human race to acquire tools and weapons, clothing and houses, furniture and decorative objects. He said that such an old castle like Vittskövle was a milestone on the way. There you could see how far humans had come three hundred and fifty years ago and judge for yourself whether things had progressed or gone backwards for them since then.

But the imp escaped listening to this, because the student who was carrying him was thirsty again and slipped into the kitchen to ask for a drink of water. Now when the imp was carried into the kitchen, he must have tried to look around for the gander. He started moving and in doing so he happened to press too hard against the cover, so that it sprang open.

Specimen-case lids always spring open, and the student did not give it any more thought, but instead simply closed it again. But then the cook asked if he had a snake in the specimen case.

'No, I just have some plants,' the student answered.

'Something moved in there,' the cook persisted.

The student then opened the lid to show her that she was mistaken. 'See for yourself if—'

But he got no further, because now the imp did not dare stay in the specimen case any longer, but instead sprang to the floor and rushed out. The maids hardly had time to see what it was that was running, but they hurried after it anyway.

The teacher was still talking, when he was interrupted by loud shouts. 'Catch him! Catch him!' the ones who had come from the kitchen screamed, and all the young men rushed after the imp, who scampered away quicker than a rat. They tried to block him at the gate, but it was not easy to get hold of someone so little and he successfully came out into the open.

The imp did not dare run down the lane, so he turned off in a different direction. He rushed through the garden into the backyard. The whole time the people were chasing after him with shouts and laughter. The poor little fellow fled for all he was worth, but it still seemed as if the humans would gain on him.

When he hurried past a small workman's dwelling, he heard a goose cackling and saw a white feather on the step. There, there was the gander! He had been on the wrong track before. He thought no more about the maids and men who were chasing him, but instead he climbed up the steps on to the landing. He could not get any farther, because the cottage door was locked. He heard the gander shrieking and complaining inside, but he could not get the door open. The big hunting party that pursued him was coming ever closer, and inside the room the gander was shrieking more and more pitifully. In this darkest hour the little fellow finally plucked up courage and pounded on the door with all his strength.

A child came and answered, and the imp looked into the room. In the middle of the floor a woman was sitting, holding the gander firmly in order to clip off his pinions. It was her child who had found him and she did not want to do him any harm. She intended to release him to her own geese once she had clipped his wings, so that he would not be able to fly away. But worse bad luck could hardly happen to the gander and he shrieked and complained with all his strength.

And lucky it was that the woman had not started the pinioning sooner. Now only two quills had fallen to the scissors when the door opened and the little imp was standing on the threshold. But the woman had never seen anyone like that before. She could only believe that it was the farm gnome himself, and she dropped the scissors in astonishment, folded her hands and forgot to hold on to the gander.

As soon as the gander noticed he was free, he ran towards the door. He did not give himself time to stop, but in passing he seized the imp by the neckband and took him with him. And on the steps he spread out his wings and went up into the air. At the same time he made a showy swing with his neck and set the little fellow upon his smooth, downy back.

Then they took off up into the air and all of Vittskövle stood and stared after them.

The Park at Övedskloster

All that day, as the geese played with the fox, the boy was lying asleep in an abandoned squirrel's nest. When he woke up towards evening, he was rather concerned. 'Now I'll soon be sent home, and then I probably can't avoid appearing before Mother and Father,' he thought.

But when he looked for the wild geese, who were swimming in Vombsjön, none of them said a word about him leaving. 'Maybe they think that the white one is too tired to go home with me this evening,' the boy thought.

The next morning the geese were awake at daybreak, long before sunrise. Now the boy felt sure that he would be going home, but strangely enough both he and the white gander got to follow the wild geese on their morning flight. The boy simply could not understand the reason for this reprieve, but then he figured out that the wild geese did not want to send the gander away on such a long trip before he had been able to eat until he was full. In any event he was just happy for every moment that passed before he had to meet his parents.

The wild geese travelled over to the manor at Övedskloster, which was situated in a magnificent park east of the lake and looked very grand with its large castle, its beautiful, stone-paved courtyard, surrounded by low walls and pavilions, and its fine, old-fashioned garden with pruned hedges, covered walk-ways, ponds, fountains, magnificent trees and immaculate lawns, whose edges were bright with spring flowers.

When the wild geese flew over the manor in the early morning, no person was yet moving. When they had carefully assured themselves of this, they flew lower towards the kennel and called, 'What kind of little hut is this? What kind of little hut is this?'

At once the watchdog came out of the kennel, angry and furious, and barked up at the air.

'Are you calling this a hut, you tramps? Don't you see that this is a tall stone castle? Don't you see what beautiful walls it has, don't you see how many windows and what large gates and what a grand terrace it has, woof, woof, woof? Are you calling this a hut, are you? Don't you see the yard? Don't you see the garden? Don't you see the greenhouses? Don't you see the marble statues? Are you calling this a hut, are you? Do huts usually have a park where there are beech forests and hazel thickets and forest mead-ows and oak groves and spruce hills and a preserve full of deer, woof, woof, woof? Are you calling this a hut, are you? Have you seen a hut that has so many outbuildings around it that it looks like a whole village? I'm sure you know of many huts that have their own church and their own parsonage, and that rule over manors and farms and tenant farms and farm workers' cabins, woof, woof, woof? Are you calling this a hut, are you? The larg-est estate in Skåne belongs to this hut, you beggars. You can't see a patch of earth from where you are hanging in the sky that isn't under the control of this hut, woof, woof, woof!'

The dog managed to call all this out in one breath, and the geese flew back and forth over the yard and listened to him, until he had to take a break. But then they shrieked, 'What are you so angry for? We weren't asking about the castle, we were just asking about your kennel.'

When the boy heard this joke, at first he laughed, but then a thought forced itself on him that made him serious at once. 'Imagine how many amusing things you would get to hear if you got to go with the wild geese through the whole country all the way up to Lapland!' he said to himself. 'Now when you're in such a bad way a trip like that would probably be the best thing you could think of.'

The wild geese flew off to one of the wide fields east of the manor to graze on grass roots, and kept at this for hours. In the meantime the boy went into the large park that bordered the field, searched for a hazel grove and started looking up at the bushes to see if there were any nuts left hanging from last autumn. But again and again while he walked in the park the thought of the journey came back to him. He imagined how nice it would be for him if he went with the wild geese. He thought he would have to starve and freeze often enough, but in return he would not have to work or study.

While he was walking there, the old grey lead goose came up to him and asked if he had found anything edible. No, he had not, he said, and then she tried to help him. She could not find any nuts either, but she found a couple of rosehips hanging on a briar bush. The boy ate them up with good appetite, but he probably wondered what his mother would have said if she knew he was now living on raw fish and old rosehips left after winter.

When the wild geese were finally full, they headed down to the lake again, and there they amused themselves by playing until almost noon. The wild geese challenged the white gander to a contest in every possible sport. They had swimming races, running races and flying races with him. The big tame gander did his best, but he was always beaten by the quick wild geese. The boy sat on the gander's back the whole time and encouraged him and had just as much fun as the others. There was shrieking and laughter and cackling, so it was strange that the people at the manor did not hear them.

When the wild geese were tired of playing, they went out on the ice and rested for a couple of hours. They spent the afternoon in almost the same way as the morning. First a couple of hours of grazing, then swimming and games in the water by the edge of the ice until sundown, when at once they settled down to sleep.

'This would be just the life that would suit me,' the boy thought, as he crept in under the gander's wing. 'But tomorrow I'll be sent home.'

Before he fell asleep, he lay there thinking that if he got to go with the wild geese he would avoid all scolding for being lazy. Then he would get to loaf all day and his only worry would be getting something to eat. But he needed so little nowadays that it would probably work out.

And then he imagined to himself what he would get to see and how many adventures he would be involved in. Yes, it would be different from the toil and moil at home. 'If I only got to go with the wild geese on their journey, I would not be sad about having been transformed,' the boy thought.

He was not afraid of anything except being sent home, but the geese did not say a word about him having to travel on Wednesday either. That day passed in the same way as Tuesday and the boy was feeling more and more comfortable with the wilderness life. He thought he had the deserted park at Övedskloster, which was big as a forest, completely to himself, and he did not feel homesick for the cramped cottage and the small fields at home.

On Wednesday he thought that the wild geese intended to keep him with them, but on Thursday he lost hope again.

Thursday started in the same way as the other days. The geese grazed on the wide fields and the boy looked for food in the park. After a while Akka came to him and asked if he had found anything edible. No, he had not, and then she found a dry caraway plant for him, with all of its little seeds intact.

When the boy had eaten, Akka said that she thought he was running around in the park much too adventurously. She wondered if he knew how many enemies he had to watch out for, being so little. No, he did not know that at all, and then Akka started listing them for him.

When he was in the park, she said, he should watch out for the fox and the marten; when he came to the lakeshore, he should keep the otters in mind; if he sat on the stone wall, he should not forget the weasel, who could creep through the smallest hole, and if he wanted to lie down to sleep in a pile of leaves, he should first investigate whether a viper was not having its winter sleep in the same pile. As soon as he came out on the open field, he should keep an eye out for hawks and buzzards, for eagles and falcons hovering in the sky. In the hazel thicket he could have been captured by the sparrowhawk; magpies and crows were everywhere, and he should not believe them too much, and as soon as it was twilight he should keep his ears pricked to listen for the large owls who flew with such silent wing strokes that they could be right on him before he noticed them.

When the boy heard that there were so many who were after his life, he realized that it was quite impossible for him to stay alive. He was not particularly afraid of dying, but he did not like being eaten up, and for that reason he asked Akka what he could do to protect himself against predators.

Akka answered at once that the boy ought to try to be on good terms with the small animals in forest and field, with squirrels and hares, finches and titmice and woodpeckers and larks. If he became their friend, they could warn him of dangers, find him hiding places and, as a last resort, they could join together and defend him.

But when the boy wanted to follow this advice later in the day and turned to Sirle, the squirrel, to ask for his assistance, it turned out that the squirrel did not want to help him. 'You mustn't expect anything good from me or the other small animals,' Sirle said. 'Don't you think we know that you are Nils the goose-boy, who last year tore down the swallow's nest, crushed the starling's eggs, threw baby crows into the marl-pit, caught thrushes in traps and put squirrels in cages? You can help yourself as best you can, and you should be happy that we don't gang up against you and chase you back to your own kind.'

This was just the sort of answer that the boy would not have left unpunished before, when he was Nils the goose-boy, but

now he was just afraid that the wild geese too would find out
how mean he could be. He had been so anxious about not getting to stay with the wild geese that he had not dared the
slightest mischief since he had been in their company. It was
true that he would not have been able to do much harm, little
as he was, but he probably could have destroyed many birds'
nests and broken many eggs, if he had wanted to. Now he had
just been nice, he had not torn a feather from a goose wing, not
given anyone an impolite answer, and every morning when he
greeted Akka, he had taken off his cap and bowed.

All of Thursday he kept on thinking that it was certainly
due to his meanness that the wild geese did not want to take
him with them up to Lapland. And when he heard in the evening that Sirle Squirrel's wife had been taken away, and that his
children were about to starve to death, he decided to help
them, and it has already been told how well he succeeded in
this.

When on Friday the boy came into the park, he heard the
chaffinches singing in every thicket about how Sirle Squirrel's
wife had been kidnapped by cruel robbers from her tender
babies and how Nils the goose-boy had ventured in among the
humans and carried the little squirrel children to her.

'Who is now so celebrated in Övedskloster's park,' the
chaffinches sang, 'as Thumbkin, he whom everyone feared
back when he was Nils the goose-boy? Sirle, the squirrel, will
give him nuts, the poor hares will play with him, the deer
will take him on their backs and fly away with him when
Smirre Fox approaches, the titmice will warn him about the
sparrowhawk, and finches and larks will sing about his heroic
deed.'

The boy was quite sure that both Akka and the wild geese
heard all this, but nonetheless all of Friday passed without
their saying anything about him being able to stay with them.

Up until Saturday the geese got to graze on the fields around
Öved, undisturbed by Smirre Fox. But when on Saturday
morning they came out on the fields, he was lying in wait for
them and followed them from one field to the next, so that they
could not eat undisturbed. When Akka realized that he did not

intend to leave them in peace, she quickly made her decision, raised herself in the air and flew with the flock many kilometres away over the plains of Färs County and the juniper-clad slopes of Linderödsåsen. They did not land until they were in the area of Vittskövle.

But here at Vittskölevel the gander was kidnapped, which has already been told. If the boy had not exerted all his strength to help him, he never would have been found again.

When on Saturday evening the boy came back with the gander to Vombsjön, he thought that he had done a good day's work, and really wondered what Akka and the wild geese would say. And the wild geese were in no way sparing of praise, but they did not say the word that he longed to hear.

Then it was Sunday again. A whole week had passed since the boy had been bewitched, and he was still just as small.

But it did not appear as if he should have any worries because of that. On Sunday afternoon he sat curled up in a large, bushy osier down by the lakeshore, blowing on a reed. Around him sat as many titmice and chaffinches and starlings as the bush could hold, chirping songs that he tried to learn to play. But the boy was not very familiar with the art. He blew so off-key that the feathers stood up on all the small instructors, and they shrieked and fluttered in despair. The boy laughed so much at their eagerness that he dropped the reed.

He started up again and it went just as badly, so that all the small birds complained. 'Today you play worse than usual, Thumbkin. You don't make a clear tone. Where are your thoughts, Thumbkin?'

'Somewhere else,' said the boy, and this was true. He was wondering about how long he would get to stay there with the wild geese or if he would be sent home, perhaps today.

Suddenly the boy threw aside the reed and jumped down out of the bush. He had seen Akka and all the geese coming up to him in a long row. They walked so unusually slowly and solemnly that the boy thought he understood at once that now he would find out what they intended to do with him.

When they finally stopped, Akka said, 'You have every good reason to wonder about me, Thumbkin, for not having thanked you for saving me from Smirre Fox. But I am the sort who prefers to say thank you with action rather than words. And now, Thumbkin, I think that I have succeeded in doing you a great favour. I have sent a message to that gnome who bewitched you. To start with he did not want to hear any talk of curing you, but I have sent message after message to him and told him how well you have conducted yourself among us. Now he says to tell you that as soon as you return home, you will get to be a human.'

But think, as happy as the boy had been when the wild goose started to speak, he was just as distressed when she ended! He did not say a word, but instead simply turned away and cried.

'What in the world is this?' said Akka. 'It looks as if you expected more from me than I have offered you.'

But the boy thought about carefree days and amusing jokes, about adventures and freedom and travels high up over the earth, which he would miss, and he really howled with distress. 'I don't care about becoming human,' he said. 'I want to go with you to Lapland.'

'I will tell you something,' said Akka. 'That gnome is very touchy and I am afraid that if you don't accept his offer now it will be hard for you to persuade him another time.'

A strange thing about this boy was that as long as he lived, he had never liked anyone. He did not like his father and mother or his schoolteachers or his schoolmates or the boys on the neighbouring farms. Everything they had wanted him to do, whether it was play or work, he had only thought was boring. For that reason now there was no one that he missed or longed for.

The only ones he could even come close to getting along with were Åsa the Goose-girl and Little Mats, a couple of children who, like him, had taken the geese to graze on the fields. But he was not really attached to them either. Far from it.

'I don't want to be a human!' the boy howled. 'I want to go with you to Lapland. That's why I've been nice a whole week.'

'I don't want to stop you going with us, as long as you want to,' said Akka. 'But first think about whether you wouldn't rather return home. There may come a day when you regret this.'

'No,' said the boy, 'there is nothing to regret. I have never had it so good as here with all of you.'

'Well, then it will be as you wish,' said Akka.

'Thank you!' said the boy, suddenly feeling so happy that he had to cry from joy, just as before he had cried from sorrow.

FOUR
Glimmingehus

Black Rats and Grey Rats

In south-eastern Skåne not far from the sea is an old castle called Glimmingehus. It consists of a single tall, large, sturdy stone building, which is visible for miles across the plains. It is no more than four storeys high, but it is so massive that an ordinary home on the same property looks like a child's playhouse.

The big stone building has such thick outer walls and interior walls and ceiling arches that inside it there is hardly room for anything other than the thick walls. The stairs are narrow, the vestibules small and the rooms few in number. In order for the walls to retain their strength, only a small number of windows are found in the upper storeys, and at the bottom there are none at all, only narrow openings for light. During wartime in the past the people were just as happy to stay inside such a strong and massive building as you are now to slip into a fur in bitter cold winter, but when the good time of peace came, they no longer wanted to live in the old castle's dark, cold stone halls. They abandoned the great Glimmingehus long ago and moved into homes where light and air could get in.

At the time when Nils Holgersson was travelling around with the wild geese, there were thus no people at Glimmingehus, but despite that it certainly did not lack inhabitants. On the roof every summer a pair of storks lived in a large nest; a pair of tawny owls lived in the attic; bats hung in the secret passageways; in the stove in the kitchen lived an old cat; and down in the cellar were several hundred of the old black rats.

Rats were not exactly held in high esteem by the other animals, but the black rats at Glimmingehus constituted an exception. They were always mentioned with respect, because they had shown great courage in battles with their enemies and great persistence during the major misfortunes that had befallen their race. You see, they belonged to a species of rat that had once been very numerous and powerful, but now was in the process of dying out. For a great many years the black rats had owned Skåne and the whole country. They had been found in every cellar, in every attic, in barns and bins, in pantries and bakehouses, in stables and stalls, in churches and castles, in breweries and mills, in every building erected by humans, but now they were expelled from all these and almost exterminated. Only in some old, deserted place or other could you happen upon a few of them, and nowhere were they in such great numbers as at Glimmingehus.

When a species dies out, humans are most often the reason for it, but that was not the case this time. True, people had struggled with the black rats, but they had not been able to do them any appreciable damage. The ones that had conquered them were a species of their own kind, called grey rats.

These grey rats had not lived in the country since ancient times like the black rats. They originated from a couple of poor immigrants, who landed a hundred years ago in Malmö from a barge from Lübeck. These were homeless, starving wretches who kept to the harbour itself, swimming around among the pilings under the piers and eating trash that was thrown in the water. They never ventured up to the city, which was owned by the black rats.

But, by and by, as the grey rats grew in number, they became bolder. To start with they moved into some deserted and condemned old buildings that the black rats had abandoned. They sought their feed in gutters and trash heaps and put up with all the rubbish that the black rats did not care to use. They were hardy, contented and fearless, and within a few years they had become so powerful that they endeavoured to chase the black rats away from Malmö. They took attics, cellars and warehouses away from them, starved them out or bit them to death, because they were not at all afraid of battle.

And when Malmö was taken, they moved off in small and large bands to conquer the whole country. It is almost impossible to understand why the black rats did not gather themselves into a large, joint war expedition and annihilate the grey rats, while these were still few in number. But the black rats were probably so sure of their power that they could not believe in the possibility of losing it. They sat quietly on their properties and in the meantime the grey rats took from them farm after farm, village after village, city after city. They were starved out, forced out, rooted out. In Skåne they had been unable to survive in a single place, except at Glimmingehus.

The old stone building had such secure walls, and so few rat passages led through them, that the black rats managed to defend it and prevent the grey rats from getting in. Year after year, night after night the battle had gone on between attackers and defenders, but the black rats kept faithful watch and fought with the greatest contempt for death and, thanks to the massive old building, they had always won.

It must be admitted that as long as the black rats were in power, they had been just as detested by all other living creatures as the grey rats are nowadays, and with good reason. They attacked poor, shackled prisoners and tormented them, they gorged on corpses, they stole the last turnip in the poor man's cellar, bit the feet off sleeping geese, stole eggs and chicks from the hens and did a thousand misdeeds. But since they had met with misfortune, all this seemed to be forgotten and no one could keep from admiring the last of the race, which had held out so long with its resistance against the enemies.

The grey rats who lived at the Glimminge estate and in the area around it still continued the struggle and tried to take advantage of every suitable opportunity to take possession of the castle. You might think they ought to have let the little band of black rats occupy Glimmingehus in peace, since they themselves had won the rest of the country, but this did not seem to occur to them. They would say that it was a point of honour for them to once again conquer the black rats, but anyone who knew the grey rats probably understood that it was because humans used Glimmingehus as a grain warehouse that the grey ones could not rest until they had taken it.

The Stork

MONDAY, 28 MARCH

Early one morning the wild geese, who were sleeping on the ice of Vombsjön, were woken by a loud call from high in the air. 'Trirop! Trirop!' it sounded. 'Trianut, the crane, sends greetings to Akka, the wild goose, and her flock! Tomorrow the great crane dance is at Kullaberg!'

Akka stretched her head up at once and answered, 'Greetings in return and thanks! Greetings and thanks!'

With that the cranes flew on, but the wild geese heard them for a long time as they travelled around, calling out over every field and every wooded slope, 'Trianut sends greetings! Tomorrow is the great crane dance at Kullaberg!'

The wild geese were very happy about this news. 'You're in luck,' they said to the white gander, 'getting to see the great crane dance.'

'Is it so remarkable to see cranes dance?' the gander asked.

'It's like nothing you've ever dreamed of,' the wild geese replied.

'Now we need to think about what to do with Thumbkin tomorrow, so that no misfortune happens to him while we travel to Kullaberg,' said Akka.

'Thumbkin doesn't need to be alone,' said the gander. 'If the cranes don't allow him to see their dance, then I'll stay with him.'

'No human has yet been allowed to be part of the animal gathering at Kullaberg,' said Akka. 'And I don't dare take Thumbkin with me there. But we can talk more about this later in the day. First and foremost now we have to think about getting something to eat.'

Akka then gave the sign for departure. This day too she sought her grazing grounds far away, because of Smirre Fox, and did not touch down until the marshy meadows some distance south of Glimmingehus.

All that day the boy sat by the shore of a little pond, blowing on reeds. He was upset about not being allowed to see the crane dance and could not make himself say a word to the gander or any of the others.

It was truly bitter that Akka should still distrust him. When a boy had given up being human to travel around with some poor wild geese, they really ought to grasp that he had no desire to betray them. And likewise they ought to grasp that when he had sacrificed so much to get to follow them, it was their duty to let him see all the remarkable things they could show him.

'I'll just have to clearly say what I think,' he thought. But hour after hour passed without him making up his mind to do that. It may sound remarkable, but the boy really had acquired a kind of respect for the old lead goose. It was not easy, he felt, setting himself against her will.

On one side of the marshy meadow where the geese were grazing was a broad stone wall, and it now happened that when towards evening the boy raised his head to finally speak with Akka, his eyes fell on this. He let out a little cry of surprise and all the geese looked up at once and turned to stare in the same direction as him. At first both they and the boy thought all the grey cobblestones that the wall was made of had grown legs and started running, but soon they saw that it was a band of rats scampering along it. They moved very quickly and ran ahead closely packed, line by line, and were so numerous that they covered the whole stone wall for some time.

The boy had been afraid of rats even when he was a big, strong human. Why shouldn't he be now, when he was so little that two or three of them could get the better of him? One shiver after another went down his spine, while he stood looking at them.

But it was remarkable that the geese seemed to share his loathing for the rats. They did not speak to them, and when they were past, they shook themselves, as if they had mud between their feathers.

'So many grey rats about!' said Yksi from Vassijaure. 'That's not a good sign.'

Now the boy meant to take the opportunity to tell Akka that he thought she ought to let him go with them to Kullaberg, but he was hindered again, because a large bird suddenly landed in the midst of the geese.

When you saw this bird, you might think he had borrowed his body, throat and head from a little white goose. But added to this he had acquired big black wings, long red legs and a long thick beak, which was too big for the little head and weighed it down, giving him a worried and mournful appearance.

Akka quickly adjusted her wing coverts and curtsied multiple times with her neck, as she walked towards the stork. She was not particularly surprised to see him in Skåne so early in the spring, because she knew that the male storks usually travel over there in good time to see that the nest has not suffered damage during the winter, before the female storks make the effort to fly over the Baltic. But she wondered why he had sought her out, because storks prefer to associate with their own kind.

'I can't believe there is anything amiss with your residence, Herr Ermenrich,' said Akka.

It turned out now that it is true, as it is said, that a stork can seldom open its beak without complaining. What made what

the stork said sound even more miserable was that he had a
hard time getting the words out. He stood for a long while and
only clattered with his beak and then spoke in a hoarse, weak
voice. He complained about everything imaginable: the nest,
which was situated at the top of the roof ridge at Glimmingehus, had been completely ruined by the winter storms, and
nowadays he could get no food in Skåne. The people in Skåne
were in the process of appropriating all of his property. They
drained his marshland and cultivated his bogs. He intended to
move out of this country and never come back.

While the stork complained, Akka, the wild goose, who had
no patronage or protection anywhere, could not help thinking
to herself, 'If I were as well off as you, Herr Ermenrich, I would
have no reason to complain. You have remained a free and
wild bird, and yet you are in such good standing with humans
that no one will fire a shot at you or steal an egg from your
nest.' But she kept all of this to herself. To the stork she said
only that she could not believe that he would want to move
away from a house where storks had sought their refuge ever
since it was built.

Then the stork quickly asked whether the geese had seen the
grey rats, who were marching towards Glimmingehus, and
when Akka replied that she had seen the scum, he started telling her about the brave black rats who for many years had
defended the castle. 'But tonight Glimmingehus is going to fall
into the hands of the grey rats,' the stork said with a sigh.

'Why tonight, Herr Ermenrich?' Akka asked.

'Because almost all the black rats went to Kullaberg yesterday evening,' said the stork. 'They were confident that all the
other animals would hurry there too. But you see that the grey
rats have stayed at home, and now they are gathering to force
their way into the castle tonight, when it is defended by only a
few old wretches who didn't feel up to going along to Kullaberg. They will probably reach their goal, but I have lived
neighbourly with the black rats for so many years that it does
not please me to live in the same place as their enemies.'

Akka now understood that the stork had become so aggravated over the grey rats' conduct that he had sought her out to

complain about them. But according to stork custom he had quite certainly done nothing to prevent the misfortune. 'Have you sent word to the black rats, Herr Ermenrich?' she asked.

'No,' the stork replied. 'That would do no good. Before they make it back, the castle will already be taken.'

'You should not be so sure of that, Herr Ermenrich,' said Akka. 'I know an old wild goose who would gladly like to prevent such villainy.'

When Akka said this, the stork raised his head and looked wide-eyed at her. And that was not strange, for old Akka had neither claws nor beak that would be good in a battle. And she was a diurnal bird to boot, and as soon as darkness came she fell helplessly asleep, while the rats fought only at night.

But Akka had evidently decided to assist the black rats. She summoned Yksi from Vassijaure and ordered him to lead the geese up to Vombsjön, and when the geese made objections, she said authoritatively, 'I think that it will be best for all of us that you obey me. I have to fly up to the great stone building, and if you follow me, it can't be avoided that the farm folk will see us and shoot us down. The only one that I want to take with me on this journey is Thumbkin. He can be very useful to me, because he has good eyes and can stay awake at night.'

The boy was in a contrary mood that day, and when he heard what Akka said, he stretched in order to be as big as possible and stepped forwards with his hands behind his back and his nose in the air and intended to say that he certainly did not want to be involved in fighting with grey rats. She would have to look for help somewhere else.

But just as the boy became visible, the stork started to move. Before, he had stood according to stork habit with his head bowed down and his beak pressed against his neck. But now gurgling was heard deep down in his throat, as if he was going to laugh. He lowered his beak at breakneck speed, grabbed the boy and threw him a couple of metres up in the air. He repeated this trick seven times, all while the boy shrieked and the geese shouted, 'What are you up to, Herr Ermenrich? That's not a frog! It's a human, Herr Ermenrich!'

At last the stork set the boy down completely unscathed anyway. After that he said to Akka, 'I am now flying back to Glimmingehus, Mother Akka. Everyone who lives there was very anxious when I left. You can be sure they will be very happy when I tell them that Akka, the wild goose, and Thumbkin, the human imp, are coming to save them.'

With that the stork extended his neck, spread his wings and set off like an arrow when it travels from a hard-drawn bow. Akka knew that he was making fun of her, but she did not let that concern her. She waited until the boy had found his wooden shoes, which the stork had shaken off him. Then she set him on her back and followed the stork. And for his part the boy did not object and did not say a word about not wanting to go along. He had become so angry at the stork that he just sat and snorted. That long red-leg thought he wasn't good for anything, because he was little, but he would show him what kind of a fellow Nils Holgersson from Västra Vemmenhög is.

A few moments later Akka was in the stork nest at Glimmingehus. It was a large, grand nest. For a base it had a wheel, and over that were several layers of twigs and tufts of grass. The nest was so old that many bushes and plants had taken root up there, and when the stork mother sat on eggs in the round hole in the middle of the nest, she not only had the beautiful view of a good part of Skåne to enjoy, she also had rosehip flowers and houseleeks to look at.

Both the boy and Akka could see at once that something was going on here that turned all normal order upside down. You see, on the edge of the stork nest were sitting two tawny owls, an old grey-striped cat and a dozen ancient rats with deformed teeth and runny eyes. These were not exactly the kind of animals that you otherwise see in peaceful coexistence.

None of them turned around to look at Akka or welcome her. They did not think about anything other than staring at some long, grey lines that were glimpsed here and there on the bare fields.

All the black rats kept silent. They were clearly in deep despair and knew well that they could defend neither their own lives nor the castle. Both of the owls sat and rolled their big eyes, turned their goggle eyes and talked in awful, sharp voices about the great cruelty of the grey rats, and that they had to move out of their nest, because they had heard that they spared neither eggs nor chicks. The old striped cat was certain that the grey rats would bite him to death, when they forced their way into the castle in such great numbers, and he quarrelled constantly with the black rats. 'How could you be so stupid and let your best warriors go away?' he said. 'How could you trust the grey rats? It's completely unforgivable.'

The twelve black rats did not say a word in reply, but the stork could not keep from teasing the cat, despite his distress. 'Don't be anxious, Måns Housecat!' he said. 'Don't you see that mother Akka and Thumbkin have come here to rescue the castle? You can be sure that they will succeed. Now I have to settle down to sleep, and I do it with the greatest calm. Tomorrow, when I wake up, there will probably not be a single grey rat at Glimmingehus.'

The boy winked at Akka and made a sign that he wanted to shove the stork to the ground, now that he had settled down to sleep on the outside edge of the nest with one leg pulled up, but Akka stopped him. She did not look at all annoyed. Instead she said in a satisfied tone, 'It would be bad if someone who is as old as I am could not get out of worse difficulties than this. If only the male and female owls, who can keep themselves awake all night, would fly off with a couple of messages on my behalf, then I think that everything will go well.'

Both the tawny owls were willing, and Akka then asked the male owl to go and find the black rats that had gone away and advise them to hurry home at once. The female owl she sent to Flammea, the barn owl, who lived in the cathedral in Lund, with a mission that was so secret that Akka dared entrust only her with it in a whisper.

The Rat-catcher

It was approaching midnight, when after much searching the grey rats managed to find a cellar aperture that was open. It

was fairly high up on the wall, but the rats set themselves on
each other's shoulders, and it did not take long before the bravest among them was in the aperture, ready to force her way
into Glimmingehus, outside whose walls so many of her ancestors had fallen.

The grey rat sat quietly in the aperture awhile and waited to
be attacked. True, the defenders' main army was away, but she
assumed that the black rats who were still in the castle would
not give up without a struggle. With beating heart she listened
for the slightest noise, but all remained silent. Then the grey
rats' leader plucked up courage and jumped down into the
coal-dark cellar.

One grey rat after another followed the leader. All kept very
quiet, and all waited for an ambush by the black rats. Not until
so many of them had forced their way into the cellar that the
floor could hold no more did they dare go further.

Although they had never been in the building before, they
had no difficulty finding their way. Very soon they located the
passages in the wall that the black rats used to get to the upper
storeys. Before they started climbing up these narrow, steep
paths, they again listened very attentively. They felt much more
terrified that the black rats held back in this way than if they
had met them in open battle. They could hardly believe their
luck when they came up to the first storey without mishap.

Immediately upon entry the grey rats were met by the smell
of the grain that was stored in large bins on the floor. But it
was not time yet for them to start enjoying their victory. First
they searched with the greatest care through the gloomy, bare
rooms. They ran up into the stove that stood in the middle of
the floor in the old castle kitchen, and came close to falling
down into the well in the inside room. They did not leave one
of the narrow light openings uninspected, but still found no
black rats. When this floor was completely in their power, they
started to take possession of the next one with the same cau-
tion. Again they had to venture a laborious and dangerous
climb through the walls, while they waited in endless anxiety
that the enemy would throw himself over them. And although
they were enticed by the most delightful aroma from the grain

bins, they forced themselves with the greatest discipline to investigate the pillared common room used by the soldiers in the past, their stone table and stove, the deep window niches and the hole in the floor that in olden days had been taken out in order thereby to be able to pour boiling pitch over an intruding enemy.

Still the black rats were nowhere to be seen. The grey rats searched up to the third storey with the castle lord's great banquet hall, which stood just as bare and plain as all the other rooms in the old building, and they even made their way up to the top storey, which consisted solely of a large, deserted room. The only place that they did not think of investigating was the large stork nest on the roof, where just at this time the female owl wakened Akka and told her that Flammea, the barn owl, had granted her request and sent her what she wanted.

Since the grey rats had investigated the whole castle so conscientiously, they felt calm. They understood that the black rats had fled and did not intend to put up resistance, and they ran with happy hearts up into the grain bins.

But the grey rats had hardly swallowed the first grains of wheat before from the yard below the sharp sound of a small, shrill pipe was heard. The grey rats raised their heads from the grain, listened worriedly, ran a couple of steps as if they intended to leave the bin, but then turned around and started eating again.

Again the pipe sounded with a sharp, cutting tone, and now something remarkable happened. One rat, two rats, yes, a whole bunch of rats left the grain, jumped out of the bin and hurried the shortest way down to the cellar to get out of the building. Yet there were still just as many grey rats left. They thought about the effort it had cost them to win Glimmingehus and they did not want to leave it. But the tones of the pipe reached them yet again and they had to follow them. They rushed out of the bins in a wild frenzy, went down through the narrow hole in the walls and tumbled over each other in their eagerness to get out.

In the middle of the courtyard stood a little imp who was blowing on a pipe. Around him he already had a whole circle of rats who listened to him, amazed and delighted, and more came with every moment. Once, he took the pipe from his mouth for a second to thumb his nose at the rats, and then it looked as if they wanted to throw themselves over him and bite him to death, but as soon as he blew, they were under his power.

When the imp had played all the grey rats out of Glimmingehus, he slowly started wandering from the courtyard out on to the road, and all the grey rats followed him, because the tones from the pipe sounded so delightful in their ears that they could not resist them.

The imp went ahead and lured them with him on the road towards Vallby. He led them on in all possible types of circles and bends and curves through hedges and down into ditches, and wherever he went, they had to follow. He blew unceasingly on his pipe, which seemed to be made of an animal horn, although the horn was so little that there is no animal in our day from whose head it could have been broken. No one knew who had made it either. Flammea, the barn owl, found it in a niche in the cathedral in Lund. She had shown it to Bataki, the raven, and together they figured out that it was the sort of horn that used to be made in the past by those who wanted to acquire power over rats and mice. But the raven was Akka's friend and it was from him that she found out that Flammea owned such a treasure.

And it was true that the rats could not resist the pipe. The boy went before them and played, as long as the starlight lasted, and they followed him the whole time. He played at daybreak, he played at sunrise, and still the whole troop of grey rats followed him and were lured farther and farther away from the great grain lofts at Glimmingehus.

FIVE

The Great Crane Dance at Kullaberg

TUESDAY, 29 MARCH

It must be said that although many magnificent buildings have been erected in Skåne, none of them has such beautiful walls as old Kullaberg.

Kullaberg is low and long. It is by no means a large or massive hill. On its broad crown there are woods and fields and an occasional heather moor. Here and there round, heather-covered mounds and bare rocks rise up. It is not particularly beautiful; it looks like any other upland ground in Skåne.

Anyone taking the road that runs straight across the hill can't help feeling a bit disappointed.

But then perhaps he turns off from the road, goes out towards the sides of the hill and looks down the rock faces, and then suddenly he finds so much worth seeing that he hardly knows how he can take it all in. For the fact is that Kullaberg is not situated with plains and valleys around it like other hills;

instead it has rushed out into the sea as far as it can go. Not the slightest stretch of land lies below the hill to protect it from the sea waves, which reach all the way up to the rock walls and can wear them and shape them as they please.

For that reason the rock walls stand there as richly ornamented as the sea and its assistant the wind have been able to accomplish. There are steep clefts deeply incised in the sides of the hill, and black promontories that have been worn smooth under the constant whiplashes of the wind. There are solitary rock pillars that stand right up out of the water, and dark grottos with narrow entries. There are vertical, bare precipices and soft, leaf-covered rises. There are small promontories and small bays and small cobblestones, which are rinsed and rattle up and down with every pounding wave. There are stately cliff gates that arch over the water, there are sharp stones constantly sprayed with white foam, and others that are reflected in black-green, changeless still water. There are giant cauldrons that are turned out in the cliff, and massive cracks that lure the wanderer to venture into the depths of the hill all the way up to the Kulla Man's cave.

And up and along all these clefts and cliffs vines and tendrils creep and crawl. Trees grow there too, but the power of the wind is so great that the trees also have to turn into creepers to survive out on the rock faces. The oaks are short and stay low to the ground, while the foliage stands over them like a narrow arch, and the short-trunked beeches cower in the clefts like big leaf tents.

These remarkable rock walls, along with the wide, blue sea beyond them and the shimmering, sharp air above them are what make Kullaberg so dear to humans that large groups of them make their way up there every day as long as summer lasts. It can be harder to see what makes it so attractive for the animals that they gather there every year for a big play date. But this is a custom that has been followed since ancient times, and you had to have been there already when the first breaker shattered into foam against the shore to be able to explain why just Kullaberg was chosen for the meeting place ahead of every other site.

When the meeting is to take place, the red deer, roe deer, hares, foxes and other wild quadrupeds make the journey to Kullaberg that very night, so as not to be noticed by the humans. Right before the sun rises, they all march up to the playground, which is a heather moor to the left of the road not far from the hill's outermost promontory.

The playground is surrounded on all sides by round rock mounds, which conceal it from anyone who does not happen to come right up to it. And in the month of March it is not very likely that any wanderer will go astray there. All the strangers that otherwise roam around on the mounds and climb up the sides of the hill, the autumn storms have already chased away many months ago. And the lighthouse keeper out on the promontory, the old woman in Kullagården farm and the Kulla farmer and his household, they go their usual ways and don't run around on the desolate heather fields.

When the quadrupeds have arrived at the playground, they settle down on the round rock mounds. Every species keeps to itself, although it is given that on a day like this general peace prevails and no one need fear being attacked. On this day a little baby hare could wander over the foxes' mound without losing so much as one of its long ears. But the animals line up anyway in separate flocks. It is ancient custom.

When all have taken their places, they start to look around for the birds. The weather is almost always beautiful on this day. The cranes are good weathermen and would not call the animals together if they expected rain. But although the air is clear and nothing obstructs the view, the quadrupeds see no birds. This is odd. The sun is high in the sky and the birds should already be on their way.

What the animals on Kullaberg do notice on the other hand is an occasional dark cloud that is slowly moving ahead over the plain. And look! One of these clouds now suddenly steers along the coast of Öresund up towards Kullaberg. When the cloud has come straight across the playground, it stops, and at the same time the whole cloud starts to ring and chirp, as if it were made up only of tones. It rises and falls, rises and falls, but still it rings and chirps. At last the whole cloud falls down over a hill, the whole cloud at once, and immediately thereafter the hill is completely covered by grey larks, showy red-grey-and-white chaffinches, speckled starlings and yellow-green chickadees.

Right after that another cloud moves across the plain. It stops over every farm, over migrant workers' huts and castles, over market towns and cities, over farms and railway stations, over fishing villages and sugar mills. Every time it stops it draws to it from the farms on the ground below a little upwardly whirling pillar of small grey specks of dust. In this way it grows and grows, and when it is finally gathered and moves up towards Kullaberg it is no longer just a cloud, but a whole cloud bank, so large that it casts a shadow on the ground all the way from Höganäs to Mölle. When it stops over the playground, it blocks the sun, and it has to rain grey sparrows down on one of the hills for a long time before the ones who have flown farthest inside the cloud once again see a glimpse of daylight.

But the largest of these bird clouds is still the one that now appears. It has been formed by flocks that have come travelling from all directions and joined up with it. It is heavy grey-blue, and not a ray of sunshine penetrates through it. It approaches, as gloomy and terrifying as a thundercloud. It is full of the most awful noise, the most horrid shrieking, the most scornful laughter and the most ominous cawing. Everyone at the playground is happy when it finally dissolves in a rain of flapping and cawing, of crows and jackdaws and ravens and rooks.

After that in the sky not only clouds, but a number of different streaks and signs are visible. Then straight, dotted lines appear in the east and north-east. These are forest birds from the counties in Göinge; black grouse and wood grouse, who come flying in long rows a few metres apart from each other. And the swimming birds who stay at the Måkläppen nature reserve outside Falsterbo now come hovering over Öresund in many peculiar flying formations: in triangles and long dashes, in tilted brackets and semicircles.

Akka and her flock came later than all the others to the great meeting that took place the year that Nils Holgersson travelled around with the wild geese, and this was not surprising, because Akka had to fly over all of Skåne to get to Kullaberg. Besides, as soon as she woke up she had been forced to go out and find Thumbkin, who for many hours had been playing for the grey rats and luring them far away from Glimmingehus. The male owl had come back with the message that the black rats would be home again right after sunrise and thus it was no longer a danger to let the barn owl's pipe fall silent and leave the grey rats free to go where they wanted.

But it was not Akka who discovered the boy, where he was going with his long retinue, and quickly descended upon him, encircled him with his beak and soared up in the air with him, but Herr Ermenrich, the stork. For Herr Ermenrich had also gone out to search for him, and once he had brought him up to the stork nest, he asked him to forgive him for having treated him with disrespect the night before.

The boy liked this a lot and he and the stork became good friends. Akka also proved to be very friendly to him, stroking her old head several times against his arm and praising him, because he had helped those who were in distress.

But it must be said in the boy's honour that he did not want to take praise that he had not earned. 'No, Mother Akka,' he said, 'you should not believe that I lured the grey rats away to help the black rats. I only wanted to show Herr Ermenrich that I was good for something.'

He had hardly said this before Akka turned to the stork and asked if he thought it was advisable to take Thumbkin along to Kullaberg. 'I think that we can rely on him like one of us,' she said. The stork at once very eagerly recommended letting Thumbkin go along. 'Of course we will take Thumbkin along to Kullaberg, Mother Akka,' he said. 'It is a joy for us that we can reward him for everything he has withstood tonight for our sake. And because it still mortifies me that last evening I did not conduct myself towards him in a suitable way, I will be the one who carries him on my back to the meeting place.'

There is not much that tastes better than getting praise from those who are themselves wise and capable, and the boy had certainly never felt so happy as when the wild goose and the stork talked about him in this way.

So the boy made the trip up to Kullaberg riding on a stork's back. Although he knew that this was a great honour, it still caused him great anxiety, because Herr Ermenrich was a master at flying and set off at quite a different speed than the wild geese. While Akka flew her direct way with even wing strokes, the stork amused himself with a lot of aerial tricks. One moment he lay quiet at an immeasurable height and floated in the air without moving his wings, the next moment he threw himself downwards at such speed that it appeared he would crash to the ground, helpless as a stone, while the next moment he amused himself by flying around Akka in big and small circles like a whirlwind. The boy had never experienced anything like this before, and although he was in constant terror, he had to admit to himself that until now he had not known what was meant by good flying.

Only a single pause was made during the flight, and that was when Akka reunited at Vombsjön with her travel companions and called to them that the grey rats had been defeated. Then they took the direct route to Kullaberg.

There they landed on top of the hill that was reserved for the wild geese, and now when the boy let his eyes wander from hill to hill, he saw that over one of them rose the many-pronged antlers of the red deer and over another the hackles of the grey herons. One hill was red with foxes, another was black and white from seabirds, one was grey with rats. One was occupied by black ravens that shrieked without ceasing, one with larks who were unable to keep still, but instead constantly threw themselves up in the air and sang with delight.

As has always been the custom at Kullaberg, it was the crows who started the day's games and tricks with their flying dance. They divided into two flocks, which flew towards each other, met, turned and started again. This dance had many turns and, to the audience, who were not initiated in the dance rules, seemed far too monotonous. The crows were very proud of their dance, but all the others were happy when it ended. It seemed to the animals just as gloomy and meaningless as a winter storm playing with snowflakes. They became dejected from watching it and waited eagerly for something that would give them a little joy.

They did not need to wait in vain, for as soon as the crows had finished, the hares came running up. They streamed forth in a long row with no apparent order. In some ranks one came alone, in others three or four ran abreast. All of them got up on two legs and rushed ahead with such speed that their long ears swung in all directions. While they ran, they twirled around, making high leaps and thumbing their front paws against their ribs to make a thumping sound. Some did a long series of somersaults, others curled up and rolled forwards like wheels, one stood on one leg and swung around, one walked on his front legs. There was no order at all, but there was a lot of amusement in the play of the hares, and the many animals who stood and observed them began to breathe faster. It was spring now, pleasure and delight were on the rise. Winter was over. Summer was approaching. Soon living would be only a game.

When the hares had finished romping, it was the big forest birds' turn to perform. Hundreds of male wood grouse in glistening black-brown garb with bright red eyebrows threw themselves up in a large oak in the middle of the playfield. The one who sat on the topmost branch ruffled up his feathers, lowered his wings and turned up his rear end so that the white wing coverts were seen. Then he extended his neck and sent out a couple of deep tones from the thickened throat. 'Sheck, sheck, sheck!' it sounded. More than that he could not get out; it gurgled only a few times deep down in his throat. Then he closed his eyes and whispered, 'Sis, sis, sis. Listen, so pretty! Sis, sis, sis.' And at the same time he fell into such rapture that he no longer knew what was happening around him.

While the first male grouse was still making his 'sis' sounds, the three who sat closest below him started singing, and before they had gone through the whole song, the ten who sat farther down started, and so it continued from branch to branch, until all hundred male grouse were singing and gurgling and making 'sis' sounds. They all fell into the same rapture during their song, and this intoxication in particular spread to the other animals as if it were contagious. Their blood, which had run happily and lightly, now started to move heavy and hot. 'Yes,

it is truly spring,' the many species thought. 'The cold of winter is gone. The fire of spring is burning over the earth.'

When the black grouse noticed that the wood grouse had
such success, they could no longer keep quiet. As there was no
tree where they could take up position, they rushed down on
the playfield, where the heather stood so high that only their
prettily swaying tail feathers and their thick beaks were visible, and started to sing: 'Coo, coo, coo!'

Just as the black grouse began to compete with the wood
grouse, something unheard-of happened. Now, while all the
animals were thinking of nothing but the grouse game, a fox
sneaked quite slowly towards the wild geese's hill. He walked
very carefully and got far up the hill before anyone noticed
him. Suddenly a goose caught sight of him and, as if she could
not believe that a fox had slipped in among the geese for any
good intention, she started calling, 'Watch out, wild geese!
Watch out!' The fox caught her by the throat, perhaps mostly
to silence her, but the wild geese had already heard the call and
all of them flew up into the air. And when they were flying, the
animals saw Smirre Fox standing on the wild geese's hill with
a dead goose in his mouth.

But because he had broken the peace of the play day in this
way, Smirre got such a harsh punishment, so that for all the
days of his life he must regret that he could not control his
desire for revenge, but instead tried to finally get at Akka and
her flock in this manner. He was surrounded at once by a band
of foxes and convicted according to ancient custom, which
enjoins that whosoever disturbs the peace on the great play
day must go into exile. No fox wanted to reduce the sentence,
because they all knew that the moment they tried anything like
that, they would be driven away from the playfield and never
be permitted to set foot on it again. Thus the sentence of exile
was incontestably pronounced over Smirre. He was prohibited
from staying in Skåne. He was exiled from wife and kinsfolk,
from hunting grounds, home, sleeping places and hiding
places, which he had heretofore owned, and must try his luck
in foreign lands. And so that all foxes in Skåne would know
that Smirre was an outlaw in the province, the oldest among

the foxes bit off the tip of his right ear. As soon as this was done, all the young foxes started to howl with bloodthirstiness and threw themselves over Smirre. For him nothing remained other than to take flight, and with all the young foxes at his heels he hurried away from Kullaberg.

All this happened while black grouse and wood grouse were busy with their game. But these birds become so absorbed in their song that they neither hear nor see. They did not let themselves be disturbed either.

The forest birds' competition was barely finished when the red deer from Häckeberga made their appearance to show their battle game. Several pairs of red deer fought at the same time. They rushed at each other with great force, struck their antlers together, thundering, so that the tines were interlaced, and tried to force each other backwards. Tufts of heather were torn up under their hooves, their breath was like smoke, awful bellowing came out of their throats, and the foam flowed down their shoulders.

All around on the hills breathless silence prevailed while the battle-hardened red deer fought each other. And new emotions were aroused in all the animals. Each and every one of them felt brave and strong, enlivened by returning strength, born again by spring, hearty and ready for all types of adventure. They felt no anger towards each other, yet everywhere wings were lifted, neck hairs raised, claws sharpened. If the Häckeberga red deer had continued a moment longer a wild struggle would have arisen on the hills, because everyone had been seized by a burning desire to show that they too were full of life, that the powerlessness of winter was over, that strength was seething in their bodies.

But the red deer stopped fighting just at the right moment, and at once a whisper went from hill to hill: 'Now the cranes are coming.'

And then came the grey, dusk-clad birds with plumes in their wings and red feather jewels on their necks. The big birds with their long legs, their slender necks, their small heads came gliding along the hill in a mysterious delirium. As they glided forward, they turned around, half-flying, half-dancing. With their wings gracefully raised they moved at inconceivable speed. There was something strange and alien about their dance. It was as if grey shadows were playing a game that the eye was barely able to follow. It was as if they had learned from the mists that hover over the lonely bogs. There was magic in this; everyone who had not been at Kullaberg before understood why the whole meeting took its name from the cranes' dance. There was wildness in it, but the feeling that it aroused was nonetheless a sweet longing. No one thought about fighting any more. Instead everyone, both those with wings and those without wings, wanted to rise up above the clouds, seek what was beyond there, leave the heavy body that pulled down towards the earth, and soar away towards the unearthly.

Such longing for the unreachable, for what is hidden behind life, the animals felt only once a year, and it was on that day when they saw the Great Crane Dance.

SIX

In Rainy Weather

It was the first rainy day during the journey. As long as the wild geese had stayed in the area of Vombsjön, the weather was beautiful, but on the day they set off on their expedition northwards it started to rain, and for several hours the boy had to sit on the goose's back soaked and shaking with cold.

In the morning when they left it was clear and calm. The wild geese flew high up in the air, evenly and without haste, in strict order with Akka in the lead and the others in two diagonal rows behind her. They did not give themselves time to call out spiteful remarks to the animals on the ground, but as they were not capable of staying completely silent, they sang out their usual call unceasingly in tempo with their wing strokes: 'Where are you? Here I am! Where are you? Here I am!'

Everyone took part in this persistent calling, and they interrupted it now and then only to show the white gander the

signposts by which they were setting course. During this journey the signs consisted of the barren hills of Linderödsåsen, the
estates of Ovesholm, the church steeples of Kristianstad, the
crown lands of Bäckaskog on the narrow isthmus between Opp-
mann Lake and Ivö Lake and the steep precipices of Ryssberg.

It had been a monotonous trip, and when the rain clouds
started to appear, the boy thought it was a real diversion.
Before, when he had seen rain clouds only from below, he
thought they were grey and boring, but it was quite different to
be up among them. Now he saw clearly that the clouds were
enormous freight wagons driving up in the air with sky-high
loads: some of them were loaded with massive, grey sacks,
some with barrels so large they could hold an entire lake, and
some with big tubs and bottles that were stacked to a tremendous height. And when so many of them had driven by that
they filled all of space, it was as if someone had given a sign,
because all at once – out of tubs, barrels, bottles and sacks –
water started flooding down over the earth.

As soon as the first spring showers pattered against the
ground, such cries of joy were raised by all the small birds in
groves and pastures that the whole air resounded with them,
and the boy jumped high up from where he sat. 'Now we get
rain, rain gives us spring, spring gives us flowers and green
leaves, green leaves and flowers give us larvae and insects, larvae and insects give us food; good and plentiful food is the best
there is,' the small birds sang.

The wild geese too were happy about the rain, which came
to waken the plants out of their slumber and poke holes in the
icy covering on the lakes. They were unable to stay as serious
as they had been so far, so they started sending humorous calls
down over the region.

As they were flying over the large potato fields, of which
there are so many in the area around Kristianstad and which
were still bare and black, they shrieked, 'Wake up and be useful! Here comes something to waken you! Now you've been
lazing long enough!'

When they saw humans hurrying to get out of the rain, they
admonished them and said, 'Why are you in such a hurry?

Don't you see that it's raining rye loaves and layer cakes, rye loaves and layer cakes?'

There was a big, thick cloud that moved quickly towards the north and followed close behind the geese. They seemed to imagine that they were pulling the cloud with them, and just now when they saw large gardens below, they cried quite proudly, 'Here we come with anemones! Here we come with roses! Here we come with apple blossoms and cherry buds! Here we come with peas and beans and turnips and cabbage! Whoever wants can take! Whoever wants can take!'

That is how it sounded while the first showers fell, when everyone was still happy about the rain. But when it continued to fall all afternoon, the geese became impatient and called to the thirsty forests around Ivö Lake, 'Haven't you had enough soon? Haven't you had enough soon?'

The sky became a more solid grey and the sun hid itself so well that no one could see where it was. The rain fell heavier, hammering hard against their wings and working its way between the oiled outer feathers all the way into their bodies. The earth was concealed by fog; lakes, hills and forests flowed together in a blurred jumble, and the signposts could not be made out. The trip went slower and slower, the happy shouts fell silent, and the boy felt the cold more and more bitterly.

But he still kept up his courage, as long as he was riding through the air. And in the afternoon, when they settled down under a little knotty pine tree out in the middle of a large bog, where everything was wet and everything was cold, where some tufts were covered with snow and others were sticking up naked out of a pool of half-melted ice, he had not felt dispirited either, but instead ran around pluckily looking for cranberries and frozen lingonberries. But then came evening and the darkness sank down so densely that even eyes like the boy's could not see through it, and the wilderness became so strangely awful and terrifying. The boy was tucked in under the gander's wing, but could not sleep, because he was cold and wet. And he heard so much rustling and whispering and stealthy steps and threatening voices that he felt such terror he did not know where he should go. He had to get near fire and light, if he was not going to be frightened to death.

'What if I were to venture up to the humans just for this one night?' the boy thought. 'Just so I could sit by a fire and get a bite of food. I could always come back to the wild geese before sunrise.'

He crawled out from under the wing and slid down to the ground. He did not waken the gander or any of the other geese, but instead slipped away, quietly and unnoticed, over the bog.

He did not know exactly where in the world he was, if it was in Skåne, in Småland or in Blekinge. But right before he had come down on the bog he had seen a glimpse of a large village and now he directed his steps there. It did not take long either before he found a road and soon he was on the village street, which was long and tree-lined and edged with farm after farm.

The boy had come to one of the large villages with a church that are so common higher up in the country, but which you don't see at all down on the plain.

The houses were wooden and very neatly built. Most had gables and frontispieces lined with carved edging and glassed-in porches with an occasional coloured pane. The walls were covered with light oil paint, doors and windowsills gleamed in blue and green or even in red. While the boy walked, observing the houses, he heard all the way out on the road how the people inside the warm cottages were talking and laughing. He could not make out the words, but he thought it was lovely to hear human voices. 'I really wonder what they would say if I pounded on the door and asked to be let in?' he thought.

This was what he intended to do, but now his fear of the dark had passed, since he saw the illuminated windows. Instead he again felt that shyness that always came over him in the vicinity of humans. 'I'll look around the village a while longer,' he thought, 'before I ask to come in to someone's house.'

On one house there was a balcony. And just as the boy walked past, the balcony doors were opened and a yellow light streamed out through fine, light curtains. Then a beautiful young woman came out on the balcony and leaned over the railing. 'It's raining, soon it will be spring,' she said. When the boy saw her, he felt a strange anxiety. It was as if he wanted to cry. For the first time he became a bit worried that he had cut himself off from the humans.

Shortly after that he went past a store. Outside the store stood a red seed-drill machine. He stopped and looked at it and finally crept up on to the driver's seat and sat down there. Once he was there, he smacked his lips and pretended he was driving. He thought about how much fun it would be to get to drive such a fine machine across a field. For a moment he forgot what he was like now, but then he remembered, and then he quickly jumped down from the machine. He felt even more worried. Someone who always had to live among animals would probably miss out on a lot. Humans were ever so remarkable and capable.

He went past the post office and thought about all the newspapers that came every day with news from the four corners of the globe. He saw the pharmacy and the doctor's house, and he thought that the power of humans was so great that they could fight against sickness and death. He came to the church and he thought that the humans had erected it so that there they could hear about a world beyond this one in which they lived, about God and resurrection and eternal life. And the farther he walked, the more he thought about humans.

The thing about children is that they think no farther than the tip of their nose. They want to have what is closest at hand without caring what it might cost them. Nils Holgersson did not understand what he had lost when he chose to remain a gnome, but now he was terribly afraid that perhaps he would never get his right form back again.

What in the world should he do to become human? That he would really like to know.

He crawled up on a step and sat down there in the midst of the pouring rain and thought. He sat there for an hour, for two hours, and he thought until his forehead was furrowed. But he was none the wiser. It was as if his thoughts simply ran around in his head. The longer he sat there, the more impossible it seemed to be to find a solution.

'This is surely far too difficult for someone who has learned as little as me,' he thought at last. 'Probably I'll get to go back to the humans in any event. I'll have to ask the minister and the doctor and the schoolteacher and others who are educated and may know the cure for something like this.'

Yes, he decided that he should do that at once, and he stood up and shook himself, because he was as wet as a dog that has been in a puddle.

Just then he saw a big owl come flying and set down in one of the trees that lined the village street. Immediately after that a tawny owl that was sitting under the cornice started moving and called, 'Kee-vit! Kee-vit! Are you home again, short-eared owl? How was it abroad?'

'Thank you very much, tawny owl! I've been fine,' said the short-eared owl. 'Has anything remarkable happened at home while I've been gone?'

'Not here in Blekinge, short-eared owl, but in Skåne it happened that a boy was transformed by a gnome and made as small as a squirrel, and then he travelled to Lapland with a domestic goose.'

'That was a strange piece of news, a strange piece of news. Can he ever be human again, tawny owl? Can he ever be human again?'

'That is a secret, short-eared owl, but you will find out anyway. The gnome said that if the boy watches over the tame gander, so that he comes home unscathed and—'

'What else, tawny owl? What else? What else?'

'Fly with me up into the church steeple, short-eared owl, then you'll find out everything! I'm afraid that there may be someone listening here on the village street.'

With that the owls flew away, but the boy threw his cap high into the air. 'If I just watch over the gander so that he comes home unscathed, then I'll get to be human! Hurrah! Hurrah! Then I'll get to be human!'

He shouted hurrah so that it was strange that they did not hear him in the houses. But they did not, and he hurried out to the wild geese in the wet bog as quickly as his legs could carry him.

SEVEN

The Staircase with Three Steps

The next day the wild geese intended to travel north through Allbo County in Småland. They sent Yksi and Kaksi there to scout, but when they came back they said that all the water was frozen and the ground all covered with snow. 'So please let us stay where we are!' the wild geese said. 'We can't travel across a country where there is neither water nor pasture.'

'If we stay where we are now, we may have to wait a whole lunar cycle,' Akka then said. 'It will be better to travel east through Blekinge and see then if we can cross Småland through Möre County, which is near the coast and where spring comes early.'

In this way the boy came to travel over Blekinge the next day. Now, when it was light, he was in his right frame of mind again and could not understand what had got into him the night before. Now he certainly did not want to give up the journey and the wilderness life.

There was a thick fog over Blekinge. The boy could not see what it looked like there. 'I wonder if it's good country or poor country that I'm riding over,' he thought, digging in his memory for what he had learned about the province in school. But at the same time he probably knew that this would be of no use, because he never used to read the lessons.

Suddenly the boy could picture the whole school before him. The children were sitting at the small desks raising their hands, the teacher sat at his desk looking dissatisfied, and he himself was up by the map and supposed to answer a question about Blekinge, but he did not have a word to say. The schoolteacher's face got darker with every second that passed, and the boy thought that the teacher was more concerned that they should learn their geography than anything else. Now the teacher also came down from his desk, took the pointer from the boy and sent him back to his seat. 'This will not end well,' the boy had thought then.

But the schoolteacher had gone up to a window and stood there for some time looking out, and then he whistled awhile. After that he went back to his desk and said that he would tell them something about Blekinge. And what he told them was so amusing that the boy listened. If he just thought about it, he could recall every word.

'Småland is a tall house with spruce trees on the roof,' the teacher said, 'and in front of it there is a wide staircase with three large steps, and that staircase is called Blekinge.

'This staircase is considerable in size. It reaches eighty kilometres along the front side of the Småland house, and anyone who wants to take the stairs all the way down to the Baltic has forty kilometres to go.

'A good long time has also gone by since the staircase was built. Both days and years have passed since the first step was cut out of granite and set down level and smooth as a comfortable route between Småland and the Baltic.

'As the staircase is so old, you can probably understand that it does not look the same now as when it was new. I don't

know how much they cared about such things at that time, but
as big as it was, no way could any broom manage to keep it
clean. After a few years moss and lichen started to grow on
it, dry grass and dry leaves blew down over it in the autumn,
and in the spring it was showered with falling stones and
gravel. And when all this had to lie there and decompose, at
last so much topsoil was collected on the steps that not only
herbs and grass, but even bushes and large trees could take
root there.

'But at the same time great differences had developed among
the three steps. The top one, which is closest to Småland, is
mostly covered with poor soil and small stones, and there no
trees will grow other than white birch and bird cherry and
spruce, which tolerate the cold at that elevation and are content with little. You can best understand how barren and poor
it is there when you see how small and narrow the fields are
that have been cleared out of the forest, and how small the cottages are that people build for themselves, and how far it is
between churches.

'On the middle step again there is better soil, and it is not
subject to such bitter cold either; there you see at once that the
trees are both taller and of finer varieties. Maple and oak and
linden, weeping birch and hazel grow there, but no conifers.
And you notice even better then that there's a lot of cultivated
ground, and likewise that the people have built big, beautiful
houses. There are many churches on the middle step, and large
villages around them, and it seems in every way better and
grander than the top step.

'But the very bottom step is still the best. It is covered with
good, rich topsoil, and where it bathes in the sea, it does not
have the slightest sensation of the Småland cold. Down here
beech and chestnut and walnut trees thrive, and they grow so
big that they reach above the church roofs. Here are also the
largest fields, but the people have not only the forest and agri-
culture to live on, but they also have fishing and trade and
navigation. For that reason the costliest homes are here and
the most beautiful churches, and the villages with churches
have grown into market towns and cities.

'But with that not all has been said about the three steps. Because you must bear in mind that when it rains up on the roof of the large Småland house, or when the snow melts up there, the water has to go somewhere, and then of course some of it rushes down the big step. In the beginning it probably flowed down over the whole step, wide as it was, but then cracks arose in it, and gradually the water has been accustomed to flowing down it in some well-developed channels. And water is water, whatever you make of it. It never takes any rest. In one place it digs and files and carries away, and in another it deposits. Those channels it has excavated into valleys, the valley walls it has covered with topsoil, and then bushes and creepers have clung firmly to them so densely and so richly that they almost conceal the stream moving along down in the depths. But when the streams come to the landings between the steps, they have to cast themselves headlong down them, and from this the water comes at such foaming speed it has the power to drive mill wheels and machines, the likes of which have sprung up by every rapids.

'But even then not all has yet been said about the country with the three steps. Instead it must also be said that up there in Småland in the big house there once lived a giant who had grown old. And it annoyed him that in his advanced age he would be forced to go down the long step to fish for salmon in the sea. It seemed to him much more suitable that the salmon should come up to him where he lived.

'For that reason he went up on the roof of his big house, and from there he threw large stones down into the Baltic. He hurled them with such force that they flew over all of Blekinge and fell down in the sea. And when the stones hit, the salmon became so afraid that they came out of the sea, fled up the Blekinge streams, rushed off through the rapids, cast themselves with high leaps up waterfalls and did not stop until they were far inside Småland with the old giant.

'How true this is, is shown by the many islands and skerries along the coast of Blekinge, which are none other than the many large stones that the giant threw.

'Along with this you also see that the salmon still enter the

Blekinge streams and work their way through rapids and calm water all the way to Småland.

'But this giant deserves much gratitude and respect from the inhabitants of Blekinge, because the trout fishing in the streams and stonecutting in the archipelago is labour that feeds many of them up to this day.'

EIGHT
By Ronneby River

Neither the wild geese nor Smirre Fox thought they would meet again, once they had left Skåne. But it so happened that the wild geese took the route over Blekinge, and Smirre Fox had also made his way there. So far he had stayed in the northern part of the province, and there he had not yet seen any manor parks or game preserves full of deer and tasty fawns. He was more dissatisfied than he could say.

One afternoon, as Smirre was prowling around in a deserted woodland in the middle region, Mellanbygden, not far from Ronneby River, he happened to see a flock of wild geese flying through the air. He noticed right away that one of the geese was white, and then he knew who he was dealing with.

Smirre started chasing after the geese at once, as much from the desire for a good meal as to get revenge on them for all the trouble they had caused him. He saw that they were travelling east until they came to Ronneby River. Then they changed direction and followed the river towards the south. He understood that they intended to find a place to sleep along the riverbank, and he thought that he could seize a couple of them without any great difficulty.

But when Smirre finally caught sight of the place where the geese had settled down, he noticed they had chosen such a well-protected place that he could not get at them.

Ronneby River is, of course, no great or mighty waterway, but nevertheless it is much talked about for its beautiful beaches. In several places it advances through steep rock walls, which stand vertically out of the water and are completely overgrown with honeysuckle and bird cherry, with hawthorn and alder, with mountain ash and willow, and there are few things more agreeable on a lovely summer day than rowing on the dark little river and looking up at all the tender greenery that clings firmly to the rough rock walls.

But now, when the wild geese and Smirre came to the river, it was cold and raw late winter, all the trees were bare and there was probably no one who had the slightest thought of whether the sandy beaches were ugly or beautiful. The wild geese praised their good fortune that under such a steep rock wall they had found a strip of sand big enough that there was room for them. In front of them roared the river, which was swift and strong now as the snow was melting, behind them they had an unscalable cliff, and hanging branches hid them. They could not have done better.

The geese fell asleep at once, but the boy could not sleep a wink. As soon as the sun was gone, he felt fear of the dark and terror of the wilderness and longed for humans. Where he was tucked in under the goose wing, he could not see anything and could hear only poorly, and he thought that if something bad happened to the gander, he would not be in a position to rescue him. He heard rustling and stirring from all directions, and he got so restless that he had to crawl out from under the wing and get on the ground alongside the goose.

Disappointed, Smirre stood on the crown of the hill and looked down on the wild geese. 'You can just as well abandon this pursuit at once,' he said to himself. 'You can't climb down

such a steep hill, you can't swim in such a wild current, and
there isn't the slightest strip of land below the rock that leads
up to their sleeping place. Those geese are too smart for you.
Don't bother hunting them any more!'

But Smirre, like other foxes, had a hard time abandoning an
enterprise once started, and therefore he lay down on the far
edge of the hill and did not take his eyes off the wild geese.
While he lay there, observing them, he thought about all the
evil they had done him. Yes, it was on their account that he
had been exiled from Skåne and had to flee to impoverished
Blekinge. He worked himself up so much while he was lying
there that he wished the wild geese were dead, even if he would
not get to eat them himself.

When Smirre's indignation had reached such a height, he
heard a rasping sound in a large pine tree growing close beside
him, and saw a squirrel come down out of the tree, fiercely
pursued by a marten. Neither of them noticed Smirre, and he
sat quietly and observed the chase, which went from tree to
tree. He watched the squirrel, who moved among the branches
as easily as if he could fly. He watched the marten, who was
not nearly as skilful a climber as the squirrel, but nonetheless
ran up and down the tree trunks as securely as if they were
smooth paths in the forest. 'If I could only climb half as well as
either of them,' the fox thought, 'those geese down here
wouldn't get to sleep peacefully for long.'

As soon as the squirrel had been captured and the hunt was
over, Smirre went up to the marten, but stopped two paces
away, as a sign that he did not want to rob him of his prey. He
greeted the marten in a very friendly way and congratulated him
on his catch. Smirre chose his words well, as foxes always do.
The marten, on the other hand, who, with his long, narrow
body, his fine head, his soft skin and the light-brown patch on
his neck looked like a minor marvel of beauty, was in reality
only a crude forest-dweller and he barely answered him. 'It sur-
prises me anyway,' said Smirre, 'that a hunter like you is content
to hunt squirrels, when there is much better game within reach.'
Here he stopped, but when the marten only sneered at him quite
shamelessly, he continued. 'Can it be possible that you haven't

seen the wild geese that are here under the rock wall? Or aren't you a good enough climber to get down to them?'

This time he did not need to wait for an answer. The marten rushed towards him with his back arched and every hair on end. 'Have you seen wild geese?' he hissed. 'Where are they? Speak up at once, otherwise I'll bite off your neck!'

'No, you have to remember that I'm twice as big as you, and be a bit respectful. I'm asking nothing more than to be able to show you the wild geese.'

The next moment the marten was on his way down the steep, and while Smirre sat and watched him swing his snake-thin body from branch to branch, he thought, 'That beautiful tree-hunter has the cruellest heart in the whole forest. I think the wild geese will have me to thank for a bloody awakening.'

But just as Smirre waited to hear the death cries of the geese, he saw the marten fall from a branch and splash down in the river, so that the water sprayed up high. Right after that there was a strong slap of hard wings and all the geese took off in urgent flight.

Smirre intended to hurry after the geese at once, but he was so curious to find out how they had been rescued that he stayed seated until the marten came climbing up. The poor thing was soaking wet and stopped now and then to rub his head with his front paws. 'I didn't expect *you* to be a clumsy oaf that would fall in the river,' Smirre said contemptuously.

'I'm not clumsy. You don't need to scold me,' said the marten. 'I was already on one of the lowest branches, thinking about how I was going to get a chance to tear a whole lot of geese apart, when a little imp, no bigger than a squirrel, rushed up and threw a rock at my head with such force that I fell into the water, and before I had time to crawl out—'

The marten did not have to continue the story. He no longer had an audience. Smirre was already far away, in search of the geese.

In the meantime, Akka had flown south, while she looked for a new place to sleep. There was still a bit of daylight and in addition the half-moon was high in the sky, so that she could more or less see. By great good luck she was well at home in that area,

because more than once she had been wind-driven towards Blekinge when she travelled over the Baltic in the spring.

She followed the river as long as she saw it wind ahead
through the moonlit landscape like a black, shiny snake. In so
doing she came all the way down to Djupafors, where the river
first hides itself in an underground channel and then, clear and
transparent, as if it were made of glass, rushes down in a narrow
ravine, against whose bottom it breaks apart in glistening drops
with foam flying around. Below the white falls were some
stones, between which the water rushed away in wild rapids,
and here Akka set down. This was once again a good sleeping
place, especially so late in the evening when no humans are
about. At sundown the geese probably could not have settled
down there, because Djupafors is not in a wilderness. On one
side of the falls is a wood-pulp mill, and on the other, which is
steep and tree-covered, is Djupadal Park, where humans are
constantly strolling around on the bare, steep paths to delight in
the turbulent motion of the wild stream down in the ravine.

It was the same way here as at the previous place, that none
of the travellers had the slightest thought that they had come
to a beautiful, renowned place. If anything, they probably
thought it was awful and dangerous to sleep on slippery, wet
stones in the middle of roaring rapids. But they had to be satisfied, because they were protected from predators.

The geese fell asleep at once, but the boy was too restless to
sleep, and sat beside them to watch over the gander.

In a while Smirre came running along the riverbank. He
caught sight of the geese at once, where they were out in the
whirling foam, and understood that he could not get at them
now either. But he could not make himself abandon them.
Instead he sat down on the shore and observed them. He felt
very humiliated and thought that his entire reputation as a
hunter was at stake.

All at once he saw an otter come crawling up out of the rapids
with a fish in his mouth. Smirre went towards him, but stayed
two paces away, to show that he did not want to take the prey
from him. 'You are a remarkable one, content to catch fish when
there are plenty of wild geese out on the stones,' said Smirre. He

was so eager that he did not have time to choose his words as well as he usually did. The otter did not even turn his head towards the stream. He was a tramp like all otters; he had fished many times at Vombsjön and knew all about Smirre Fox. 'I think I know how you go about getting a salmon by trickery, Smirre,' he said.

'I see, it's you, Gripe,' Smirre said happily, because he knew that this otter was a bold, skilful swimmer. 'I'm not surprised that you don't want to look at the wild geese, when you're unable to get out to them.' But the otter, who had webbed toes, a stiff tail that was as good as an oar, and fur impervious to moisture, did not want it said about him that there was a rapids he could not deal with. He turned towards the stream and as soon as he caught sight of the wild geese, he threw the fish away and rushed down the steep bank into the river.

If it had been later in the spring, so that the nightingales in Djupadal Park had been at home, they would have sung for many nights about Gripe's struggle with the rapids. Because the otter was carried off several times by the waves and conveyed down the river, but he steadily fought his way back up again. He swam ahead in the backwater, he crawled over stones and gradually got closer to the wild geese. It was a perilous journey that deserved to be celebrated in song by the nightingales.

Smirre followed his route with his eyes as best he could. At last he saw that the otter was in the process of climbing up to the wild geese. But just then there was a shrill, wild scream. The otter fell backwards down into the water and was carried away, as if he had been a blind kitten. Immediately after that there was a hard flapping of goose wings. They took off and went away to find a different place to sleep.

The otter soon came up on land. He did not say anything and started licking one of his front paws. When Smirre mocked him because he hadn't succeeded, he burst out, 'There was nothing wrong with my swimming, Smirre. I made it all the way up to the geese and was about to reach them, when a little imp came running and cut me on the paw with some sharp iron. It hurt so much that I lost my footing and then the rapids took me.'

He did not need to say more. Smirre was already far away, in search of the geese.

Yet again Akka and her flock had to fly away into the night. By great good luck the moon had not gone down, and with the help of its light she succeeded in finding another of the sleeping places that she knew about in that area. She again followed the glistening river towards the south. Over Djupadal's estate and over the dark roofs and white waterfalls of Ronneby she soared ahead without setting down. But a bit south of the city, not far from the sea, are the Ronneby mineral springs with bathhouse and well-house, with large hotels and summer lodgings for visitors. All of this is empty and deserted throughout the winter, which every bird knows, and many are the flocks of birds that seek shelter during heavy storms in the abandoned buildings' terraces and verandas.

Here the wild geese settled down on a balcony, and as usual they fell asleep at once. The boy, on the other hand, could not sleep, because he did not want to crawl in under the gander's wing.

The balcony faced south, so that the boy had a view of the sea. And now when he could not sleep, he sat and looked at how nice it was when sea and land met here in Blekinge.

You see, it is the case that sea and land can meet in many different ways. In many places the land comes down to the sea with flat, grassy meadows, and the sea meets the land with drift sand which it sets up in walls and dunes. It is as if they both thought so badly of each other, that they only wanted to show the worst they have. But it can also happen that when the land comes down towards the sea, it raises up a wall of rock in front of it, as if the sea were something dangerous; and when the land does that, the sea comes against it with angry breakers, whipping and roaring and striking against the rocks and looking as if it wants to tear apart the shore.

But in Blekinge it is completely different when sea and land meet. There the land splits apart in promontories and islands and islets, and the sea divides itself into fjards and bays and sounds, and perhaps it is because of this that it looks as if they are meeting in joy and concord.

Now think first and foremost about the sea! Far out it is deserted and empty and large and has nothing to do other than roll its grey waves. When it comes in towards land, it encounters the first skerry. This it takes possession of at once, tearing off every-thing green and making it just as bare and grey as itself. Then it meets another skerry. It does the same with this one. And yet another. Yes, it does the same with this one too. It is disrobed and plundered, as if it has fallen into the hands of pirates. But then the skerries become ever denser and then the sea must understand that the land is sending out its smallest children to move it to leniency. It becomes more and more friendly too, the farther in it comes, rolling its waves less high, subduing its storms, leaving the greenery alone in cracks and crevasses, dividing itself into small sounds and bays and at last near land becoming so harmless that small boats venture out on it. It can certainly not recognize itself, so light and friendly has it become.

And then think about the land! It is monotonous and the same almost everywhere. It consists of flat fields with an occasional meadow covered with birches between them or else of extended forest ridges. It looks as if it only thinks about oats and turnips and potatoes and spruce and pine. Then comes a bay, which cuts far into it. It does not care about that, but instead borders it with birch and alder, as if it were an ordinary freshwater lake. Then another bay makes an entry. The land does not bother to make a fuss about this either, instead it gets the same covering as the first one. But then the fjards start to expand and break up. They split up the fields and forests, and then the land cannot avoid noticing them. 'I think it's the sea itself that is coming,' says the land, and then it starts to dress up. It wreathes itself with flowers, goes up and down in hills and casts islands out into the sea. It no longer wants to hear about spruce and pine, instead it casts them aside like old everyday clothes and shows off with oak trees and linden and chestnut and with flowering meadows and becomes as grand as a country estate. And when it meets the sea, it is so trans-formed that it cannot recognize itself.

You cannot really see all that until it is summer, but the boy noticed anyway how mild and friendly nature was, and he started to feel calmer than earlier in the night. Then suddenly he heard a loud and awful howl from down in the bathhouse park. And when he jumped up he saw a fox standing in the white moonlight on the open area under the balcony. For

Smirre had followed the geese yet again. But when he found the place where they had settled down, he understood that now it was impossible for him to get at them in any way, and then he could not keep from howling in frustration.

When the fox howled like that, old Akka, the lead goose, woke up and, although she could see almost nothing, she thought she recognized the voice. 'Is that you, Smirre, who is out tonight?' she said.

'Yes,' said Smirre, 'it's me, and now I want to ask you geese what you think about the night that I've arranged for you.'

'Do you mean to say that you're the one who sent both the marten and the otter?' Akka asked.

'A good deed should not be denied,' said Smirre. 'Once you played the goose game with me. Now I've started playing the fox game with you, and I am of no mind to stop, as long as a single one of you is alive, if I am forced to follow you all over the country.'

'Smirre, you ought to think about whether it is right of you, who is armed with both tooth and claw, to persecute us, who are defenceless, in this way,' said Akka.

Smirre thought that Akka sounded scared, and he said quickly, 'Akka, if you want to throw that Thumbkin down to me, who has opposed me so many times, then I promise to make peace with you. I will never again persecute either you or any of yours.'

'I cannot give you Thumbkin,' said Akka. 'From the youngest to the oldest of us we will gladly give our lives for his sake.'

'If you're so fond of him,' said Smirre, 'then I promise you that he will be the first among you that I take revenge on.'

Akka said no more, and after Smirre had let out a few more howls, everything was silent. The boy was still awake. Now it was Akka's words to the fox that kept him from sleeping. He never would have thought that he would hear something so grand, that someone would risk their life for his sake. From that moment it could no longer be said of Nils Holgersson that he did not like anyone.

NINE
Karlskrona

It was a moonlit evening in Karlskrona, beautiful and calm. Earlier in the day it had stormed and rained, and the humans must have thought that the bad weather still continued, because hardly any of them had ventured out on to the street.

While the city was so deserted, Akka, the wild goose, and her flock came flying down towards it over the islands of Vämmön and Pantarholmen. They were out in the late evening to find a safe place to sleep in the archipelago. They could not stay on land, because they were harassed by Smirre Fox wherever they settled down.

As the boy now rode along high up in the air and looked at the sea and the archipelago spread out in front of him, he thought that everything seemed strange and spooky. The sky was no longer blue, but instead arched over him like a cover of green glass. The sea was milky white. As far as he could see

small white waves were rolling with a silver shimmer at their
tops. In the midst of this whiteness the numerous archipelago
islands were completely coal black. Whether they were large or
small, even if they were like meadows or full of cliffs, they
appeared equally black. Yes, even houses and churches and
windmills, which are usually white or red, were outlined in
black against the green sky. The boy thought that it was as if
the earth had been exchanged below him, and that he had
come to another world.

He was just thinking that this night he would stay brave and
not be afraid, when he saw something that really frightened
him. It was a high rocky island covered with large, angular
blocks, and between the black blocks were shining flecks of
bright, shimmering gold. He could not keep from thinking
about Maglestenen at Trolle-Ljungby, the big stone the trolls
sometimes raised up on high gold pillars, and he wondered
whether this was something along the same lines.

But it probably would have been all right anyway with the
stones and the gold, if there hadn't been so many monsters in
the water around the island. They looked like whales and
sharks and other large sea creatures, but the boy understood
that it was the sea trolls who had gathered around the island
and intended to crawl up on it to fight with the land trolls who
lived there. And the ones on land were probably afraid, because
he saw how a large giant stood at the very top of the island and
raised his arms, as if in despair at all the misfortune that would
befall him and his island.

The boy became more than a little terrified when he noticed
that Akka started to descend right over this island. 'No, not
that! We can't very well land there!' he said.

But the geese continued to descend, and soon the boy was
surprised at how he could have been so wrong. For one thing,
the big stone blocks were nothing more than buildings. The
whole island was a city, and the shining gold patches were lan-
terns and illuminated rows of windows. The giant that stood
at the top of the island, reaching out his arms, was a church
with two steep towers, and all the trolls and monsters of the
sea that he thought he saw were boats and vessels of every type

moored all around the island. On the side that was towards
land were mostly rowboats and sloops and small coastal
steamers, but on the side that faced towards the sea were
armour-clad warships, some broad with enormously thick,
backward-leaning chimneys, others long and narrow and
shaped so that they could glide through the water like fish.

What kind of city could this be? Well, the boy could figure
that out because he saw the many warships. He had been inter-
ested in ships his whole life, although he had not dealt with
any other than the galleons he sailed in the ditch by the road.
He knew very well that the city where there were so many warships could be none other than Karlskrona.

The boy's grandfather had been an old sailor, and as long as
he lived every day he talked about Karlskrona, about the big
naval shipyard and about everything else there was to see there
in the city. Here the boy felt completely at home and he was
happy to be able to see everything he had heard so much about.

But he got only a glimpse of the towers and the fortifications
that closed the entrance to the harbour, and of the many buildings at the shipyard, before Akka settled down on one of the
flat church towers.

It was probably a safe place for anyone who wanted to get
away from a fox, and the boy started to wonder if he dared to
creep in under the gander's wing for this one night. Yes, he definitely did; it would be good for him to sleep a bit. He would
try to see a little more of the shipyard and the vessels when it
was light.

The boy thought that it was strange that he could not stay still
and wait until the morning to see the ships. He had probably
not slept for five minutes before he slid out from under the
wing and climbed down the lightning rod and the gutters all
the way to the ground.

He was soon standing on a large square that spread out in
front of the church. It was paved with cobblestones and just as
difficult for him to walk across as it is for big people to walk
on a brush-covered meadow. Those who are used to being in
the wilderness or who live far out in the country always feel

anxious when they come into a city, where the buildings stand
straight and stiff and the streets are open, so that each and
every one can see anyone who is walking there. And it was the
same way now for the boy. As he stood on the big Karlskrona
square and looked at the German church and city hall and the
big church he had just come down from, he wished for nothing
more than to be back up on the tower with the geese.

It was fortunate that the square was completely empty. There
was not a person, if you didn't count a statue that stood there
on a tall pedestal. The boy looked for a long time at the statue,
which depicted a large, burly man in a three-cornered hat, long
coat, knee breeches and rough shoes, and wondered what kind
of person he was. He held a long stick in his hand and looked
as if he was about to make use of it too, because he had a dreadfully stern face with a big, crooked nose and an ugly mouth.

'What's this long-lip doing here?' the boy said at last. He
had never felt so little and pitiful as that evening. He tried to
cheer himself up by saying an impertinent word. Then he
thought no more about the statue, but instead turned on to a
broad street that led down to the sea.

But the boy had not walked far before he heard that someone was coming after him. Someone was walking behind him
who stamped on the stone pavement with heavy feet and struck
the ground with a tipped cane. It sounded as if the bronze fellow himself up on the square had gone out for a walk.

The boy listened for the steps while he ran down the street,
and he became more and more certain that it was the bronze
fellow. The ground trembled and the buildings shook. It could
be none other than him who walked so heavily, and the boy
was afraid when he thought about what he had just said to him.
He did not dare turn his head to see whether it really was him.

'Maybe he's just out walking for the fun of it,' the boy
thought. 'He can't very well be after me because of what I said.
I didn't mean it badly at all.'

Instead of walking straight ahead and trying to get down to
the shipyard, the boy turned off on a street that led to the
east. First and foremost he wanted to get away from whoever
was walking after him.

But right after that he heard that the bronze fellow had turned on to the same street, and the boy got so scared he did not know right off where he should look. And it was hard to find any hiding places in a city where all the gates are closed! Then to his right he saw an old wooden church that was a bit off the street in the middle of a large garden. He did not consider for a moment, but rushed towards the church. 'If I just get there, I'm sure I'll be protected from all evil,' he thought.

As he ran ahead, he suddenly caught sight of a fellow standing on a sandy path waving to him. 'That may be someone who wants to help me,' the boy thought, and happily hurried in that direction. He was truly so scared that his heart was pounding in his chest.

But when he came up to the fellow who stood at the edge of the sandy path on a little stool, he was quite alarmed. 'This can't very well be the one who waved at me,' he thought, because he saw that the entire fellow was made of wood.

He stood there and stared at him. He was a rough fellow on short legs with a broad, ruddy face, shiny, black hair and full black beard. On his head he wore a black wooden hat, on his body a brown wooden coat, around his waist a black wooden sash, on his legs he had wide, grey wooden knee breeches and wooden stockings and on his feet black wooden boots. He was freshly painted and newly varnished, so that he glistened and shone in the moonlight, and this probably helped give him such a good-natured appearance that the boy immediately felt confidence in him.

In his left hand he held a wooden slate, and there the boy read:

> I very humbly beg you,
> Although my voice is flat:
> Please drop a coin inside,
> But first lift up my hat!

So, the fellow was only a poor box. The boy felt disappointed. He had expected it to be something really remarkable. And now he remembered that Grandfather had also talked about this wooden fellow and said that all the children in Karlskrona liked him very much. And this was probably true, because he also had a hard time separating himself from the wooden fellow. There was something so old-fashioned about him that you could easily take him to be hundreds of years old, and at the same time he looked so strong and plucky and full of life, just as you might imagine that people were in the past.

The boy was enjoying looking at the wooden fellow so much that he completely forgot the other one that he was fleeing from. But now he heard him. He turned off from the street and came into the churchyard. He was after him here too! Where should the boy go?

At once he saw the wooden fellow bend down towards him and reach out his big, broad hand. It was impossible to think him other than good, and with a hop the boy was standing in his hand. And the wooden fellow lifted him to his hat and stuck him in under it.

The boy was only just hidden and the wooden fellow had only just got his arm down in the right place again when the bronze fellow stopped in front of him and pounded his cane on the ground so that the wooden fellow shook on his stool. Then the bronze fellow said in a strong, ringing voice, 'Who are you?'

The wooden fellow's arm went upwards, so that the old lumber creaked, and he touched the brim of his hat as he answered, 'Rosenbom, if I may say so, Your Majesty. At one time petty officer first class on the ship of the line *Daring*, after completion of military service sexton at the Admiralty Church, most recently carved in wood and set out on the churchyard as a poor box.'

The boy gave a start when he heard the wooden fellow say 'Your Majesty'. Because now when he thought about it, he knew that the statue on the square depicted the person who had founded the city. It was probably no less than Charles XI himself that he had come up against.

'You give a good account of yourself,' said the bronze fellow. 'Can you also tell me now if you've seen a little lad running around the city tonight? He's an impudent scoundrel and if I just get hold of him I'll teach him some manners.' With that he once again pounded the cane on the ground and looked terribly angry.

'If I may say so, Your Majesty, I just saw him,' the wooden fellow said, and the boy became so scared that he started trembling where he sat, curled up under the hat, looking at the bronze fellow through a crack in the wood. But he calmed down when the wooden fellow continued: 'Your Majesty is on the wrong track. That lad surely had the intention of running into the shipyard and hiding there.'

'Do you say so, Rosenbom? Yes, don't stand there any longer on your stool, but come with me and help me find him! Four eyes are better than two, Rosenbom.'

But the wooden fellow answered in a mournful voice, 'I would most humbly ask to stay here where I am. I look fresh and shiny because of the paint, but I am old and rotten and don't tolerate moving around.'

The bronze fellow was probably not one of those who likes to be contradicted. 'What sort of talk is that? Come on now, Rosenbom!' And he raised his long cane and gave the other one a thundering blow across the shoulder. 'You see, you hold up just fine, Rosenbom!'

With that they departed and went along the streets of Karlskrona, great and mighty, until they reached a high gate that led into the shipyard. Outside there one of the fleet's sailors was on watch, but the bronze fellow simply strode past him and kicked open the gate, without the sailor taking any notice.

As soon as they had come into the shipyard, they saw before them an extensive harbour, divided with pile bridges. In the various wet docks were warships that looked bigger and more frightful close up than earlier when the boy had seen them from above. 'It wasn't so crazy to think that they were sea trolls,' he thought.

'Where do you find it most advisable that we begin the search, Rosenbom?' the bronze fellow said.

'Someone like him could probably most easily hide himself in the model hall,' the wooden fellow answered.

On a narrow strip of land that extended to the right from the gate all along the harbour were old-fashioned buildings.

The bronze fellow went up to a building with low walls, small windows and a good-sized roof. He thrust his staff against the door so that it sprang open and stamped up a stairway with worn steps. After that they came into a large hall that was filled with full-rigged small vessels. The boy realized, without anyone telling him, that these were models of the ones that had been built for the Swedish navy.

There were many different types. There were old ships of the line with their sides studded with cannon, with high structures fore and aft and the masts weighed down by a jumble of sails and ropes. There were small archipelago vessels with rowing benches along the sides of the ship, there were undecked cannon sloops and richly gilded frigates, which were models of those that the kings had used on their journeys. Finally there were also the heavy, broad armoured vessels with towers and cannon on the deck, which are in use nowadays, and narrow, shiny torpedo boats, which resembled long, slender fish.

When the boy was carried around among all of this, he was quite astounded. 'That such big and grand vessels have been built here in Sweden!' he thought to himself.

He had plenty of time to observe what was in there, because when the bronze fellow saw the models, he forgot everything else. He looked at them all, from the first to the last, and asked about them. And Rosenbom, petty officer first class on the *Daring*, told as much as he knew about the ships' builders and about those who had guided them, and about the fates they had met. He told about Chapman and Puke and Trolle, about Hogland and Svensksund, all the way up to 1809, because after that he had no longer been involved.

Both he and the bronze fellow had the most to say about the grand old wooden ships. They did not seem to really understand the new armoured ships.

'I hear that you don't know anything about these new ones, Rosenbom,' the bronze fellow said. 'So let's go and look at something else! Because this amuses me, Rosenbom.'

Now he had surely completely stopped looking for the boy, who could feel secure and calm in his place in the wooden hat.

After that the two fellows wandered through the large installations: the sailmaker's workshop and the anchor smithy, machine and carpentry shops. They saw the mast cranes and the docks, the large warehouses, the artillery yard, the armoury, the long ropewalk and the large, abandoned dock that had been blasted out of the rock. They went out on the pile bridges where the naval vessels were tied up, climbed on board and inspected them like two old salts, asking and rejecting and approving and getting aggravated.

The boy sat securely under the wooden hat and heard about how they had worked and struggled at this place to equip all the fleets that had departed from here. He heard how life and blood had been ventured, how the last mite had been sacrificed in order to build the warships, how ingenious men had exerted all their energy to improve and complete these vessels, which had safeguarded the fatherland. There were a couple of times when the boy got tears in his eyes when he heard about all this. And he was happy to learn so much.

At the very last they went into an open yard where the figureheads from old ships of the line were set up. And the boy had never seen a more remarkable sight, because these figureheads had incredibly powerful, terrifying faces. They were large, daring and wild, filled with the same proud spirit that had equipped the big ships. They were from a different time than his. He thought he shrivelled up in front of them.

But when they got here, the bronze fellow said to the wooden fellow, 'Take off your hat, Rosenbom, for those who stand here! They have always been in battle for the fatherland.'

And Rosenbom had forgotten why they had started the tour, he and the bronze fellow. Without stopping to think he raised the wooden hat from his head and called out, 'I raise my hat to the one who chose the harbour and founded the shipyard and recreated the fleet, for the king who has brought all this to life.'

'Thanks, Rosenbom! That was well said. You're a splendid fellow, Rosenbom. But what's this, Rosenbom?'

For there stood Nils Holgersson in the middle of Rosenbom's bald pate. But he was no longer afraid, instead he raised his white cap and shouted, 'Hurrah for you, Long-Lip!'

The bronze fellow pounded his cane hard on the ground, but the boy never found out what he meant to do, because now the sun came up and with that both the bronze fellow and the wooden fellow disappeared, as if they had been made of mist. While he was still standing and staring after them, the wild geese flew up from the church tower and floated back and forth over the city. Suddenly they caught sight of Nils Holgersson and then the big white goose shot down out of the sky and picked him up.

TEN

Journey to Öland

The wild geese went out to an island in the archipelago to graze. They encountered some grey geese there who were astonished to see them, because they knew very well that their kinsfolk, the wild geese, prefer to travel over the interior of the country. They were curious and inquisitive and were not content until the wild geese told them about the persecution they had to endure from Smirre Fox. When they had finished, one grey goose, who seemed to be as old and as wise as Akka herself, said, 'It was a great misfortune for you that the fox was declared an outlaw in his own country. He will certainly keep his word and follow you all the way up to Lapland. If I were you I would not travel north over Småland, but instead take the outer route to Öland, so that he loses the trail completely. In order to really confound him you should stay on the south cape of Öland for a few days. There's plenty of food and plenty of company there. I don't think you'll regret it if you travel that way.'

This was truly wise advice, which the wild geese decided to follow. As soon as they had eaten their fill they started the journey to Öland. None of them had ever been there before, but the grey geese had given them good markers. They had only to travel straight south, until they encountered the big flyway that passed outside the Blekinge coast. All the birds that spent the winter by the North Sea and now were going to Finland and Russia flew there, and in passing they would all land in Öland to rest. The wild geese would have no difficulty finding guides.

That day it was completely still and hot, as on a summer's day, the best weather you could imagine for a sea journey. The only disquieting thing was that it was not completely clear; the sky was grey and hazy. Here and there were huge masses of clouds that hung all the way down to the surface of the sea and blocked the view.

When the travellers had passed the skerries the sea broadened out so smooth and reflective that the boy, when he happened to look down, thought the water had disappeared. There was no longer any earth below him. He had nothing but clouds and sky around him. He became quite dizzy and clung firmly to the goose's back, more anxious than when he first sat there. It was as if he could not possibly hold on; he had to fall in some direction.

It got even worse when they reached the great flyway that the grey goose had talked about. There, truly, flock after flock came flying in the very same direction. It was as if they followed a staked-out path. There were ducks and grey geese, velvet scoters and guillemots, divers and long-tailed ducks, mergansers and grebes, oystercatchers and common scoters. When the boy leaned forwards and looked in the direction where the sea ought to be, he saw the whole bird train reflected in the water. But he was so dizzy that he did not understand how this happened; he thought that the whole band of birds was flying with their bellies facing up. He did not think much about this anyway, because he himself did not know what was up and what was down.

The birds were exhausted and impatient to arrive. None of them shrieked or said a funny word, which meant that everything seemed strangely unreal.

'What if we've travelled away from the world?' he said to himself. 'What if we're on our way up to heaven?'

He saw nothing but clouds and birds around him and started to think it was reasonable that they were travelling towards heaven. He was happy and wondered what he would see up there. His dizziness went away at once. He was so terribly happy at the thought that he was on his way up to heaven and leaving the Earth.

Just then he heard the crack of a couple of shots and saw several small white pillars of smoke rise up.

There was worry and commotion among the birds. 'Hunters! Hunters! Hunters in boats!' they cried. 'Fly high! Fly away!'

Then the boy finally saw that they were still travelling over the surface of the sea, and that they were not in heaven at all. There were small boats in a long row, filled with hunters who were firing shot after shot. The flocks of birds in the forefront had not noticed them in time. They had stayed too low. Several dark bodies sank down towards the sea, and for each and every one that fell, loud cries of distress were raised by the living.

It was strange for anyone who had just believed himself to be in heaven to wake up to such terror and lamentation. Akka shot towards the heights as fast as she could, and then the flock set off at the greatest possible speed. The wild geese also got away unscathed, but the boy could not recover from his astonishment. Imagine that someone would want to shoot at the likes of Akka and Yksi and Kaksi and the gander and the others! The humans had no idea what they were doing.

Then they were moving ahead again in the still air, and it was quiet like just before, with the exception that a few exhausted birds shouted now and then, 'Will we be there soon? Are you sure we're going the right way?' With that the ones who were flying in the lead answered, 'We're right by Öland! Right by Öland!'

The mallards were tired, and the divers went past them. 'Don't be in such a hurry!' the ducks called. 'You'll eat up all our food!'

'There's enough for all of us!' the divers answered.

Before they had gone far enough that they could see Öland, a faint wind came towards them. It brought with it something that resembled masses of white smoke, as if there were a great fire somewhere.

When the birds saw the first white whirls, they became anxious and increased their speed. But whatever it was that was like smoke billowed forth even denser and finally enveloped them completely. No smell was detected and the smoke was not dark and dry, but white and damp. The boy suddenly understood that it was nothing other than fog.

When the fog became so dense that you could not see a goose-length in front of you, the birds started to behave like real lunatics. All of them, who had flown along before in such good order, started playing in the fog. They flew this way and that to lead each other astray. 'Watch out!' they called. 'You're just flying aimlessly! Turn around, for goodness' sake! You won't get to Öland that way!'

Everyone knew very well where the island was, but they did their best to mislead each other. 'Look at those long-tailed ducks!' voices sounded in the fog. 'They're flying back to the North Sea!'

'Watch out, greylags!' another shrieked from a different direction. 'If you continue that way, you'll go all the way to Rügen!'

There was, as said, no danger that the birds who were used to travelling here would let themselves be fooled into going in the wrong direction. But what made it difficult was the wild geese. The practical jokers noticed that they were not sure about the way and did everything they could to confuse them.

'Where are you going, good folk?' called a swan. He came right up to Akka and looked sympathetic and serious.

'We're travelling to Öland, but we've never been there before,' said Akka. She thought that this was a bird that could be trusted.

'That's too bad,' said the swan. 'They've lured you astray. You're on your way to Blekinge. Come with me now, I'll show you the right way!'

And then he set off with them, and when he had led them so far away from the main thoroughfare that they heard no calls, he disappeared in the fog.

Now they flew around for a while completely at random. They had barely managed to find the birds again, before a duck came up to them. 'It's best that you settle down on the water, until the fog goes away,' the duck said. 'It shows that you aren't used to finding your way while travelling.'

It cannot be denied that the rogues succeeded in making Akka dizzy. As far as the boy could tell, the wild geese flew around a long time.

'Watch out! Don't you see that you're flying upside down?' called a diver as he rushed past. The boy involuntarily took hold of the gander's neck. That was something he had feared for a long time.

No one can say when they would have got there if a muffled rolling shot had not been heard far away.

Then Akka stuck out her neck, flapped her wings hard and hurried up. Now she had something to be guided by. The grey goose had just told her that she should not settle down at the far end of Öland's south cape, because there was a cannon there that the humans use to shoot at the fog. Now she knew the direction and no one in the world could lure her astray.

ELEVEN
The South Cape of Öland

At the southernmost part of Öland is an old royal estate called
Ottenby. It is quite a large property, extending straight across
the island from shore to shore, and remarkable because it has
always been a refuge for large groups of animals. In the seven-
teenth century, when the kings used to come over to Öland to
hunt, the whole property was nothing but one large deer park.
In the eighteenth century there was a stud farm where thor-
oughbred race-horses were raised, and a sheep farm where
several hundred sheep were kept. In our days at Ottenby there
are neither thoroughbreds nor sheep. Living there in their place
are several large herds of young horses, which will be used by
our cavalry regiments.

There is surely no farm in the whole country that can be a
better place for animals to stay. Along the east coast lies the
old sheep meadow, which is ten kilometres long, the largest

meadow on all of Öland, where the animals can graze and play and roll over and over as free as in the wild. And there is the renowned Ottenby grove with the hundred-year-old oaks, which provide shade from the sun and shelter from the harsh Öland wind. And then you can't forget the long Ottenby wall, which goes from shore to shore and divides Ottenby from the rest of the island, so that the animals know how far the old royal estate extends and can avoid going on to other land, where they are not as well protected.

But it is not enough that there are plenty of domestic animals at Ottenby. You might almost believe that the wild animals also had a sense that on an old crown estate animals both wild and domestic ought to be able to count on kindness and protection, and that is why they venture there in such large groups. Besides the fact that deer are still there from the old breed and that hares and shelducks and partridges love living there, in the spring and late summer it constitutes a resting place for many thousands of migratory birds. Mainly it is on the marshy eastern shore below the sheep meadow that the migratory birds settle down to graze and rest.

When the wild geese and Nils Holgersson had finally found their way to Öland, like all the others they landed on the shore below the sheep meadow. The fog was dense over the island as it had been over the sea. But the boy was still astonished at all the birds that he could make out on the little patch of shore that he could look out over.

It was a low seashore with stones and pools of water and a lot of washed-up seaweed. If the boy could have chosen, he never would have thought about setting down there, but the birds seemed to consider it a real paradise. Ducks and grey geese walked and grazed on the meadow, sandpipers and other shore birds ran closer to the water. The divers were in the sea, fishing, but the most life and movement was on the long banks of seaweed along the coast. There the birds stood close beside each other and gathered up larvae, of which there must have been a limitless quantity, because no complaints were heard about lack of food.

The great majority would travel on and had settled down simply to get some rest, and as soon as the leader of a flock

thought that his comrades had revived sufficiently, he said, 'If
you're ready, then we should probably take off.'

'No, wait, wait! We're far from being full yet,' the followers
said.

'You don't think I intend to let you eat so much that you
can't move, do you?' said the leader, flapping his wings
and setting off. But it happened more than once that he had
to turn around, because he could not get the others to follow him.

Beyond the outermost seaweed banks was a flock of swans.
They did not care to go ashore, but instead they rested by rocking on the water. Now and then they stuck their necks down
and gathered food from the seabed. When they got hold of
something really good, they let out loud shouts, which sounded
like trumpet blasts.

When the boy heard that there were swans on the shoals, he
hurried out on the seaweed banks. He had never seen wild
swans close up before. He was lucky, so that he came right up
to them.

The boy was not the only one who had heard the swans.
Wild geese and grey geese and ducks and divers all swam out
between the banks, placing themselves like a ring around the
flock of swans and staring at them. The swans puffed up their
feathers, raised their wings like sails and lifted their necks high
in the air. Sometimes one or two of them swam up to a goose
or black-throated diver or sea duck and said a few words. And
then it seemed as if the one addressed hardly dared to raise his
beak to answer.

But then there was a red-throated diver, a little black mischief-
maker, who could not put up with all this solemnity. He dived
suddenly and disappeared under the surface of the water. Right
after that one of the swans let out a shriek and swam away so
quickly that the water foamed. Then he stopped and started
looking majestic again. But soon another shrieked the same as
the first, and then a third shrieked.

Now the red-throated diver was unable to stay underwater
any longer and he appeared on the surface, small and black
and spiteful. The swans rushed towards him, but when they

saw what a little wretch he was, they turned abruptly, as if they considered themselves too good to quarrel with him. Then the red-throated diver dived again and nipped them on the feet. It must have hurt, and the worst thing was that they could not maintain their dignity. Suddenly they settled the matter. They started whipping the air with their wings so that it thundered, moved ahead a long way as if running on the water, finally got air under their wings and took off.

When the swans were gone, their absence was greatly felt, and the ones who had been amused by the red-throated diver's pranks now criticized him for his insolence.

The boy went back towards land. There he placed himself to watch how the sandpipers played. They resembled tiny, tiny cranes; like them they had small bodies, long legs, long necks and made light, hovering movements, but they were not grey, but brown. They stood in a long row on the shore, where it was washed by the waves. As soon as a wave streamed in, the whole row ran backwards. As soon as it was drawn out, they followed. And they kept on like that for hours.

The showiest of all the birds were the shelducks. They were probably related to common ducks, because like them they had a heavy, squat body, broad beak and webbed feet, but they were much more splendidly dressed up. Their plumage itself was white; around their necks they wore a broad yellow band; the speculum shone in green, red and black; the wing tips were black; and the heads were black green and changed like silk.

As soon as any of them appeared on the shore, the other birds said, 'Look at them! They know how to dress up!'

'If they weren't so showy, they wouldn't need to dig their nests down into the ground, instead they could stay in the daylight like anyone else,' said a brown mallard.

'However hard they try, they're never going to get anything out with a beak like that,' said a grey goose. And this was really true. The shelducks had a large bump on the root of the beak that spoiled their appearance.

Beyond the shore, seagulls and terns passed over the water and fished. 'What kind of fish are you bringing up?' a wild goose asked.

'It's stickleback. Öland's stickleback. It's the best stickleback in the world,' a gull said. 'Would you like a taste?' And
he flew towards the goose with his mouth full of the small fish
and wanted to give her some.

'Yuck! Do you think I want to eat anything so disgusting?'

The next morning it was still just as foggy. The wild geese
grazed on the meadow, but the boy had gone down to the
shore to gather mussels. There were plenty of them, and when
he thought that the next day perhaps he would be at a place
where he could not get any food at all, he decided that he
would try to make himself a little pouch that he could fill with
mussels. On the meadow he found old sedge that was tough
and strong, and from it he started weaving a knapsack. He
worked on this for several hours, but he was very satisfied with
it when it was finished.

At noon all the wild geese came running and asked if he had
seen the white gander. 'No, he hasn't been with me,' said the boy.

'We had him with us until just recently,' said Akka, 'but
now we don't know where he is.'

The boy jumped up and was terribly afraid. He asked if any
fox or eagle had appeared, or if any human had been seen in
the area. But no one had noticed anything dangerous. The gander had probably simply got lost in the fog.

But however the white gander had got lost, it was just as
great a misfortune for the boy and he took off at once to search
for him. The fog protected him, so that he could run unseen
anywhere at all, but it also prevented him from seeing. He ran
south along the coast all the way down to the lighthouse and
the mist cannon on the outermost cape of the island. Everywhere was the same throng of birds, but no gander. He
ventured up to Ottenby Farm, and he searched through every
one of the old hollow oaks in Ottenby Grove, but found no
trace of the gander.

He searched until it started to get dark. Then he had to
make his way back to the eastern shore. He walked with heavy
steps and was in a dreadfully gloomy mood. He did not know
what would become of him if he did not find the gander. There
was no one he needed more.

But as he wandered across the sheep meadow, what kind of large white object was coming towards him in the fog, if not the gander? He was completely unscathed and very happy that he had finally been able to make his way back to the others. The fog made him so dizzy, he said, that he had walked around the big meadow all day. The boy threw his arms around his neck in happiness and asked him to watch what he was doing and not go away from the others. And he promised firmly that he would never do so again. No, never again.

But the next morning, when the boy went down to the water's edge to look for mussels, the geese came running and asked if he had seen the gander.

No, he had certainly not. Yes, the gander was gone again. He had got lost in the fog in the same way as the day before.

The boy ran off in great dismay and started searching. He found a place where the Ottenby wall was so crumbling that he could climb over it. Then he walked around both down at the water's edge, which gradually widened and became so large that there was room for fields and meadows and farms, and up on the flat highland that occupied the middle of the island, where there were no buildings other than windmills, and where the ground cover was so thin that the white limestone was visible below.

He could not find the gander, however, and as evening approached and the boy had to return to the shore, he could only believe that his travelling companion was lost. He was so dispirited that he did not know what he should do.

He had already climbed over the wall again, when he heard a stone slide down right beside him. When he turned around to see what it was, he thought he could make out something moving on a pile of stones by the wall. He crept closer and then saw the white gander come laboriously up the pile of stones with several large root bundles in his mouth. The gander did not see the boy and the boy did not call to him, but instead thought that he should first find out why the gander disappeared like this again and again.

He soon found out the reason too. Up on the mound of stones was a young grey goose, who shouted with joy when the

gander came. The boy sneaked closer, so that he heard what
they said, and then found out that one of the grey goose's
wings was injured so that she could not fly, and that her flock
had departed and left her behind. She had been close to dying
from hunger when the day before the white gander heard her
call and found her. Ever since he had been occupied with carrying food to her. Both of them hoped that she would get healthy
before he left the island, but she could still neither fly nor walk.
She was very distressed about this, but he consoled her that he
would not be leaving for a long time. At last he bade her good
night and promised he would come back the next day.

The boy let the gander go, and as soon as he was gone, he in
turn sneaked up to the mound of stones. He was angry that he
had been fooled and now he wanted to tell that grey goose that
the gander was his property. He was going to take the boy up
to Lapland, and there could be no talk of him staying here for
her sake. But now when he saw the young goose close up, he
understood both why the gander had carried food for her for
two days and why he had not wanted to tell anyone that he was
helping her. She had the most beautiful little head, her plumage
was like soft silk, and her eyes were gentle and pleading.

When she saw the boy she wanted to run away. But her left
wing was out of joint and dragged against the ground, so that
it obstructed all her movements.

'You shouldn't be afraid of me,' the boy said, not looking
angry at all, as he had intended to. 'I am Thumbkin, Martin
Gander's travelling companion,' he continued. And then he
stood there not knowing what he should say.

Sometimes there is something about an animal that makes
you wonder what kind of being they are. You almost feel afraid
that they could be a transformed human. There was something
like that about the grey goose. As soon as Thumbkin said who
he was, she lowered her neck and her head very gracefully
before him and said in a voice so beautiful that the boy could
not believe it was a goose speaking, 'I am very happy that you
have come here to assist me. The white gander has told me that
no one is as wise and as good as you.'

She said this with such dignity that the boy became very shy.

'This can't be a bird,' he said. 'This must be an enchanted princess.'

He had a great desire to help her and stuck his little hands under her feathers and felt along the wing-bone. The bone was not broken, but there was something out of order with the joint. He got his finger down in an empty joint socket. 'Watch out now!' he said, took firm hold of the bone shaft and set it in where it should be. He did this very fast and well, considering it was the first time he had attempted something like that, but it must have hurt a lot, because the poor young goose let out a single shrill shriek, and then she sank down among the stones without giving any sign of life.

The boy was terribly frightened. He had wanted to help her, but now she was dead. He took a long leap from the mound of stones and ran away. He thought it was as if he had killed a human.

The next morning was clear and free of fog and Akka said that now they would continue the journey. All the others were willing to leave, but the white gander made objections. The boy understood that he did not want to leave the grey goose. But Akka did not listen to him and took off.

The boy jumped up on the gander's back and the white bird followed the flock, though slowly and unwillingly. The boy was really happy that they could leave the island. He had pangs of conscience about the grey goose and did not want to tell the gander what had happened when he tried to treat her. It was probably best if Martin Gander never found out, he thought. At the same time he wondered that the white bird had the heart to leave the grey goose.

But suddenly the gander turned. The thought of the young goose was too much for him. Never mind the Lapland journey, he could not follow the others when he knew that she was lying alone and sick and would starve to death.

With a few wing strokes he was up at the mound of stones. But there was no grey goose lying among them. 'Downy! Downy! Where are you?' the gander asked.

'The fox has probably been here and taken her,' the boy thought. But just then he heard a beautiful voice answer the gander, 'I'm here, gander! I'm here! I've just been taking a morning bath.' And up out of the water came the little grey goose, healthy and sound, and she explained that Thumbkin had put her wing back in its joint and that she was completely fine and ready to follow on the journey.

The water drops were like pearls on her silky feathers and Thumbkin thought once again that she was a real little princess.

TWELVE

The Big Butterfly

The geese travelled along the lengthy island, which was clearly visible below them. The boy felt happy and light-hearted during the journey. He was just as content and pleased as he had been gloomy and downhearted the day before, when he had wandered around on the island looking for the gander.

He now saw that the interior of the island consisted of a bare plateau with a broad wreath of good, fruitful land along the coasts, and he started to understand the meaning of something he had heard during the night.

He had just sat down to rest by one of the many windmills that were erected on the plateau, when a couple of shepherds came walking along with their dogs by their sides, accompanied by a large flock of sheep. The boy had not been scared, because he was sitting well hidden under the windmill steps. But it turned out that the shepherds came and sat down on the same steps, and then there was nothing for the boy to do other than stay still.

One of the shepherds was young and looked like most people, while the other was old and strange. His body was big and bony, but his head was little and his face had soft, gentle features. It seemed as if body and head did not fit together at all.

He sat silently for a while and stared into the fog with an indescribably tired expression. Then he started talking with his comrade. The younger man took bread and cheese out of his bag to have his evening meal. He hardly said anything in response, but he listened very patiently, as if he were thinking, 'I might as well give you the pleasure of letting you talk awhile.'

'Now I'm going to tell you something, Erik,' the old shepherd said. 'I've figured out that in the past, when both humans and animals were much bigger than they are now, the butterflies must have been incredibly big too. And once there was a butterfly that was dozens of kilometres long and had wings as broad as lakes. Those wings were shiny blue and silver, and so magnificent that when the butterfly was out flying all the other animals stopped and stared.

'The problem, of course, was that it was too big. Its wings had a hard time carrying it. But it probably would have been fine if it had been wise enough to stay over the land. But it wasn't. Instead it took off out over the Baltic. And it did not get far before a storm came towards it and started tearing at its wings. Yes, it's easy for you to understand, Erik, how it would turn out when a Baltic storm gets to play with delicate butterfly wings. It didn't take long before they were torn off and whirled away, and then, of course, the poor butterfly fell down into the sea. It was tossed back and forth in the waves to start with and then it was stranded on some submerged rock outside Småland. And there it lay, as big and long as it was.

'Now I'm thinking, Erik, that if the butterfly had been lying on land, soon it would have decomposed and fallen apart. But because it fell into the sea, it was imbued with lime and as hard as stone. You probably know that we've found stones on the shore that are nothing but hardened worms. And now I think that the same thing happened with the big butterfly body. I think it became a long, narrow rock where it lay out in the Baltic. Don't you think so too?'

He paused to get a response and the other man nodded at him. 'Keep on now, so I get to hear where you're going with this!' he said.

'And take heed now, Erik, that this Öland, on which you and I live, is nothing other than the old butterfly body. If you just think about it, then you notice that the island is a butterfly. To the north is the narrow forepart and the round head, and to the south you see the abdomen, which first spreads out and then narrows off to a sharp point.'

Here he paused again and looked at his comrade, as if anxious as to how he would take this assertion. But the young man continued to eat calmly and nodded at him to continue.

'As soon as the butterfly had been transformed into limestone, many sorts of seeds from plants and trees came travelling with the wind and wanted to take root in it. But they had difficulty getting a footing on the bare, smooth rock. It took a long time before anything other than sedge could grow there. Then came the sheep fescue and rock rose and thorn. But even today there isn't enough vegetation on the Alvar to really cover the rock, so it shows here and there. And no one can imagine ploughing and sowing up here, where the crust is so thin.

'But now if you accept that the Alvar and the sea cliffs around it are formed by the butterfly's body, then you have the right to ask where the land that lies below the sea cliffs came from.'

'Yes, that's exactly right,' said the one who was eating. 'I'd really like to know that.'

'Well, you have to remember that Öland has been in the sea for a good many years, and during that time all the sorts of things that toss around with the waves – seaweed and sand and snails – gathered around it and stayed. And then stone and gravel have slid down from both the eastern and western sea cliffs. In that way the island has gained broad beaches, where grain and flowers and trees can grow.

'Up here on the hard butterfly back only sheep and cows and small horses go, only lapwings and golden plovers live here, and there are no buildings other than windmills and a few poor stone huts that we shepherds crawl into. But down on the shore are large farming villages and parsonages and fishing villages and a whole city.'

He looked inquisitively at the other one. He had stopped eating and was in the process of tying up his food sack. 'I wonder where you're going with all this,' he said.

'Yes, it's just this that I want to know,' said the shepherd, while he lowered his voice so that he almost whispered the words, looking into the fog with his small eyes, which appeared to be exhausted by looking for everything that does not exist. 'I just want to know this: if the farmers who live in the surrounding farms down under the sea cliffs, or the fishermen who take the herring out of the sea, or the merchants in Borgholm, or the vacationers who come here every summer, or the travellers who wander around in the Borgholm castle ruins, or the hunters who come here in the autumn and hunt partridge, or the painters who sit here at the Alvar and paint the sheep and the windmills – I would like to know if any of them understand that this island was once a butterfly, which flew around with big, shiny wings.'

'I see,' the young shepherd said suddenly. 'It must have occurred to some of them, sitting here one evening on the edge of the sea cliff and hearing the nightingales warble in the forest meadow below and looking over Kalmar Sound that this island cannot have come about like any other.'

'I wanted to ask,' the old man continued, 'if no one has had the idea of putting wings on the windmills so big that they could reach up to the sky, so big that they would be able to lift the whole island up out of the sea and let it fly like a butterfly among butterflies.'

'There may well be something in what you say,' the young shepherd said. 'Because on summer nights, when the sky arches high and open over the island, sometimes I've thought that it was as if it wanted to raise itself out of the sea and fly away.'

But now when the old man had finally got the young man to speak, he did not listen to him much. 'I would really like to know,' he said in a lower voice, 'if anyone can explain why such longing lives up here on the Alvar. I've felt it every day of my life, and I think that it makes its way into the heart of anyone who has to be here. I'd like to know whether anyone else has realized that all that yearning comes from the fact that the whole island is a butterfly, longing for its wings.'

THIRTEEN
Lilla Karlsön

The Storm

FRIDAY, 8 APRIL

The wild geese had spent the night on the north cape of Öland and were now en route to the mainland. A strong southerly wind was blowing over Kalmar Sound, tossing them north-wards. They still worked their way at good speed towards land. But as they were approaching the first skerry they heard a mighty rumbling, as if a large number of birds with strong wings had come flying, and the water below suddenly turned completely black. Akka pulled in her wings so quickly that she almost remained stationary in the air. After that she descended to land on the surface of the sea. But before the geese had reached the water, the western storm caught up with them. It was already chasing clouds of dust, salt foam and small birds ahead of it, and now it also tore the wild geese with it, threw them backwards and heaved them out towards the sea.

It was a dreadful storm. Again and again the wild geese tried to turn, but they were unable to, instead being driven out towards the Baltic. The storm had already cast them past Öland, and the sea lay empty and desolate before them. They could do nothing other than run before the wind.

When Akka noticed that they were unable to turn, she thought it was unnecessary to let the storm drive them over the entire Baltic. For that reason she descended on to the water. The seaway was already rough and growing more so every moment. The waves rolled ahead, sea-green with sputtering foam on the crests. One wave heaved up higher than the next. It was as if they were competing over which could raise itself highest and foam the wildest. But the wild geese were not afraid of the surging sea. On the contrary, it seemed to give them great enjoyment. They did not exert themselves by swimming, but instead let themselves be washed up on the crests and down in the troughs of the waves and had as much fun as children on a swing. Their only worry was that the flock would be scattered. The poor land birds, who drove past up in the storm, shouted enviously, 'You've got nothing to complain about, since you can swim!'

But the wild geese were certainly not out of all danger. For one thing the rocking made them hopelessly sleepy. They kept wanting to turn their heads backwards, stick their beaks in under their wings and sleep. Nothing can be more dangerous than falling asleep like that, and Akka called constantly, 'Don't fall asleep, wild geese! Anyone who falls asleep will be separated from the flock! Anyone who is separated from the flock is lost!'

Despite all attempts to resist, one after the other fell asleep, and Akka herself was very close to slumbering when suddenly she saw something round and dark rise over the top of a wave. 'Seals! Seals! Seals!' Akka called in a loud, shrill voice, raising herself in the air with flapping wing strokes. It was at the very last moment. Before the last wild goose had managed to get up out of the water, the seals were so close that they were snapping at their feet.

So the wild geese were again up in the storm, which drove

them ahead of it out to sea. No rest was granted either to it or
to them. And they saw no land, only desolate sea.

They settled down on the water again as soon as they dared.
But when they had rocked on the water awhile, they got sleepy
again. And when they fell asleep, the seals came swimming. If
old Akka had not been so watchful, not one of them would
have escaped.

The storm continued all day and it caused dreadful havoc
among the masses of birds migrating at this time of year. Some
were driven off course, away to distant lands where they died
of starvation, others were so exhausted they sank down in the
sea and drowned. Many were crushed against the cliff walls
and many became prey for the seals.

The storm lasted all day, until Akka started to wonder if she
and the flock would be lost. They were now dead tired and she
could see nowhere they might rest. Towards evening she no
longer dared settle down on the sea, because now it was suddenly filled with large ice floes which collided with each other,
and she feared that they would be crushed between them. A
couple of times the wild geese tried to set down on the ice floe.
But one time the storm swept them into the water. Another
time the merciless seals came crawling up on the ice.

At sundown the geese were once again high in the air. They
flew forwards, anxious about the night. The darkness seemed
to come over them much too quickly this evening, which was
so full of dangers.

It was dreadful that they still did not see land. What would
happen to them if they were forced to stay out on the sea the
whole night? They would either be crushed between the ice
floes or bitten to death by the seals or scattered by the storm.

The sky was cloud-covered, the moon stayed hidden and
darkness came quickly. At the same time all of nature was
filled by a ghastliness that struck the bravest hearts with terror. The cries of migratory birds in distress had sounded over
the sea the whole day without anyone paying them any heed,
but now, when you no longer saw who was making them, they
seemed dismal and frightening. Down on the sea the floes of
drift ice bumped against each other with a strong rumbling.

The seals struck up their wild hunting songs. It was as if sky and earth were about to collide.

The Sheep

The boy had been looking down at the sea for a while. Suddenly he thought that it started to roar more than before. He looked up. Right in front of him, only a few metres away, a rough, bare rock wall rose up. Down at its foot the waves were struck into high-spraying foam. The wild geese were flying straight towards the cliff, and the boy's only thought was that they would be crushed against it.

He barely had time to wonder that Akka had not seen this danger in time before they were at the rock. Then he also noticed that ahead of them the semicircular entrance to a grotto opened. The geese steered into it and the next moment they were in safety.

The first thing the travellers thought about, before they took a moment to rejoice over their rescue, was to see whether all their comrades were also saved. Then there were Akka, Yksi, Kolme, Neljä, Viisi, Kuusi, all six goslings, the gander, Downy and Thumbkin, but Kaksi from Nuolja, the first goose on the left, was missing, and no one knew anything about her fate.

When the wild geese noticed that no one except Kaksi had been separated from the flock, they took the matter lightly. Kaksi was old and wise. She knew all their paths and habits, and she would probably know how to find her way back to them.

Then the wild geese started looking around inside the cavern. Enough daylight still came in through the opening that they could see that the grotto was both deep and wide. They were happy to have found themselves such a splendid lodging, when one of them caught sight of some glistening green dots that shone out of a dark corner. 'Those are eyes!' Akka called. 'There are large animals in here.' They rushed towards the exit, but Thumbkin, who saw better in the dark than the wild geese, called to them, 'It's nothing to flee from! It's only some sheep lying along the grotto wall.'

When the wild geese had got used to the dim light in the grotto, they saw the sheep very well. There might be roughly as many adults as themselves, but in addition there were some small lambs. A big ram with long, twisted horns seemed to be the leader of the flock. The wild geese went towards him with much curtsying. 'Wilderness salutations!' they greeted, but the big ram lay quietly and did not say a word of welcome.

Then the wild geese thought the sheep were unhappy that they had made their way into their grotto. 'Perhaps it is not pleasing to you that we've come into the house here?' said Akka. 'But we can't help it, because we are wind-driven. We have travelled around in the storm the whole day and it would be very good to be able to stay here tonight.' After this it took a long while before any of the sheep answered with words, but on the other hand it was clearly heard that a couple of them let out long sighs. Akka knew that sheep are always shy and peculiar, but these did not seem to have any concept at all of how to behave. Finally an old ewe, who had a long-set, mournful face and a whining voice, said, 'None of us will refuse to let you stay, but this is a house of mourning and we cannot receive guests like in the past.'

'You don't need to be worried about any such thing,' Akka said. 'If you knew what we've been subjected to today, you would probably realize that we will be satisfied just to get a safe spot to sleep on.'

When Akka said this, the old ewe got up. 'I believe that it would be better for you to fly around in the strongest storm than to stay here. But you will not leave here anyway before we've been able to offer you such good cheer as the house can provide.'

She showed them to a hole in the ground, which was full of water. Beside it was a pile of husks and chaff, and she asked them to be content with that. 'We've had a lot of snow this year on the island,' she said. 'The farmers who own us came out with hay and oat straw, so that we wouldn't starve to death. And this rubbish is all that is left of the fodder.'

The geese pounced on the food at once. They thought that they had been fortunate and were in a good mood. They noticed, however, that the sheep were anxious, but they knew how easily frightened sheep usually are and did not think that there was any real danger imminent. As soon as they had eaten, they intended to settle down to sleep as usual. But then the big ram got up and came over to them. The geese thought that they had never seen a sheep with such long, rough horns. He was striking in other ways too. He had a large, bulging forehead, wise eyes and good posture, as if he were a proud, courageous animal.

'I cannot be held accountable for letting you fall asleep without telling you that it is unsafe here,' he said. 'We cannot receive overnight guests nowadays.' Finally Akka started to understand that this was serious.

'We'll go our way, because you absolutely wish it,' she said. 'But won't you first tell us what is tormenting you? We don't know a thing. We don't even know where we are.'

'This is the island of Lilla Karlsön,' said the ram. 'It is located outside Gotland, and nothing but sheep and seabirds live here.'

'Perhaps you are wild sheep?' said Akka.

'Not far from it,' the ram answered. 'We basically have nothing to do with humans. There is an old agreement between us and the farmers in a place on Gotland that they will supply us with fodder in case there is snow in the winter, and in return they get to take away those of us who are excess. The island is small, so it can't feed all that many of us. But otherwise we take care of ourselves year-round, and we don't live in houses with doors and locks, instead we stay in grottos like this.'

'Do you stay out here in the winter too?' Akka asked, surprised.

'Yes, we do,' the ram answered. 'We have good grazing up here on the hill year-round.'

'I think it sounds as if you have it better than other sheep,' said Akka. 'But what kind of misfortune has befallen you?'

'There was severe cold last winter. The sea froze and then three foxes came over here on the ice and they've stayed here ever since. Otherwise there is not a dangerous animal here on the island.'

'I see, the foxes dare to attack the likes of you?'

'Oh no, not during the day, when I can probably defend myself and my flock,' the ram said, shaking his horns. 'But they sneak up on us at night, when we are sleeping in the grottos. We try to stay awake, but sometimes you have to sleep and then they attack us. They've already killed every single sheep in the other grottos and those were flocks that were just as big as mine.'

'It's not pleasant to say that we are so helpless,' the old ewe now said. 'We can't take care of ourselves any better than if we were domestic sheep.'

'Do you think they will come here tonight?' said Akka.

'There's nothing to do but wait,' the old ewe answered. 'They were here last night and stole a lamb from us. They will probably come again, as long as any of us are still alive. That's what they've done at other places.'

'But if they are allowed to carry on like this, then you'll be completely wiped out,' said Akka.

'Yes, it probably won't be long before it's the end of all the sheep on Lilla Karlsön,' said the ewe.

Akka stood there, quite uncertain. It wasn't pleasant to head out into the storm again, and it wasn't good to stay in a house where such guests were expected. When she had thought for a while, she turned to Thumbkin. 'I wonder if you will help us, as you have done many times before?' she said.

Yes, the boy answered, of course he would.

'It's too bad for you not to get to sleep,' the wild goose said, 'but I wonder if you are able to keep watch until the foxes come, and then wake us so that we can fly away?'

The boy was not overly happy about this, but anything was better than going out into the storm again, so he promised that he would stay awake.

He went up to the grotto opening, crept down behind a stone so that he would have shelter from the storm, and sat down to keep watch.

When the boy had been sitting there a while, the storm seemed to abate. The sky became clear and the moonlight started playing on the waves. The boy went to the grotto opening to look out. The grotto was situated quite high up on the hill. A narrow, steep trail led up to it. It was probably there that he could expect the foxes.

He saw no foxes yet, but on the other hand something which at first he was much more afraid of. On the strip of shore below the hill stood some big giants or other stone trolls, or perhaps it was even humans. At first he thought he was dreaming, but now he was quite certain that he had not fallen asleep. He saw the big fellows so clearly that it could not be an optical illusion. Some stood out on the water's edge and others right next to the rock, as if they intended to climb up it. Some had big, thick heads and others had none at all. Some were one-armed and some had humps both front and back. He had never seen anything so strange.

The boy was scaring himself about these trolls, so that he almost forgot to watch out for the foxes. But now he heard a claw scraping against a stone. He saw three foxes come up the precipice, and as soon as he knew that he had something real to deal with, he became calm again and not a bit scared. It struck him that it was a shame to simply wake the geese and leave the sheep to their fate. He thought he would like to arrange things differently.

He quickly ran into the grotto, shaking the big ram by the horn so that he woke up, and at the same time swung himself up on his back. 'Get up, Father, let's try to scare the foxes a little!'

He tried to be as quiet as possible, but the foxes must have heard all the commotion. When they came to the opening of the grotto they stopped and considered. 'There was definitely something moving in there,' said one. 'I wonder if they're awake.'

'Oh, just get on with it!' said another. 'They can't do anything to us anyway.'

When they came farther into the grotto, they stopped and sniffed. 'Who shall we take tonight?' whispered the fox who went first.

'Tonight we'll take the big ram,' said the last one. 'Then we'll have an easy time with the others.'

The boy sat on the old ram's back and saw how they were sneaking up. 'Now lunge straight ahead,' the boy whispered. The ram lunged and the first fox was thrown headlong back towards the opening.

'Lunge now to the left!' the boy said, turning the ram's big head in the right direction. The ram aimed a terrible blow, which struck the second fox on the side. He rolled around several times, before he got on his feet again and could flee. The boy would have liked to have shoved the third one too, but he had already taken off.

'Now I think they've had enough for tonight,' the boy said.

'I think so too,' said the big ram. 'Now lie on my back and crawl down into the wool! You deserve to be nice and warm after all the wind you've been out in.'

The Hell Hole

SATURDAY, 9 APRIL

The next day the big ram went around with the boy on his back and showed him the island. It consisted of a single massive cliff. It was like a big house with vertical walls and a flat roof. The ram first went up on the rocky roof and showed the boy the good grazing grounds there, and the boy had to admit that the island seemed to be specially created for sheep. Not much grew on the rock other than sheep fescue and the kind of small, dry, spicy-smelling plants that sheep like.

But to be sure, there was more besides sheep grazing to see once someone had come up the precipice. For one thing the whole sea was visible, now lying blue and sunlit and rolling along in shining swells. Only at an occasional promontory did it spray up in foam. Due east was Gotland with its even, long coast and in the south-west Stora Karlsön, which was constructed the same way as the smaller island. When the ram went all the way to the edge of the roof, so that the boy could look down the rock walls, he noticed that they were full of birds' nests, and in the blue sea below him were velvet scoters and eider ducks and kittiwakes and guillemots and razorbills so beautiful and peaceful, busy fishing for herring.

'This is really a promised land,' said the boy. 'You live in such a beautiful place, you sheep.'

'Yes, it's definitely beautiful here,' said the big ram. It was as if he wanted to add something, but he did not say anything, only sighed. 'But if you walk here alone, you have to watch out for all the cracks that run across the rock,' he continued after a while. And this was a good warning, because there were deep and wide cracks in several places. The biggest of them was called the Hell Hole. That crack was several fathoms deep and almost a fathom wide. 'If someone were to fall down here, it would be all over for him,' the big ram said. The boy thought it sounded as if he had a particular meaning in what he said.

Then he brought the boy down to the water's edge. He could see those giants close up that had frightened him the night before. It was nothing other than big cliff pillars. The big ram called them 'raukar'. The boy could not stop looking at them. If trolls had ever been turned into stone, he thought, they would look just like that.

Although it was beautiful down at the water's edge, the boy still liked it better up on the summit. It was awful down here, because they encountered dead sheep everywhere. Here was where the foxes had their dinner. He saw skeletons completely picked clean, but also bodies that were only half-eaten, and others they had hardly tasted, but instead left untouched. It was quite heart-rending to see that the wild animals had thrown themselves over the sheep only for sport, only to get to hunt and kill.

The big ram did not stop in front of the dead, but instead went calmly past them. But the boy could not avoid seeing all the unpleasantness in any event.

Now the big ram went back up to the summit, but when he got there, he stopped and said, 'If anyone who was capable and wise had to see all the misery that prevails here, he would probably not rest until those foxes got their punishment.'

'Foxes have to live too,' the boy said.

'Yes,' said the big ram. 'Those who don't kill more animals than they need for their sustenance, they may well live. But these are miscreants.'

'The farmers who own the island ought to be able to come here and help you,' the boy said.

'They've rowed over here several times,' the ram answered, 'but the foxes hid in grottos and cracks, so they didn't get a chance to shoot them.'

'You can't very well mean that a little wretch like me should be able to get the better of those that you and the farmers haven't been able to overcome.'

'Someone who is small and quick-witted can put many things right,' said the big ram.

They spoke no more about this, but the boy went and sat down with the wild geese, who were grazing up on the highland. Although he had not wanted to show it to the ram, he was very distressed for the sheep's sake and he really wanted to help them. 'I'll at least talk with Akka and Martin Gander about it,' he thought. 'Perhaps they can assist me with some good advice.'

Later the white gander took the boy on his back and went over the plateau beyond the Hell Hole.

He wandered carefree on the open summit and did not seem to think about how white and big he was. He did not seek shelter behind grassy hillocks or other elevations, instead he walked straight ahead. It was strange that he was not more careful, because he seemed to have been badly knocked about during yesterday's storm. He limped on his right leg and his left wing hung and dragged, as if it were broken.

He behaved as if there was no danger, nibbling a blade of grass here and another there and not looking around in any direction. The boy was stretched out on the gander's back, looking up towards the blue sky. He was now so used to riding that he could both stand and lie on the goose's back.

When the gander and the boy were so carefree, they did not notice, of course, that the three foxes had come up on the plateau. And the foxes, who knew that it is almost impossible to get close to a goose on open ground, did not think about chasing the gander at all to start with. But as they had nothing else to do, they finally went down into one of the long cracks anyway and tried to sneak up on him. They set about it so carefully that the gander could not catch a glimpse of them.

They were not far away when the gander made an attempt to raise himself in the air. He flapped his wings, but he was unable to take off. When the foxes thought this meant that he could not fly, they hurried ahead with greater eagerness than before. They no longer kept themselves hidden in the crevice, but instead went out on the plateau. They concealed themselves as best they could behind tussocks and rocks and got ever closer to the gander, without him seeming to notice that he was being hunted. At last the foxes were so close that they could take a run for the final leap. All three threw themselves at one time at the gander in a long leap.

At the last moment the gander must have noticed something anyway, because he ran away, so that the foxes missed him. This did not mean that much in any case, because the gander's head start was only a couple of fathoms, and he was limping besides. The poor thing ran off anyway, as quickly as he was able.

The boy was sitting backwards on the gander's back and called and shouted at the foxes, 'You've got too fat on mutton, foxes! You can't even catch up with a goose!' He made fun of them, so that they were crazed with fury and only thought about rushing ahead.

The white one ran towards the big crevice. When he came up to it, he made a flap with his wings so that he went over. Just then the foxes were right behind him.

The gander hurried ahead at the same speed as before, even after he had crossed over the Hell Hole. But he had only run a couple of metres before the boy tapped him on the neck and said, 'Now you can stop, gander.'

At the same moment they heard behind them some wild howls and scraping with claws and heavy falls. But they saw no more of the foxes.

The next morning the lighthouse keeper at Stora Karlsön found a piece of bark stuck under the front door, and on it was carved in crooked, block letters: 'The foxes on the small island fell down into the Hell Hole. Take care of them!'

And the lighthouse keeper did that too.

FOURTEEN
Two Cities

The City at the Bottom of the Sea

SATURDAY, 9 APRIL

It turned out to be a calm, clear night. The wild geese did not bother to seek shelter in any of the grottos. Instead they slept up on the summit, and the boy settled down in the short, dry grass alongside the geese.

There was bright moonlight that night, so bright that the boy had a hard time falling asleep. He lay there thinking about how long he had been away from home, and he worked out that it was three weeks since he had started the journey. At the same time he remembered that it was Easter Eve that night.

'Tonight is when all the witches come home from Blåkulla,' he thought, laughing to himself. Because he was a bit afraid of both the water sprite and the gnome, but he did not have the slightest belief in witches.

If there had been witches out that evening, he would have seen them. There was such bright light up in the sky that the smallest black dot could not move in the air without him noticing it.

While he was lying there with his nose in the air, thinking about this, he caught sight of something beautiful. The disc of the moon stood whole and round rather high up, and in front of it a large bird came flying. It was not flying past the moon, but it was approaching as if it could have flown out of it. The bird appeared black against the light backdrop, and its wings extended from one edge of the disc to the other. It flew so evenly ahead in the same direction that the boy thought it was drawn on the moon. Its body was small, its neck long and slender, its legs hung down, long and thin. It could be nothing other than a stork.

A few moments later Herr Ermenrich, the stork, set down beside him. He bent over the boy and bumped him with his beak to get him awake.

The boy sat up at once. 'I'm not sleeping, Herr Ermenrich,' he said. 'Why are you out in the middle of the night and how are things at Glimmingehus? Do you want to speak with Mother Akka?'

'It's too light to sleep tonight,' Herr Ermenrich answered. 'For that reason I decided to make the journey over here to Karlsön and call on you, my friend Thumbkin. I found out from a gull that you were here tonight. I haven't flown over to Glimmingehus yet, I'm still staying in Pomerania.'

The boy was incredibly happy that Herr Ermenrich had sought him out. They talked about everything imaginable like old friends. At last the stork asked if the boy didn't want to go out and ride for a while in the beautiful night.

Yes, the boy would like that very much, if the stork only arranged it so that he came back to the wild geese before sunrise. He promised to, and then they were off.

Herr Ermenrich again flew right towards the moon. They climbed and climbed, the sea sank down deep, but the flight was so strangely easy that it seemed almost as if they were lying still in the air.

The boy thought that the flight had lasted an incredibly short time when Herr Ermenrich descended to set down.

They landed on a deserted beach that was covered with even, fine sand. Along the coast was a long row of sand dunes with lyme grass on the top. They were not very high, but they prevented the boy from seeing any of the inland.

Herr Ermenrich positioned himself on a sand hill, pulled up one leg and bent his neck backwards to stick his beak under his wing. 'You can wander around here on the beach a while, while I rest,' he said to Thumbkin. 'But don't go too far, so you can find your way back to me!'

The boy intended first to climb up on a sand dune to see what the country looked like beyond it. But when he had taken a few steps, the front edge of his wooden shoe bumped into something hard. He leaned over and saw that on the sand there was a small copper coin so corroded with verdigris it was almost transparent. It was in such poor condition that he did not even think about picking it up, but instead just kicked it away.

But when he was standing upright again, he was quite surprised, because two steps away rose a high, dark wall with a large gate topped by a tower.

The moment before, when the boy leaned down, the sea had spread out glistening and bright, and now it was concealed by a long wall with towers and pinnacles. And right in front of him, where before there had been only a few banks of seaweed, the large gate was opening.

The boy probably understood that there was spookery involved. But this was nothing to be afraid of, he thought. It was not some dangerous trolls or other evil, which he always feared encountering at night. Both the wall and the gate were so splendidly constructed that he had only a desire to see what might be behind them. 'I have to find out what this might be,' he thought, making his way through the gate.

In the deep archway sat watchmen dressed in motley, puffed clothing with long-shafted halberds beside them, playing dice. They were thinking only about the game and paid no attention to the boy, who quickly hurried past them.

Inside the gate he found an open plaza, paved with large, even slabs of stone. All around stood tall, magnificent houses, and between them were long, narrow streets.

The plaza before the gate was swarming with people. The men wore long, fur-lined coats over silk undergarments, plume-adorned berets sat askew on their heads, on their chests hung thick chains. All of them were so impressively dressed up that they could have been kings.

The women wore conical hats, long skirts and narrow sleeves. They were also grandly dressed, but their finery did not nearly approach the men's.

This was just like in the old fairy-tale book that Mother took out of the chest once and showed him. The boy could simply not believe his eyes.

But what was more remarkable to see than the men and the women was the city itself. Every house was built so that one gable faced towards the street. And the gables were decorated so that you might believe that they wanted to compete with each other over who could show the loveliest decorations.

Anyone who suddenly sees so many new things cannot manage to preserve everything in memory. But afterwards the boy could still recall that he had seen stepped gables that bore pictures of Christ and his apostles on the various landings, gables where pictures stood in niches up the entire wall, gables that were inlaid with multicoloured pieces of glass, and gables that were striped and checked with white and black marble.

While the boy marvelled at all this, an intense urgency came over him. 'My eyes have never seen anything like this before. They will never see anything like this again,' he said to himself. And he started running into the city, up and down the streets.

The streets were cramped and narrow, but not empty and gloomy like in the cities he knew about. There were people everywhere. Old women sat by their doors spinning without spinning wheels, using only a spindle. The merchants' shops were like market stalls, open to the street. All the craftsmen did their work outside. In one place cod-liver oil was being boiled, at another skins were being dressed, in a third was a long ropeyard.

If the boy had only had the time he could have learned to manufacture everything imaginable. Here he saw how armourers hammered out thin breastplates, how silversmiths set precious stones in rings and bracelets, how turners wielded their iron, how shoemakers soled soft red shoes, how the goldsmith twisted gold wire into thread, and how the weavers added silk and gold to their weavings.

But the boy did not have time to stop. He just rushed ahead to be able to see as much as possible, before all of it disappeared again.

The high wall ran around the whole city, enclosing it like a stone wall surrounds a field. At the end of every street he saw it, crowned with pinnacles and adorned with towers. Up on the wall the soldiers marched in shining breastplates and helmets.

When he had run straight through the whole city, he came to yet another gate in the wall. Beyond it was the sea with the harbour. The boy saw old-time ships with rowing benches in the middle and high structures fore and aft. Some were taking in cargo, others were just casting anchor. Carriers and merchants hurried past each other. Urgency and life prevailed everywhere.

But he did not think he had time to linger here, either. He hurried in towards the city again, and now he came up to the main square. There was the cathedral with three high towers and deep archways adorned with images. The walls were so ornamented by sculptors that there was not a stone that did not have a decoration. And such magnificence was glimpsed through the open gate: golden crosses and gilded altars and priests in golden vestments! Across from the church was a building that had pinnacles on the roof and a single, narrow, sky-high tower. It was probably the city hall. And between the church and the city hall, around the whole square, lovely gabled houses rose in the most varied decoration.

The boy had been running, so that he was hot and tired. He now thought he had seen what was most remarkable and so he started to walk more slowly. The street on to which he had turned was surely the one where the city-dwellers bought their magnificent clothing. He saw throngs of people standing in front of the small shops, where over the counters the merchants spread out flowery, stiff silk, thick gold cloth, shot velvet, light gauze and lace as thin as spider webs.

Before, when the boy ran so fast, no one paid any attention to him. The people probably thought it was just a little grey rat scampering past them. But now, when he was walking along the street quite slowly, one of the merchants caught sight of him and started waving.

The boy was anxious at first and wanted to hurry away, but the merchant just waved and smiled and spread a grand piece of silk damask out on the counter as if to entice him.

The boy shook his head. 'I'll never be so rich that I can buy a yard of that fabric,' he thought.

But now they had caught sight of him in every shop all along the street. Wherever he looked a shopkeeper stood waving to him. They left their rich customers and only thought about him. He saw how they hurried into the most hidden corners of the shop to get the best they had to sell, and how their hands trembled with urgency and eagerness, while they set it out on the counter.

When the boy continued to walk ahead, one of the merchants threw himself over the counter, caught up with him and set down silver fabric and woven tapestries, radiant with colours, in front of him. The boy could do nothing but laugh. The shopkeeper must understand that a poor wretch like him could not buy such things. He stopped and held out his empty hands, so that they would understand that he had nothing and leave him in peace.

But the merchant raised one finger and nodded and pushed the whole pile of magnificent goods towards him.

'Can he mean that he wants to sell all this for one gold coin?' the boy thought.

The merchant took out a little, worn coin in poor condition, the most insignificant you could see, and showed it to him. And he was so eager to sell that he added to his pile a couple of large, heavy silver beakers.

Then the boy started digging in his pockets. He knew, of course, that he did not have a single coin, but he could not keep from looking.

All the other merchants stood trying to see how the transaction would turn out, and when they noticed that the boy was starting to dig in his pockets, they threw themselves over the counters, took handfuls of gold and silver jewellery and offered it to him. And they all showed him that what they requested in payment was only a single small coin.

But the boy turned both his vest and trouser pockets inside out, so that they would see he had nothing. Then they got tears in their eyes, all of these stately merchants, who were so much richer than he. At last he was so moved by their anxiety that he thought about whether he could not help them in some way. And then he happened to think about that patinated coin that he had just seen on the beach.

He took off running down the street, and luck was with him, so that he came to the same gate that he had first happened upon. He rushed through it and started searching for the little verdigris-green copper coin that had been lying on the shore a while ago.

He found it too, quite rightly, but when he had picked it up and wanted to hurry back into the city with it, he saw only the sea before him. No city wall, no gate, no watchmen, no streets, no buildings were seen now, only the sea.

The boy could not help getting tears in his eyes. To start with he had thought that what he saw was nothing but an optical illusion, but he had managed to forget that. He had only thought how beautiful everything was. He felt a very deep sorrow that the city had disappeared.

At the same moment Herr Ermenrich awakened and came up to him. But he did not hear him, instead the stork had to bump him with his beak to make himself noticed. 'I think that you're standing here sleeping, like me,' said Herr Ermenrich.

'Oh, Herr Ermenrich!' the boy said. 'What kind of city was it that was just here?'

'Did you see a city?' said the stork. 'You fell asleep and were dreaming, like I said.'

'No, I wasn't dreaming,' said Thumbkin, and he told the stork everything he had experienced.

Then Herr Ermenrich said, 'For my part, Thumbkin, I think you fell asleep here on the beach and dreamed all this. But I don't want to hide from you that Bataki, the raven, who is the most learned of all birds, once told me that on this shore in the past there was a city, which was called Vineta. It was so rich and fortunate that no city has even been more glorious, but unfortunately its inhabitants abandoned themselves to arrogance and a love of display. As punishment for this, says Bataki, the city of Vineta was flooded by a storm and sank into the sea. But its inhabitants cannot die, nor can their city be destroyed. And one night every hundred years it rises up in all its glory out of the sea and is on the earth's surface for exactly one hour.'

'Yes, it must be true,' said Thumbkin, 'because I saw it.'

'But when the hour is past, it sinks down into the sea again if, during that time, a merchant in Vineta has not been able to sell something to a living being. If you, Thumbkin, only had ever so small a coin to pay the merchant, Vineta would have been able to stay here on the shore and its people would be able to live and die like other people.'

'Herr Ermenrich,' said the boy, 'now I understand why you came and got me in the middle of the night. It was because you believed that I could save the old city. I'm so sorry it didn't work out as you wanted, Herr Ermenrich.'

He put his hands before his eyes and wept. It was not easy to say who looked most distressed, the boy or Herr Ermenrich.

The Living City

MONDAY, 11 APRIL

In the afternoon on the day after Easter the wild geese and Thumbkin were out flying. They swept along over Gotland.

The large island was big and level below them. The ground was chequered just like in Skåne, and there were plenty of churches and farms. But the difference was that there were more forest meadows between the fields here, and the farms were not enclosed. And there were no large estates at all, with old castles, towers and extensive grounds.

The wild geese had taken the route over Gotland for Thumbkin's sake. He had not been himself for two days and had not said a happy word. The reason for this was that he was thinking about that city, which in such a peculiar way had appeared to him. He had never seen anything so beautiful and magnificent, and he could not come to terms with the fact that he had not been able to rescue it. He was not sensitive by nature otherwise, but he really grieved over the lovely buildings and the stately people.

Both Akka and the gander tried to convince Thumbkin that he'd had a dream or an optical illusion, but the boy did not want to hear any such thing. He was so sure he had really seen what he saw that no one could budge him from this conviction. He was acting so distressed that his travelling companions became worried about him.

Just as the boy was at his most downhearted, old Kaksi returned to the flock. She had been thrown towards Gotland and had to travel across the whole island before she heard from some crows that her travelling companions were on Lilla Karlsön. When Kaksi found out what Thumbkin was missing, she said quite suddenly, 'If Thumbkin is grieving over an old city, we can soon console him. Just come along, I will lead you to a place that I saw yesterday! He won't have to be distressed for long.'

With that the geese said goodbye to the sheep, and now they were on their way to the place that Kaksi wanted to show Thumbkin. As sad as he was, he could not help looking down as usual at the land over which he was travelling.

He thought it looked as if the whole island to start with must have been a high, steep cliff like Karlsön, although much bigger, of course. But then it had somehow been flattened. Someone had taken a big rolling pin and rolled it out, as if it were a lump of dough. Not because it had become completely even and smooth like a loaf of bread, it definitely had not. While they had travelled along the coast, in several places he had seen high, white limestone walls with grottos and *raukar*, but in the majority of places they were erased and the shore sank humbly down to the sea.

On Gotland they had a beautiful, peaceful holiday afternoon. Mild spring weather prevailed, the trees had large buds, spring flowers covered the ground in the forest meadows, the long, thin curtains of the poplars swayed, and in the small gardens that were found by every cottage the gooseberry bushes were completely green.

The warmth and the budding spring had lured humans out on to roads and yards, and wherever any of them were gathered they were playing. It was not only the children who played but the grown-ups too. They threw stones at targets, and they hit balls up into the air so high that they almost reached the wild geese. It looked merry and pleasant to see big people playing, and the boy probably would have been happy about it if he could have forgotten his annoyance that he had not been able to save the old city.

He had to admit anyway that this was a lovely flight. There was so much song and sound in the air. Small children played a circle game and sang along. And the Salvation Army was out. He saw a whole crowd of people, dressed in black and red, sitting on a wooded hillside, playing guitars and brass instruments. There were Good Templars, who had been on a pleasure outing. He recognized them by the large banners with gold inscriptions that swayed over them. And they sang song after song, as long as he could hear them.

The boy could never remember Gotland later without also thinking of games and songs.

For a long time he sat looking down, but now he happened to raise his eyes. No one can describe how surprised he was. Without his having noticed it, the geese had left the interior of the island and travelled west towards the coast. Now the wide, blue sea lay before him. But it was not the sea that was remarkable, but a city that rose up from the seashore.

The boy came from the east and the sun had started to go down in the west. As he approached the city, its walls and towers and high-gabled houses and churches stood completely black against the light evening sky. For that reason he could not see what they were like in reality, and for a few moments he thought that it was as grand a city as the one he had seen on Easter Eve.

When he really came up to it, he saw that it was both like and unlike that city from the bottom of the sea. It was the same difference as if on one day you saw a man dressed in purple and jewellery and another day saw him destitute and in rags.

Yes, this city had probably once been like the one he was thinking about. This one was also surrounded by a city wall with towers and gates. But the towers in this city, which had been able to remain on land, were roofless, hollow and empty. The gates were without doors, watchmen and soldiers were missing. All the shining splendour was gone. It was only the bare, grey stone structure that was there.

As the boy came farther in over the city, he saw that for the most part it was built up with small, low houses, but here and there some of the high-gabled houses were still there and some churches from the old times. The walls of the gabled houses were whitewashed and completely without decoration, but because he had so recently seen the sunken city, he thought he could understand how they had been adorned: some with statues and others with black-and-white marble. And it was the same way with the old churches. Most of them had no roof with bare interiors. The window openings stood empty, the floors were grass-covered, and ivy climbed up the walls. But now he knew how they had once looked, that they had been covered with images and paintings, that the chancel had decorated altars and gilded crosses, and that priests had moved about dressed in golden vestments.

The boy also saw the narrow streets, almost empty of people on the holiday afternoon. He knew what a stream of stately people had once swarmed on them. He knew that they had been like large workshops, full of all kinds of workers.

But what Nils Holgersson did not see was that even today the city was both beautiful and remarkable. He saw neither the pleasant cottages on the back streets with black walls, white corners and red geraniums behind the sparkling windowpanes, nor the many lovely gardens and lanes, nor the beauty of the ruins draped in creepers. His eyes were so filled by the magnificence of the past that he could not see anything good in the present.

The wild geese flew back and forth a few times over the city, so that Thumbkin could get to see everything really well. At last they descended on to the grass-covered floor in a church ruin to stay there overnight.

When they had already settled down to sleep, Thumbkin was still awake and looked through the broken roof arches up towards the pale red evening sky. When he had been sitting there a while, he thought that he did not want to fret any more that he had not been able to save the sunken city.

No, he did not want to, since he got to see this. If the city that he had seen did not have to sink down to the seabed again, perhaps in time it would be just as dilapidated as this one. Perhaps it would have been unable to withstand time and transiency, but soon would have stood with roofless churches and unadorned houses and deserted, empty streets like this. Then it was better that it was still there in all its magnificence down in the depths.

'It was best that it happened the way it did,' he thought. 'If I had the power to rescue the city, I don't think I would.' Then he no longer grieved about it.

And there are probably many of those who are young who think the same way. But when people get old and are used to being content with little, then they are happier about the Visby that exists than a grand Vineta at the bottom of the sea.

FIFTEEN
The Tale of Småland

TUESDAY, 12 APRIL

The wild geese had a good journey over the sea and landed in the county of Tjust in northern Småland. That county couldn't seem to decide whether it was land or sea. The bays divided the land everywhere into islands and peninsulas, into promontories and spits. The sea was so intrusive that the only things that could stay above water were hills and rocky slopes. All the lowland was hidden away under the surface.

It was evening when the wild geese came in from the sea, and the rolling country was beautifully situated between the glistening bays. Here and there on the islands the boy saw cabins and cottages, and the farther in towards land he came, the bigger and better the houses became. At last they grew into big, white manor houses. Along the shoreline there was usually a wreath of trees, beyond which were strips of fields, and up on the top of the small hills the trees took off again. He could not help but think of Blekinge. This was once again a place where land and sea met in such a beautiful, quiet way, as if trying to show each other their best and loveliest side.

The wild geese landed on a bare islet far inside the Gås-fjärden. At first glance towards the shore they noticed that spring had made major advances while they had been away on the islands. There were no leaves yet on the big, magnificent trees, but the ground beneath them was dotted with wood anemone, yellow star of Bethlehem and blue anemone.

When the wild geese saw the carpet of flowers, they were afraid they had lingered too long in the southern part of the country. Akka said at once that there was no time to visit any of the resting places in Småland. Already the next morning they had to head northwards over Östergötland.

Thus the boy would not see any of Småland and this annoyed him. He had not heard any other province talked about as much as Småland and he wanted to see it with his own eyes.

The previous summer, when he had a job as a goose-boy with a farmer in the vicinity of Jordberga, almost every day he had encountered a couple of poor Småland children, who were also tending geese. The children had teased him quite terribly about their Småland.

Although you probably can't really say that Åsa the Goose-girl teased him. She was much too sensible for such things. But the one who could be annoying with a vengeance was her brother, Little Mats.

'Have you heard, Nils the goose-boy, what happened when Småland and Skåne were created?' he would ask, and if Nils Holgersson said no, he started telling the old folk tale at once.

'Well, it was at the time when Our Lord was creating the world. While he was busy working, St Peter came walking past. He stopped and watched, and then he asked if it was a hard job. "Oh well, it's not so easy either," said Our Lord. St Peter stood there a while longer, and when he noticed how easy it was to set out one land after the other, he wanted to give it a go himself. "Perhaps you need to rest a little," St Peter said. "Then I could manage the work for you in the meantime." But Our Lord did not want that. "I don't know if you are so practised in the art that I can trust you to take over while I stop," he answered. Then St Peter got angry and said that he thought he could create countries just as good as Our Lord Himself.

'The fact of the matter is that just then Our Lord was in the process of creating Småland. It was not even half- finished, but it appeared to be an indescribably beautiful and fruitful country. It was hard for Our Lord to say no to St Peter, and besides he probably thought that no one could spoil what was so well begun. For that reason he said, "If you agree, then let's test which of us is best at this sort of work. You, who are only a beginner, can continue with what I've started, and I will create a new country." St Peter agreed to this at once, and then they each started working in their own place.

'Our Lord moved a section southwards, and there he set about creating Skåne. It did not take long before he was done, and immediately he asked whether St Peter had finished and wanted to come and look at his work. "I had mine done long ago," said St Peter, and his tone of voice told how satisfied he was with what he had achieved.

'When St Peter saw Skåne, he had to admit that there was nothing but good to be said about that country. It was a fertile, easily cultivated land with large plains wherever he looked, and hardly a hint of hills. It seemed that Our Lord had really thought about making it so that people would thrive there. "Yes, this is a good country," said St Peter, "but I do think that mine is better."

' "Then let's go take a look at it," said Our Lord.

'The country was already finished in the north and east when St Peter started his work, but he got to shape the southern and western part and the whole interior alone. Now when Our Lord came up to where St Peter had worked, He was so startled that He stopped abruptly and said, "What in the world have you done to this country, St Peter?"

'St Peter also stood and looked around, quite surprised. He'd had the notion that nothing could be so good for a country as a lot of heat. For that reason he had dragged together an incredible mass of stone and rock and built up a highland, and he had done this so that it would come close to the sun and get a lot of the sun's heat. Above the heaps of stones he had spread out a thin layer of topsoil, and then he thought that everything was in good order.

'But now a couple of strong rain showers had come while he was down in Skåne, and it took no more than this to show what his work was good for. When Our Lord came to inspect the country all the topsoil had been washed away and bare bedrock was sticking out everywhere. At its best there was clay and heavy gravel over the rocks, but it looked so meagre that it was obvious that scarcely anything could grow there other than spruce and juniper and moss and heather. What there was plenty of, was water. It had filled up all the crevices in the bedrock, and lakes, rivers and creeks were seen everywhere, not to mention marshes and fens, which extended over large areas. And the most mortifying thing was that while some areas had more than enough water, it was so scarce in other places that large fields were like dry moors, where sand and dirt whirled up in clouds with the slightest breeze.

'"What was the idea of creating a country like this?" said Our Lord, and St Peter excused himself and said that he had wanted to build up the country so high that it would get a lot of heat from the sun. "But then it will also get a lot of cold at night," said Our Lord, "because that too comes from the sky. I am afraid that the little that can grow here is going to freeze."

'Of course, St Peter had not thought about that.

'"Yes, this will be a poor, frost-bound country," said Our Lord. "It can't be helped."'

When Little Mats got that far in his story, Åsa the Goose-girl interrupted him. 'Little Mats, I can't stand you saying that it's so miserable in Småland,' she said. 'You completely forget how much good soil there is there. Just think about Möre County over by Kalmar Sound! I wonder where there is a richer district for grain. There is field upon field, just like here in Skåne. There is such good soil there that I don't know what couldn't grow there.'

'I can't help it,' said Little Mats. 'I'm just repeating what others have said before.'

'And I've heard many people say that a more beautiful coastland than Tjust does not exist. Think about the bays and the islets and the estates and the groves!' said Åsa.

'Yes, I'm sure that's true,' Little Mats admitted.

'And don't you remember,' Åsa continued, 'that the school-teacher said that such a lively and beautiful region like the bit of Småland that is south of Vättern is not to be found in all of Sweden? Think about the beautiful lake and the yellow shore rocks and about Gränna and Jönköping with the match factory, and Munksjö, and think about Huskvarna and all the big factories there!'

'Yes, I'm sure that's true,' Little Mats said again.

'And think about Visingsö, Little Mats, with the ruins and the oak forest and the sagas! Think about the valley the Emån River runs through, with all the villages and mills and wood-pulp factories and sawmills and carpentry shops!'

'Yes, that's all true,' Little Mats said, looking quite distressed.

Suddenly he looked up. 'Now we are all really dumb,' he said. 'All of that, of course, is in Our Lord's Småland, in the part of the country that was already finished before St Peter went to work. It's only right that it should be beautiful and grand there. But in St Peter's Småland everything looks as it says in the story. And it was not strange that Our Lord became distressed when he saw it,' Little Mats continued, as he resumed his story. 'St Peter did not lose courage in any event. Instead he tried to console Our Lord. "Don't get so upset about this!" he said. "Just wait until I have time to create people who can cultivate the marshes and plough up fields out of the stony hills!"'

'Then Our Lord's patience had finally run out, and he said, "No. You can go down to Skåne, which I have made into a good, easily cultivated land, and create the people there, but I want to create the people of Småland myself." And so Our Lord created the people of Småland and made them clever and contented and happy and diligent and enterprising and capable, so that they could make a livelihood for themselves in their poor country.'

With that Little Mats fell silent, and if Nils Holgersson had also kept quiet now, everything would have gone well, but he could not possibly keep from asking how St Peter had done in creating the people of Skåne.

'Yes, what do you think yourself?' said Little Mats and looked so scornful that Nils Holgersson lunged at him to hit him. But Mats was only a little fellow and Åsa the Goose-girl, who was one year older, ran at once to help him. As good-tempered as she was, she reared up like a lioness as soon as anyone touched her brother. And Nils Holgersson did not want to fight with a girl, so instead he turned his back on them and went away and did not look at those Småland children the whole day.

SIXTEEN
The Crows

The Clay Pot

In the south-west corner of Småland is a county called Sunnerbo. It is a rather flat and level area, and anyone who sees it in the winter, when it is covered with snow, would simply assume that under the snow is an expanse of ploughed, fallow ground, green rye fields and mown clover fields, the way it usually is in a flat country. But when the snow finally melts away in Sunnerbo in early April, it turns out that what lies hidden beneath it is nothing but dry sand moors, bare rocks and large, swampy marshes. There are no doubt fields here and there, but they are so insignificant that you hardly notice them, and there are small grey or red peasant cottages too, but they are usually set back on some birch-covered hill, almost as if they were afraid to show themselves.

Where Sunnerbo County bumps against the border with the province of Halland, there is a sandy moor so extensive that anyone standing at its edge cannot see over to the opposite side. Nothing but heather grows on the whole moor, and it would be difficult to get other plants to thrive there. The very first thing then would be to root out the heather, because the fact is that although it only has a small stunted trunk, small stunted branches and dry, stunted leaves, it imagines that it is a tree. For that reason it behaves the same way as real trees, spreading out in forests over wide stretches, keeping faithfully together and causing all foreign plants that want to intrude on its area to die out.

The only place on the moor where the heather is not all-powerful is a low, stony ridge that sweeps across it. There one finds juniper bushes, mountain ash and some large, beautiful birches. At the time when Nils Holgersson was travelling around with the wild geese there was also a cottage with a little bit of cleared ground around it, but the people who once lived there had moved away for some reason or other. The little cottage stood empty and the field was untilled.

When the people left the cottage, they closed the damper, put on the window catches and locked the door. But they had not thought that a pane in the window was broken and only stopped up with a rag. After a couple of summer rain showers that rag had decayed and crumpled up, and at last a crow managed to peck it away.

The ridge on the heather moor was not as deserted as you might think; it was populated by a large group of crows. Naturally the crows did not live there all year round. They moved abroad in the winter; in the autumn they swept across one field after the next all over the Götaland region and picked grain; in the summer they dispersed to the farms in Sunnerbo County and lived off eggs, berries and chicks; but every spring when they were going to build nests and lay eggs, they came back to the heather moor.

The one who plucked the rag out of the window was a male crow whose name was Garm White-Feather, although he was never called anything but Fumle or Drumle or even Fumle-Drumle, because he always acted stupid and awkward and was not good for anything but being made fun of. Fumle-Drumle was bigger and stronger than any of the other crows, but that did not help him in the least; instead he was and remained an object of ridicule. It was of little avail to him either that he was from a very good family. If everything had gone right, he should even have been leader of the whole flock, because that dignity had since time immemorial belonged to the oldest of the White-Feathers. But long before Fumle-Drumle was born, the power had gone from his family and was now held by a cruel and wild crow, whose name was Wind-Ile.

That transfer of power happened because the crows on Kråkåsen felt like changing their way of life. Many believe that all crows live the same way, but this is completely incorrect. There are entire groups of crows that lead an honourable life, that is, they eat only seeds, worms, larvae and already dead animals, and there are others who lead a real robbers' life, who swoop down on young hares and small birds and plunder every bird's nest they catch sight of.

The old White-Feathers had been strict and moderate, and as long as they led the flock, they had forced the crows to conduct themselves such that other birds did not have anything bad to say about them. But the crows were numerous and there was great poverty among them. In the long run they could not stand leading such a strict life and instead revolted against the White-Feathers and gave the power to Wind-Ile, who was the worst nest-plunderer and robber that could be imagined, if his wife, Wind-Kåra, weren't worse. Under their control the crows started to lead such a life that they were now more feared than goshawks and great horned owls.

Fumle-Drumle naturally had no say in the flock. Everyone was in agreement that he did not resemble his ancestors in the slightest, and that he was not cut out to be the leader. No one would have talked about him if he had not constantly made new blunders. A few who were really wise sometimes said that perhaps it was good fortune for Fumle-Drumle that he was such a clumsy wretch, otherwise Wind-Ile and Wind-Kåra probably would not have let him, who was of the old chieftain clan, remain with the flock.

Now on the contrary they were quite friendly towards him

and happily took him along on their hunts. There everyone could see how much more skilful and bold they were than him.

None of the crows knew that it was Fumle-Drumle who had plucked the rag out of the window, and if they had known this they would have been incredibly surprised. Such boldness – to approach a human dwelling – they would not have believed of him. He himself carefully concealed the matter and had his good reasons for it. Wind-Ile and Kåra always treated him well during the day and when the others were present, but one very dark night, when their comrades were already sitting on the night perch, he had been attacked by a pair of crows and almost murdered. After this, every evening after it had become dark he moved from his usual sleeping place into the empty cottage.

It happened now one afternoon, when the crows had already got their nests in order on Kråkåsen, that they made a remarkable find. Wind-Ile, Fumle-Drumle and a few others had flown down into a large hollow which was in one corner of the moor. The hollow was nothing but a gravel pit, but the crows could not be content with such a simple explanation. Instead they kept flying down into it, turning over every grain of sand to figure out why humans had dug it. While the crows were there, a mass of gravel tumbled down from one side. They hurried and had the good fortune to find among the fallen stones and tufts of grass a rather large clay pot, which was closed with a wooden lid. Naturally they wanted to know if there was anything in it, and they tried both hacking holes in the pot and prising up the lid, but neither succeeded.

They stood there quite perplexed and observed the pot, when they heard someone say, 'Shall I come down and help you, crows?' They looked up quickly. On the edge of the hollow a fox sat looking down at them. He was one of the most beautiful foxes they had ever seen, in both colour and shape. The only fault with him was that he had lost one ear.

'If you want to do us a favour,' said Wind-Ile, 'we won't say no.' At the same time both he and the others flew up out of the hollow. The fox jumped down in their place, bit on the pot and pulled on the lid, but he could not open it either.

'Can you figure out what's in it?' Wind-Ile said. The fox

rolled the pot back and forth and listened attentively. 'It can't be anything other than silver coins,' he said.

This was more than the crows had expected. 'Do you think it can be silver?' they said, and their eyes were about to pop out of their heads with greed, because, however strange it may sound, there is nothing in the world that crows love as much as silver coins.

'Hear how they jingle!' the fox said, rolling the pot around again. 'I just can't understand how we're going to get at them.'

'No, it's probably impossible,' said the crows.

The fox stood and rubbed his head with his left leg and thought. Perhaps he would succeed now with the crows' help to be master over that imp who always evaded him. 'I think I know someone who would be able to open the pot for you,' the fox said.

'Say it, then! Say it!' the crows called and were so eager that they fluttered down into the hollow.

'I'll do that, only first you have to agree to my terms,' he said.

The fox now told the crows about Thumbkin and said to them that if they could bring him to the moor he could probably open the pot for them. But as reward for this advice he demanded that they turn Thumbkin over to him as soon as he had got them the silver coins. The crows had no reason to spare Thumbkin, so they immediately agreed.

This was all easily settled, but it was harder to find out where Thumbkin and the wild geese were.

Wind-Ile himself took off with fifty crows and said that he would soon be back. But one day passed after the next, without the crows on Kråkåsen seeing a glimpse of him.

Kidnapped by Crows

WEDNESDAY, 13 APRIL

The wild geese were up at the crack of dawn to have time to get a little food before starting their journey towards Östergötland.

The islet in Gåsfjärden they had slept on was small and bare, but in the water around it there were plants they could fill up on. It was worse for the boy. He was unable to find anything edible.

As he stood that morning, hungry and cold, looking around in all directions, his eyes fell on a couple of squirrels playing on a tree-covered promontory right in front of the rocky islet. He wondered whether the squirrels did not still have some of their winter stores left, and he asked the white gander to carry him over to the promontory so that he could beg a couple of hazel-nuts from them.

The large white gander swam at once across the sound with him, but as bad luck would have it, the squirrels were having so much fun chasing each other from tree to tree that they did not bother to listen to the boy. Instead they went farther into the grove. He hurried after and soon went out of sight of the gander, who was still by the shore.

The boy waded forth between some wood anemone plants, which were so tall they reached all the way up to his chin, when he felt someone take hold of him from behind and try to lift him up. He turned around and saw that a crow had seized hold of his neckband. He tried to tear himself loose, but before he had succeeded another crow hurried up, took hold of his one sock and pulled him down.

If Nils Holgersson had immediately called for help, the white gander would certainly have been able to free him, but the boy probably thought that he ought to be able to manage alone against a couple of crows. He kicked and hit, but the crows did not let go, and they succeeded in getting up in the air with him. In doing so they proceeded so carelessly that his head struck against a branch. He got a hard blow across the top of his head, it turned black before his eyes and he lost consciousness.

When he opened his eyes again he found himself high above the ground. He slowly returned to consciousness and at first he did not know either where he was or what he was seeing. When he looked down, he thought that below him an incredibly large, woolly carpet spread out, which was woven from green

and brown in large, irregular shapes. The carpet was very
thick and strong, but he thought it was a shame it was so much
the worse for wear. It was really ragged, long tears ran along it
and in some places large pieces were torn away. And the strangest thing was that it seemed to be lying over a mirrored floor,
because under the holes and tears in the carpet shiny, glistening glass shimmered forth.

What the boy noticed next was that the sun came rolling up
in the sky. Immediately the mirrored glass under the holes and
tears in the carpet started to glisten in red and gold. It looked
very splendid and the beautiful shifts in colour pleased the boy,
although he did not really understand what it was he was seeing. But now the crows descended and at once he noticed that
the large carpet under him was the earth, which here was clad
with green pine forest and brown, bare deciduous forest, and
that the holes and tears were glistening fjords and small lakes.

He recalled that the first time he had travelled up in the air
he thought that the ground in Skåne looked like a piece of chequered cloth. But this, which resembled a torn carpet, what
kind of country could it be?

He started asking himself a lot of questions. Why wasn't he
sitting on the gander's back? Why was a large swarm of crows
flying around him? And why was he being jerked and tossed
here and there, so that he was about to fall off?

Then it all became clear to him at once. He had been kidnapped by a couple of crows. The white gander was still
waiting by the shore and the wild geese would be travelling up
to Östergötland today. He himself was being taken to the
south-west, which he understood because the sun was behind
him. And the large forest carpet which lay below him was
surely Småland.

'What will happen to the white gander when I can't take
care of him?' the boy thought, and he started shouting at the
crows that they should take him back to the wild geese at once.
He was not a bit worried for his own sake. He thought it was
out of sheer mischief that they carried him away.

The crows did not respond to his requests at all, but instead
flew ahead as fast as they were able. But after a while one of

them flapped its wings in the way that means, 'Look out! Danger!' Right after that they dived down into a spruce forest, squeezed between the scrubby branches all the way to the forest floor and set the boy down under a dense spruce, where he was so well hidden that not even a hawk could have caught sight of him.

Fifty crows lined up around the boy with their beaks aimed towards him to guard him. 'Now, crows, maybe I can find out what your intentions are in taking me away,' he said. But he had hardly finished what he was saying before a big crow hissed at him, 'Just keep quiet! Otherwise I'll peck your eyes out!'

It was clear the crow meant what he said, and the boy could do nothing other than obey. So he sat there and stared at the crows, and the crows stared at him.

The longer he looked at them, the less he liked them. It was terrible how dusty and badly battered their plumage was, as if they didn't know about either bathing or oiling. Their toes and claws were soiled with dried dirt, and the corners of their mouths were covered with food scraps. This was a different sort of bird than the wild geese, he noticed. He felt they had a cruel, greedy, watchful and bold appearance, just like scoundrels and tramps.

'I've definitely fallen into the hands of a band of robbers,' he thought.

Just then he heard the call of the wild geese above him. 'Where are you? Here am I! Where are you? Here am I!'

He realized that Akka and the others had gone out to search for him, but before he had time to answer them, the big crow, who seemed to be the leader of the band, hissed in his ear, 'Think about your eyes!' And there was nothing for him to do other than to keep silent.

The wild geese could not have known that he was so close to them, but instead only by chance happened to fly over this forest. He heard their calls a few more times, then they died away. 'Yes, now you have to manage on your own, Nils Holgersson,' the boy then said to himself. 'Now you get to show whether you've learned anything during these weeks in the wilderness.'

Shortly thereafter the crows made signs of departing, and as they now seemed intent on carrying him with one holding on to his neckband and one on to his sock, the boy said, 'Aren't any of you crows strong enough to carry me on her back? You've already treated me so roughly that it feels as if I were torn in two. Just let me ride! I won't throw myself down from a crow's back, I promise you that.'

'You shouldn't think we care about how you feel,' the leader said, but now the biggest of the crows, a dishevelled and ungainly one with a white feather on his wing, came up and said, 'It would probably be better for us all, Wind-Ile, if Thumbkin arrived whole rather than in half, and for that reason I will try to carry him on my back.'

'If you're able, Fumle-Drumle, then I have nothing against it,' said Wind-Ile. 'But don't lose him!'

This in itself was a major gain and the boy felt satisfied once more. 'It's not worth it to lose my temper because I've been kidnapped by the crows,' he thought. 'I think I'll get the better of these wretches.'

The crows were still flying towards the south-west over Småland. It was a splendid morning, sunny and calm, and the birds down on the ground were busy singing their best court-ing songs. In a high, dark forest the thrush himself sat with drooping wings and thickened throat up in the top of a spruce and warbled over and over. 'How lovely you are! How lovely you are! How lovely you are!' he sang. 'No one is so lovely! No one is so lovely! No one is so lovely!' And as soon as he had finished this song, he started it again.

But the boy was riding over the forest just then, and when he had heard the song a few times and noticed that the thrush did not know any others, he put both his hands around his mouth like a horn and called downwards, 'We've heard that before! We've heard that before!'

'Who is it? Who is it? Who is it? Who's making fun of me?' the thrush asked, trying to catch sight of whoever was calling.

'It's Abducted-by-Crows who's making fun of your song!' the boy answered. The crow chieftain turned his head at once and said, 'Watch your eyes, Thumbkin!' But the boy thought, 'No, I don't care about that. I just want to show you that I'm not afraid of you.'

They were travelling farther up country and there were forests and lakes everywhere. In a birch grove the stock dove was sitting on a bare branch and in front of her stood the male. He puffed up his feathers, crooked his neck and raised and lowered his body, so that his breast feathers buzzed against the branch. All the while he cooed, 'You, you, you are the loveliest in the forest! No one in the forest is as lovely as you, you, you!'

But up in the air the boy went past, and when he heard the male dove he could not keep quiet. 'Don't believe him! Don't believe him!' he shouted.

'Who, who, who is it who is lying about me?' the male dove cooed, trying to catch sight of whoever had yelled at him.

'It's Taken-by-Crows who is lying about you!' the boy answered. Once again Wind-Ile turned his head towards the boy and ordered him to be silent, but Fumle-Drumle, who was carrying him, said, 'Let him talk, then the small birds will think that we crows have become quick-witted, funny birds!'

'Maybe that's not such a bad idea,' said Wind-Ile, but he must have liked the idea, because then he let the boy shout as much as he wanted.

It was mostly forest and woodland that they flew over, but of course there were also churches and villages and small cottages at the forest edge. In one place they saw a nice old estate. It was situated with the forest behind it and the lake in front of it, with red walls and a gambrel roof, massive maple trees around the yard and large, scrubby gooseberry bushes in the garden. At the top of the weathervane the starling sat and sang so that every note was heard by the female, who was sitting on eggs in the nesting box over in the pear tree. 'We have four beautiful little eggs!' the starling sang. 'We have four beautiful, round little eggs! We have a whole nesting box full of splendid eggs!'

As the starling was singing the song for the thousandth time, the boy passed over the farm. He put his hands around his mouth and shouted, 'The magpie will take them! The magpie will take them!'

'Who is it who wants to frighten me?' the starling asked, worriedly flapping his wings.

'It's Captured-by-Crows who is scaring you!' the boy said. This time the crow chieftain did not try to silence him. Instead, both he and the whole flock were having such fun that they cawed with contentment.

The farther up country they came, the larger the lakes became, and the richer they became in islands and promontories. And on one lakeshore a drake was standing, fawning for the female duck. 'I will be faithful to you for all my days! I will be faithful to you for all my days!' the drake said.

'Won't last beyond the end of summer!' the boy shouted as they passed.

'Who is that?' the drake called.

'My name is Stolen-by-Crows!' the boy shouted.

At midday the crows landed in an enclosed pasture. They went around gathering food, but none of them thought about giving the boy anything. Then Fumle-Drumle came rushing up to the chieftain with a twig from a briar bush, on which there were some red rose hips. 'Here you go, Wind-Ile,' he said. 'This is some nice food just for you.'

Wind-Ile snorted contemptuously. 'Do you think I want to eat old, dried-up rose hips?' he said.

'And here I thought you'd be happy about them!' Fumle-Drumle said, tossing away the rose-hip twig as if in dejection. But it fell down right in front of the boy, and he was not slow to take hold of it and eat until he was full.

When the crows had eaten, they started talking. 'What are you thinking about, Wind-Ile? You're so quiet today,' one of them said to the leader.

'I'm thinking that once in this area lived a hen who was very fond of her mistress and to really please her she went and laid a batch of eggs, which she hid under a barn floor. The whole time she sat on the eggs she delighted in the thought of how happy her mistress would be about the chicks. Her mistress wondered, of course, where the hen was keeping herself for such a long time. She searched for her, but didn't find her. Can you guess, Long-Beak, who found her and the eggs?'

'I think I can guess, Wind-Ile, but now that you mention it, I'll tell you something similar. Do you remember the big, black cat in Hinneryd parsonage? She was dissatisfied with the master and mistress, because they always took her newborn kittens from her and drowned them. She managed to keep them hidden no more than once and that was when she placed them in a haystack out in the field. She was probably very satisfied with those kittens, but I think I got more joy from them than she did.'

Now they all got so excited that they started talking at once. 'What art is there in stealing eggs and kittens?' said one. 'Once I chased a young hare who was almost full-grown. I had to follow him from thicket to thicket.' She got no further, before another took over. 'It may be fun to annoy hens and cats, but I find it even more remarkable that a crow can cause a human trouble. Once I stole a silver spoon—'

But now the boy thought that he was too good to sit and listen to such talk. 'No, listen up, crows!' he said. 'I think you ought to be ashamed, talking about all your meanness. I have lived among wild geese for three weeks and I have never seen or heard anything but good from them. You must have a bad chieftain, who lets you rob and murder like this. You all ought to change your ways, because I can tell you that the humans are so sick and tired of your evil that they are trying with all their might to eradicate you. And then it will probably soon be the end of you.'

When Wind-Ile and the crows heard this, they became so angry that they intended to throw themselves on to the boy and tear him apart. But Fumle-Drumle laughed and cawed and placed himself in front of him. 'No, no, no!' he said, seeming to be quite terrified. 'What do you think Wind-Kåra will say if you tear Thumbkin apart before he has got us the silver coins?'

'Fumle-Drumle, you should be the one who is afraid of womenfolk,' Ile said, but in any event both he and the others left Thumbkin alone.

Shortly after that the crows continued. So far the boy had thought to himself that Småland was not such a poor country as he had heard. To be sure it was woody and full of ridges, but along rivers and lakes was cultivated land, and he had not encountered any real desolation. But as they came farther into the country, there were fewer and fewer villages and cottages. At last he thought that he was travelling over a real desert, where he saw nothing other than marshes and moors and juniper-clad hills.

The sun had gone down, but it was still light out when the crows reached the large heather moor. Wind-Ile sent one crow in advance to report that he had had success, and when it became known, Wind-Kåra took off with several hundred crows from Kråkåsen to meet the arrivals. In the middle of the deafening cawing raised by the reception of the crows, Fumle-Drumle now said to the boy, 'You've been so amusing and happy during the journey that I really like you. For that reason I'll give you some good advice. As soon as we set down, you will be asked to perform a task that may seem very easy to you. But be careful about doing it!'

Right after that Fumle-Drumle set Nils Holgersson down on the bottom of a sandpit. The boy threw himself down and remained lying there, as if he were exhausted. So many crows flapped around him that the air was roaring like a storm, but he did not look up.

'Thumbkin!' said Wind-Ile. 'Get up now! Now you will help us with something that will be very easy for you.'

But the boy did not move. Instead, he pretended to be asleep. Then Wind-Ile took him by the arm and dragged him across the sand to an old-fashioned clay pot in the middle of the pit. 'Get up, Thumbkin,' he said, 'and open this pot!'

'Why can't you let me sleep?' the boy said. 'I'm too tired to do anything tonight. Wait till tomorrow!'

'Open the pot!' Wind-Ile said, shaking him. The boy then sat up and carefully examined the pot. 'How can I, a poor child, open such a pot? It's as big as I am.'

'Open it!' Wind-Ile ordered again. 'Otherwise you'll be in big trouble.'

The boy stood up, staggered over to the pot, felt the lid and dropped his arms. 'I'm not usually this weak,' he said. 'If you'll just let me sleep until tomorrow, I think I can probably manage the lid.'

But Wind-Ile was impatient, and he rushed over and nipped the boy on the leg. The boy would not tolerate such treatment from a crow. He quickly pulled himself loose, ran a couple of steps backwards, pulled his knife from its sheath and held it stretched out in front of him. 'Watch out now!' he called to Wind-Ile.

Wind-Ile was nevertheless so embittered that he did not dodge the danger. As if he had been blind, he rushed towards the boy and ran right against the knife so that it penetrated through his eye into his brain. The boy quickly pulled the knife back, but Wind-Ile only flapped his wings. Then he sank down dead.

'Wind-Ile is dead! The stranger has killed our chieftain, Wind-Ile!' the crows closest by called and then a terrible racket arose. Some wailed, others called for revenge. All of them ran or flapped towards the boy, with Fumle-Drumle in the lead. But as usual he behaved crazily. He just flapped with outspread wings over the boy and prevented the others from coming up and drilling their beaks into him.

Now the boy really thought that he was in a bad way. He could not run away from the crows and there was no place where he could hide. But then he happened to think about the clay pot. He took a firm hold on the lid and pulled it off. Then he jumped up into the pot to hide himself in it. But it was a bad hiding place, because it was almost filled to the brim with small, thin silver coins. The boy could not get deep enough down into it. Then he leaned over and started throwing out the coins.

So far the crows had been flapping around him in a dense swarm, hacking at him, but when he threw out the coins they suddenly forgot their desire for revenge and hurried to gather them. The boy threw out fistfuls of coins and all the crows – yes, even Wind-Kåra – caught them up. And each and every one of them who managed to get hold of a coin, went off in the greatest haste to their nest to hide it.

When the boy had thrown all the silver coins out of the pot, he looked up. Not more than a single crow was still in the sandpit. It was Fumle-Drumle with the white feather in his wing, the one who had carried him. 'You've done me a greater service, Thumbkin, than you yourself understand,' the crow said in a quite different voice and tone than before. 'And I want to save your life. Get up on my back, then I will carry you to a hiding place where you will be safe tonight! Tomorrow I will arrange it so that you get back to the wild geese.'

The Cottage

THURSDAY, 14 APRIL

The next morning when the boy woke up he was in a bed. When he saw that he was indoors with four walls around him and a roof over him, he thought he was home.

'I wonder if Mother is coming with coffee soon?' he mumbled, half-asleep. But then he remembered that he was in an abandoned cottage on Kråkåsen, and that Fumle-Drumle with the white feather had carried him there the night before.

The boy's whole body was sore after the journey he had made the day before and he thought it was nice to lie still while he waited for Fumle-Drumle, who had promised to come and get him.

Chequered cotton curtains were hanging in front of the bed, and he pushed them to the side to see out into the cottage. It was clear to him at once that he had never seen the likes of a building like this. The walls consisted of only a few rows of logs; then the roof started. There was no ceiling; he could see all the way to the roof ridge. The whole cottage was so small that it seemed to be made for someone like him rather than for real people, but even so the stove and hearth were larger than any he had ever seen. The entry door was on the end wall beside the stove and was so narrow it was more like a hatch. On the wall at the other end he saw a low, wide window with many small panes. There was almost no movable furniture in the cottage. The bench on the one long side and the table under the window were built-in, as was the motley cupboard and the big bed where he was lying.

The boy could not help wondering who owned the cottage and why it was abandoned. To be sure, it looked as if the people who had lived there intended to come back. The coffee kettle and porridge pot were still on the stove, and there was a little wood in the stove corner. The oven rake and bread peel were standing in a corner, the spinning wheel had been moved on to a bench, on the shelf above the window were flax and tow, a couple of skeins of yarn, a tallow candle and a bundle of matches.

Yes, it certainly appeared as if those who owned the cottage intended to come back. There was bedding on the bed and on the wall there were still long strips of fabric, where three men on horseback, whose names were Caspar, Melchior and Balthasar, were painted. The same horses and the same riders were depicted many times. They rode around the whole cottage and continued their journey even up the roof beams.

But by the ceiling the boy caught sight of something that got him on his feet in no time. It was a couple of dry loaves of bread that were hanging there on a spit. To be sure, they looked mouldy and old, but it was still bread. He gave them a hit with the bread peel, so that one fell to the floor. He ate and filled his bag. It was incredible how good bread was in any event.

He looked around the cottage once again to try to discover if there was anything else that might be useful for him to take along. 'I guess I can take what I need, when no one else cares about it,' he thought. But most of what was there was too big and heavy. The only thing he could manage would be a few matches.

He climbed up on the table, then swung up on the window shelf with the help of the curtain. While he stood there, putting matches into his bag, the crow with the white feather came in through the window.

'See, here I am now!' Fumle-Drumle said, landing on the table. 'I wasn't able to come earlier, because today we crows have elected a new chieftain after Wind-Ile.'

'So who have you elected?' the boy said.

'Well, we have elected one who will not allow robbery and injustice. We have elected Garm White-Feather, who was called Fumle-Drumle before,' he answered and stretched so that he looked quite majestic.

'That was a good choice,' the boy said, congratulating him.

'Yes, you probably should wish me luck,' said Garm, who started telling the boy about how he was treated before by Wind-Ile and Kåra.

In the midst of this the boy heard a voice outside the window, which he thought he recognized. 'Is this where he is?' Smirre Fox asked.

'Yes, he's hiding in here,' a crow voice answered.

'Be on your guard, Thumbkin!' Garm called. 'Wind-Kåra is standing outside with that fox who wants to eat you up.' He did not have time to say more, because Smirre made a leap towards the window. The rotten old window casements gave way, and the next moment Smirre was standing on the table by the window. Garm White-Feather did not have time to fly away and he bit him to death at once. After that he jumped down on the floor and looked around for the boy.

The boy tried to hide behind a large blue morning glory, but Smirre had already seen him and curled up to get ready for a leap. And as little and low as the cottage was, the boy understood that the fox could reach him without the slightest difficulty. But at this moment the boy was not without defensive weapons. Quickly he lit a match, guided it up to the flax, and when it flared up he threw it down on to Smirre Fox. When the fire came over the fox, he was seized by an insane terror. He thought no more about the boy, but instead frantically fled the cottage.

But it appeared as if the boy had escaped one danger by casting himself into an even greater one. From the tuft of flax he had thrown at Smirre, the fire had managed to spread to the bed curtain. He ran down and tried to put it out, but it was already flaming far too intensely. The cottage was suddenly filled with smoke and Smirre Fox, who had stopped outside the window, started to understand what was going on inside. 'Well, Thumbkin,' he called, 'which do you choose now, letting yourself be cooked or coming out to me? To be sure, I would probably prefer to eat you, but whatever way death befalls you is fine by me.'

The boy began to think that the fox was right, because the fire spread terribly quickly. The whole bed was already burning, smoke rose up from the floor, and along the painted fabric borders the fire crept from rider to rider. The boy had jumped up on the stove and was trying to open the cover to the baking oven, when he heard a key in the lock slowly turning. It must be humans that were coming, and in such distress as he now found himself, he was not afraid, but only happy. He was already at the threshold when the door finally opened. He saw a couple of children in front of him. He did not take time to look at their expressions when they saw the cottage all ablaze, but instead rushed past them and out into the open.

He did not dare run far. He knew that Smirre Fox was waiting for him, and he realized that he had to stay near the children. He turned around to see what kind of people they were, but he had not observed them for a second before he rushed towards them and shouted, 'Good day to you, Åsa the Goose-girl! Good day to you, Little Mats!'

Because when the boy saw those children, he completely forgot where he was. Crows and a burning cottage and talking animals disappeared from his memory. He was on a stubble field in Västra Vemmenhög tending a flock of geese, and on the adjacent field those Småland children were walking with their geese. And as soon as he saw them, he ran up on the stone wall and called, 'Good day to you, Åsa the Goose-girl! Good day to you, Little Mats!'

But when the two children saw such a little imp come towards them with outstretched hand, they grabbed each other, took a few steps backwards and looked mortally terrified.

When the boy saw their terror, he came to and remembered who he was. And then he thought that nothing worse could happen to him than for just those children to see that he had been enchanted. Shame and sorrow that he was no longer human overwhelmed him. He turned around and fled. He did not know where.

But the boy made a good encounter when he came down to the moor. For there in the heather he glimpsed something white, and towards him the white gander came in the company of Downy. When the white gander saw the boy come running at such speed, he thought that dangerous enemies were pursuing him. He threw him quickly up on his back and took off with him.

SEVENTEEN
The Old Farmwoman

Three tired travellers were out late in the evening, looking for lodging. They were travelling in a poor, desolate part of northern Småland, but they should have been able to find a suitable place to rest, because they weren't weaklings who asked for soft beds or cosy rooms. 'If one of these long ridges had a top so steep and high that a fox could not climb up it from any side, then we'd have a good place to sleep,' said one of them.

'If just one of the big marshes was thawed out and so swampy and wet that a fox would not venture out on to it, then that would be really good accommodation too,' said the other.

'If the ice on one of the frozen lakes that we are passing was separate from the land, so that a fox could not get out on to it, then we would have found just what we're looking for,' said the third.

The worst thing was that once the sun had gone down two of the travellers got so sleepy that at any moment they were about to drop to the ground. The third, who could keep himself awake, became more worried as night approached. 'It was unfortunate,' he thought, 'that we've come to a country where lakes and marshes are frozen, so that the fox can get across everywhere. The ice has thawed away in other places, but now we're well up in the very coldest part of Småland, where spring has not yet arrived. I don't know how I'm going to find a good place to sleep. If I don't find a place that's well protected, we'll have Smirre Fox on us before morning.'

He peered in all directions, but he did not see a lodging where he could enter. And a dark and chilly evening it was, with wind and pouring rain. The surroundings got more awful and more unpleasant with every moment.

It may sound peculiar, but the travellers did not seem to have any desire at all to ask for shelter at a farm. They had already gone past many villages without knocking on a single door. Small crofts at the forest's edge, which all poor wanderers are happy to encounter, they pretended not to see either. You might almost be tempted to say that they deserved to have a hard time, as they did not ask for help where it was at hand.

But at long last, when it was so dark there was hardly a sliver of daylight left in the sky, and the two who needed to sleep were shuffling along half-awake, they happened upon a farm that stood alone, far from any neighbours. And not only was it isolated, but also it appeared to be completely uninhabited. No smoke rose from the chimney, no candlelight shone from the windows, no one was moving on the farmyard. When the one of the three who could keep awake saw the place, he thought, 'Now things will turn out as they will, but we have to try to go into this farm. We're not likely to find anything better.'

Right after that all three of them were standing in the farmyard. The two fell asleep the moment they stopped, but the third looked eagerly around to figure out where he could come in under a roof. It was not a small farm. Besides the dwelling house and stable and cowshed there were long rows with barns and bins and storehouses and tool sheds. But everything looked dreadfully poor and dilapidated. The buildings had grey, moss-covered, leaning walls that seemed about to fall down. In the roofs were gaping holes and the doors were hanging crooked on broken hinges. It was evident that no one had bothered to hammer a nail in the wall here for a long time.

However, the one who was awake had figured out which building was the cowshed. He shook his travelling companions out of their slumber and led them up to the cowshed door. Fortunately it was closed with nothing but a hook, which he could easily poke up with a twig. He was already heaving a sigh of relief at the thought that they would soon be safe. But when the cowshed door swung open with a shrill screech, he heard a cow start mooing. 'Are you finally coming, mistress?' the cow said. 'I thought you weren't going to give me any food this evening.'

The one who was awake stopped at the door in terror when he noticed that the cowshed was not empty. But he soon saw that there was no more than a single cow and three or four hens, and then he plucked up courage again. 'We are three poor travellers who wish to come in to a place where no fox can attack us and no human can catch us,' he said. 'We wonder whether this might be a good place for us.'

'I can't see why not,' the cow answered. 'To be sure, the walls are poor, but the fox can't walk through them anyway, and no one lives here but an old woman who is certainly unable to take anyone captive. But what sort of thing are you?' she continued, as she twisted in the stall to catch sight of the new arrivals.

'Yes, I am Nils Holgersson from Västra Vemmenhög, who has been turned into a gnome,' he answered, the first of those entering, 'and I have with me a domestic goose that I ride on and a grey goose.'

'Such delightful strangers have not been within my walls before,' said the cow, 'and you are welcome, although I would have preferred it to be my mistress coming to give me my supper.'

The boy now led the geese into the cowshed, which was rather large, and placed them in an empty stall, where they immediately fell asleep. For himself he pulled together a little bed of straw and expected that he too would drift off at once.

But nothing came of that, because the poor cow, who had not had her supper, would not keep quiet for a moment. She shook on her neck chain, moved around in the stall and complained about how hungry she was. The boy could not get a wink of sleep, but instead lay there, going over everything that had happened to him in the past few days.

He thought about Åsa the Goose-girl and Little Mats, whom he had so unexpectedly encountered, and he worked out that the little cottage he happened to set fire to must have been their old home in Småland. He recalled that he had heard them talk about just that sort of cottage and about the large heather moor below it. Now they had come to see their home again, and it had been in flames, just as they reached it! It was probably a great sorrow he had caused them, and that made him very angry. If he ever became human again, he would try to compensate them for their injury and disappointment.

Then his thoughts went to the crows, and when he thought about Fumle-Drumle, who had rescued him and met death so soon after having been chosen as chieftain, he became so distressed that tears came to his eyes.

It had been a very difficult time for him, those past few days. But it had still been good luck that the gander and Downy had found him.

The gander had told him that as soon as the wild geese had noticed Thumbkin was missing they asked the small animals in the forest about him. They soon found out that a flock of Småland crows had carried him away. But the crows were already out of sight and no one could say where they were headed. In order to find the boy as soon as possible, Akka then ordered the wild geese to take off, two by two, in separate directions and search for him. But after two days of searching, whether they had found him or not, they were to meet in north-west Småland at a high hilltop, which resembled a sheared-off tower and was called Taberg. And after Akka had given them the best signposts and carefully described to them how to get to Taberg, they went their separate ways.

The white gander had chosen Downy as a travelling companion and they flew around here and there, very worried about Thumbkin. During this roving about they heard a thrush, who was sitting in a treetop, shout and scream about the fact that someone who called himself Abducted-by-Crows had made fun of him. They struck up a conversation with the thrush and he had shown them in which direction this Abducted-by-Crows had gone. Later they encountered a male dove, a starling and a mallard, all of whom complained about a malefactor who had interrupted their song, and whose name was Taken-by-Crows, Captured-by-Crows and Stolen-by-Crows. In this way they had been able to track Thumbkin all the way down to the heather moor in Sunnerbo County.

As soon as the gander and Downy found Thumbkin, they had taken off for the north to get to Taberg. But it was a long way to go and darkness came over them before they caught sight of the hilltop. 'But if we just get there tomorrow, all our worries will probably be over,' the boy thought, burrowing himself deep down in the straw to get warmer.

The cow had been making a fuss in the stall the whole time. Now she suddenly started talking with the boy. 'I thought that one of them who came in here said he was a gnome. If that is so, he surely must understand how to take care of a cow.'

'What is it you're lacking?' the boy asked.

'I'm lacking everything imaginable,' the cow said. 'I haven't been milked or groomed. I haven't got any night fodder in the manger, and I haven't got bedding under me. Mistress came in here at twilight to get things ready for me like she always does, but she felt so sick that she had to go in again right away, and she hasn't come back.'

'It's really too bad that I should be so little and powerless,' the boy said. 'I don't think I'm able to help you.'

'Don't expect me to believe that you're powerless just because you're little,' the cow said. 'All gnomes that I've heard about have been so strong they can pull a whole load of hay and kill a cow with a single punch.'

The boy could not keep from laughing at the cow. 'Those were probably gnomes of a different type than me,' he said.

'But I'll loosen your neck chain and open the door for you so that you can go out and drink in one of the puddles in the yard, and then I'll try to climb up into the hayloft and toss down hay into your manger.'

'Yes, that would be some help,' the cow said.

The boy did as he had offered, and when the cow was standing with a full manger in front of her, he thought that he would finally get to sleep. But he had hardly crept down in the bed before she started talking again.

'I'm sure you'll be very tired of me if I ask you for one more thing,' the cow said.

'I won't be, just so it's something I can manage,' the boy said.

'Then I want to ask you to go into the cottage across from here and see how my mistress is doing. I'm afraid that she's had an accident.'

'No, I can't,' the boy said. 'I don't dare show myself to people.'

'You don't have to be afraid of a sick old woman,' said the cow. 'But you don't need to go into the cottage, either. Just stand outside and look in through the chink in the door.'

'Yes, if there isn't anything else you ask of me, then I suppose I can do that,' the boy said.

With this he opened the cowshed door and made his way to the farmyard. It was a terrible night to go out. Neither moon nor stars were shining, the wind howled and the rain was pouring down. But the worst thing was that seven large owls were sitting in a row on the roof ridge of the house. It was eerie just to hear them as they sat and complained about the weather, and it was even worse to think that if a single one of them caught sight of him, it would be the end of him.

'Pity anyone who is small!' the boy said as he made his way out on to the farmyard. And he had reason to say so. He was blown over two times before he came up to the house, and one time the wind swept him into a puddle so deep that he almost drowned. But he made it there in any event.

He climbed up a couple of steps, wriggled over a threshold and came on to the landing. The cottage door was closed, but down in one corner a large piece had been removed, so that the cat could go in and out. Thus there was no difficulty for the boy to see what was going on in the cottage.

He had hardly glanced in before he gave a start and drew back his head. An old, grey-haired woman lay stretched out on the floor inside. She neither moved nor complained, and her face shone strangely white. It was as if an invisible moon had cast a pale light over it.

The boy remembered that when his grandfather died, his face had also turned strangely white like that. And he understood that the old person who was lying on the floor in the cottage must be dead. Death must have come over her so quickly that she did not even have time to lie down in her bed.

He became terribly afraid when he found himself in the middle of the dark night alone with a dead person. He threw himself headlong down the steps and rushed back to the cowshed.

When he told the cow what he had seen in the cottage, she stopped eating. 'I see, Mistress is dead,' she said. 'Then it will probably soon be the end of me too.'

'There will always be someone to take care of you,' the boy said consolingly.

'You don't know, do you,' the cow said, 'that I am already twice as old as a cow usually is before she is put on the slaughtering block. But I don't care to live any longer either, since the woman in there can no longer come and look after me.'

She said no more for a while, but the boy noticed that she was neither sleeping nor eating. It did not take long before she started talking again. 'Is she lying on the bare floor?' she asked.

'Yes, she is,' the boy said.

'She had the habit of coming out in the cowshed,' the cow continued, 'and talking about everything that worried her. I understood what she said, although I could not answer her. These past few days she was saying that she was afraid that she would not have anyone with her when she died. She was anxious that no one would be able to close her eyes or cross her hands over her chest when she was dead. Perhaps you will go in and do that?'

The boy was hesitant. He remembered that when his grand-father died, his mother had been careful to arrange him. He knew that this was something that had to be done. But on the other hand he felt that he did not dare go to the dead woman in the awful night. He did not say no, but neither did he take a step towards the cowshed door.

For a few moments the old cow stood silently, as if waiting for an answer. But when the boy said nothing, she did not repeat her request. Instead she started to talk about her mistress.

There was a lot to talk about. First and foremost, there were all the children she had brought up. They had been in the cow-shed every day, and in the summer they tended the cattle in the bog and in the pastures, so the old cow knew them well. All of them had been strong and cheerful and industrious. A cow knew well enough what her keepers were good for.

And likewise there was plenty to say about the farm. It had not always been as poor as it was now. It was very extensive, although for the most part it consisted of bogs and stony pas-tures. There was not much room for fields, but there was abundant grazing everywhere. At one time there had been a cow in every stall in the cowshed, and the ox stall, which was now completely empty, had been full of oxen. And then joy and happiness had prevailed in both the cottage and the barns. When the mistress opened the cowshed door, she hummed and sang, and all the cows bellowed with delight when they heard her coming.

But the farmer died while the children were too small to be of any help, and the mistress had to take over the farm and all the work and worries. She had been as strong as a man and she had both ploughed and harvested. In the evenings, when she came in to the cowshed to milk, she was sometimes so tired that she cried. But when she thought about her children, she became happy again. Then she wiped away the tears in her eyes and said, 'It's nothing. I too will have good days, after my children grow up. Yes, after they grow up.'

But as soon as the children were grown, a strange longing came over them. They did not want to stay at home, but instead they went away to a foreign land. Their mother never got any help from them. A couple of the children had managed to marry before they went and they left their small children behind at home. And these children now followed the mistress into the cowshed, as her own had done. They tended the cows and they were good and fine folk. And in the evenings, when the mistress was so tired that she could fall asleep in the middle of milking, she instilled fresh courage in herself by thinking about them. 'I'm sure I'll have good days, even me,' she said, shaking off sleep, 'when they grow up.'

But once these children were grown, they left to go to their parents in the foreign land. No one came back, no one stayed at home. The old mistress remained alone on the farm.

She probably never asked them to stay behind with her. 'Do you think, Rödlinna, that I should ask them to stay here with me, when they can go out into the world and do well?' she used to say when she stood in the stall with the old cow. 'Here in Småland they can expect only poverty.'

But when her last grandchild had left, it was all over for the mistress. She suddenly became stooped and grey, and she staggered when she walked, as if she no longer had the energy to move. And she stopped working. She did not want to tend the farm, but instead let everything deteriorate. She no longer improved the buildings and she sold off both oxen and cows. The only one she kept was the old cow, who was now talking with Thumbkin. She let her live, because all the children had gone to pasture with her.

She probably could have taken maids and farmhands into service, who would have helped her with the work, but she could not tolerate seeing strangers around, since her own kin had abandoned her. And perhaps she was mostly content to let the farm deteriorate, when none of the children were going to take it over. She did not care that she herself became poor because she did not take care of what was hers. But she was anxious that the children might find out how hard it was for her. 'Just so the children don't find out! Just so the children don't find out!' she sighed as she staggered through the cowshed.

The children wrote regularly and asked her to come to them,

but she did not want to. She did not want to see the country that had taken them from her. She was angry with it. 'It's probably stupid of me that I don't like the country that has been so good for them,' she said. 'But I don't want to see it.'

She never thought about anything other than the children and about the fact that they had to leave. When it was summer, she led the cow out so that she could graze on the big bog. She sat for entire days by the edge of the bog with her hands in her lap, and when she went home she said, 'You see, Rödlinna, if there had been big, fertile fields instead of this infertile bog here, then they wouldn't have had to leave.'

She could get furious at the bog, which was so big and did no one any good. She could sit and say it was the bog's fault that the children had gone away from her.

This last evening she had been shakier and weaker than ever before. She could not even manage the milking. She leaned against the stall and said that two farmers had been to see her and asked to buy the bog. They wanted to drain it and sow and harvest on it. This had made her both anxious and happy. 'Do you hear, Rödlinna,' she had said, 'do you hear that they said that rye can be grown on the bog? Now I'll write to the children, that they should come home. Now they don't need to stay away any longer, now they can get their bread here at home.'

This was what she had gone into the cottage to do.

The boy heard no more of what the cow was telling. He had opened the cowshed door and crossed the yard to the dead woman, of whom he had been so afraid just before.

First he stood quietly a moment and looked around.

It was not as poor in the cottage as he had expected. It was richly supplied with the kinds of things that are usually found among those who have relatives in America. In one corner was an American rocking chair, on the table in front of the window was a multicoloured plush cloth, a lovely cover was spread over the bed, on the walls hung photographs of the children and grandchildren who had gone away in fine, carved frames, on the chest of drawers were tall vases and a pair of candlesticks with thick, twisted candles.

The boy searched for a matchbox and lit those candles, not because he needed to see better than he already did, but because he thought that this was a way of honouring the dead woman.

Then he went up to her, closed her eyes, crossed her hands over her chest and stroked the thin, grey hair away from her face.

He no longer thought about being afraid of her. He was so sincerely distressed that she had had to live out her old age in loneliness and longing. Now at least he would watch over her dead body this night.

He searched for the hymn book and sat down to read a couple of hymns half out loud. But in the midst of reading he stopped, because he happened to think about his mother and father.

Just think, that parents can long so for their children! He had never known that. Just think, that it can be as if life is over for them when their children are gone! What if those there at home were longing for him the same way as this old woman had longed!

That thought made him happy, but he did not dare believe it. He had not been the sort that anyone would long for.

But what he had not been, perhaps he could become.

Around him he saw the portraits of those who had left. There were big, strong men and women with serious faces. There were brides in long veils and gentlemen in fine clothes, and there were children who had curly hair and beautiful, white dresses. And he thought that they were all staring blindly out into space and did not want to see.

'You poor things!' the boy said to the portraits. 'Your mother is dead. You can no longer make good the fact that you left her. But my mother is alive!'

Here he interrupted himself and nodded and smiled. 'My mother is alive,' he said. 'Both Father and Mother are alive.'

EIGHTEEN

From Taberg to Huskvarna

FRIDAY, 15 APRIL

The boy sat awake almost all night, but towards morning he fell asleep, and then he dreamed about his father and mother. He barely recognized them. Both of them had grey hair and old, wrinkled faces. He asked why this was and they answered that they had both aged so much because they had been missing him. He was both moved and surprised, because he thought they would be happy to escape him.

When the boy woke up, morning had already arrived with beautiful, clear weather. He first had a slice of bread that he found in the cottage, then he gave morning fodder to both the geese and the cow and opened the cowshed door, so that the cow could take off to the nearest farm. When they saw her walking alone, the neighbours would probably understand there was something the matter with her mistress. They would hurry to the deserted farm to see how the old woman was doing, and then they would find her dead body and bury it.

The boy and the geese had hardly ascended into the air before they caught sight of a tall hill with almost vertical walls and a sheared-off top, and they realized that this must be Taberg. And at the top of Taberg stood Akka with Yksi and Kaksi, Kolme and Neljä, Viisi and Kuusi and all six goslings waiting for them. There was joy and a cackling and flapping and calling impossible to describe when they saw that the gander and Downy had succeeded in finding Thumbkin.

Forest grew relatively high up on the sides of Taberg, but the very top was bare, and from there you could see far in all directions. If you looked to the east, to the south or to the west, there was almost nothing to see other than poor highland with dark spruce forests, brown bogs, ice-covered lakes and mountain ridges turning blue. The boy could not help thinking that it was true that whoever had created this had not taken great pains with his work, but instead had hacked it out in haste. But if you looked to the north, it was quite a different thing. Here the country looked as if it had been shaped with the greatest love and care. In that direction nothing but beautiful hills, gentle valleys and winding rivers were seen up to the large Lake Vättern, which was ice-free and dazzlingly clear and shone as if it were not filled with water but with blue light.

It was just Vättern that made it so beautiful to look towards the north, because it seemed as if a blue shimmer had risen up from the lake and also spread out over the land. Groves and heights and the roofs and spires of the city of Jönköping, which was glimpsed on the shore of Vättern, were wrapped in a light blue that caressed the eye. If there were countries in heaven, they would probably also be this blue, the boy thought and felt that he had a little glimpse of what it looked like in Paradise.

When towards day the geese continued their flight, they went up the blue valley. They were in the very best spirits, shrieking and making noise, so that no one who had ears could avoid noticing them.

Now this happened to be the first really beautiful spring day they had had in this area. Up until now spring had done its work under rain and foul weather, and now when the weather had suddenly become beautiful, the humans were filled with such a longing for summer warmth and green forests that they had a hard time tending to their chores. And when the wild geese came past, free and merry, high over the earth, there was not a single person who did not drop what they were doing to watch them.

The first ones who saw the wild geese that day were the mineworkers on Taberg, who were extracting ore from the rock surface. When they heard them cackling, they stopped drilling their blasting holes, and one of them called to the birds, 'Where are you going? Where are you going?' The geese did not understand what he was saying, but the boy leaned out over the gander's back and answered in their stead, 'To where there is neither pickaxe nor hammer!'

When the mineworkers heard those words, they thought it was their own longing that made the goose cackling sound like human speech. 'Let us go with you! Let us go with you!' they called.

'Not this year!' the boy shouted. 'Not this year!'

The wild geese followed the Taberg River down towards a lake called Munksjö, and they still made the same noise. Here on the narrow strip of land between Munksjö and Vättern was Jönköping with its large factories. The wild geese first flew over Munksjö paper mill. The midday break was just over then and large groups of workers were streaming towards the factory gate. When they heard the wild geese they stopped a moment to listen to them. 'Where are you going? Where are you going?' one worker called. The wild geese did not understand what he was saying, but the boy answered in their place, 'To where there are neither machines nor boilers!'

When the workers heard this response, they thought it was their own longing that made the goose cackling sound like human speech. 'Let us go with you!' a whole group of them called. 'Let us go with you!'

'Not this year!' the boy answered. 'Not this year!'

Next the geese travelled over the renowned match factory on the shore of Vättern, as big as a fortress, raising its tall chimneys towards the sky. No people were moving on the courtyards, but some young female workers were sitting in a large hall, filling matchboxes. They had opened a window because of the beautiful weather, so the calls of the wild geese made their way in to them. The woman sitting closest to the window leaned out with a matchbox in her hand and called, 'Where are you going? Where are you going?'

'To the land where neither candles nor matches are needed!' the boy said. The girl probably assumed that what she heard was only goose cackling, but because she thought she made out a few words, she called in response, 'Let me go with you! Let me go with you!'

'Not this year!' the boy answered. 'Not this year!'

East of the factories, Jönköping rises up on the most delightful place that any city can occupy. Narrow Lake Vättern has high, steep sand beaches both on the eastern and western side, but right to the south the sand walls are broken down, as if to make room for a large gate through which you can reach the lake. And in the middle of the gate, with hills to the right and hills to the left, with Munksjön behind it and Vättern before it, is Jönköping.

The geese travelled over the long, narrow city, making the same noise here as out in the countryside. But in the city there was no one to answer them. It was not to be expected that city-dwellers would stand out on the street and call at the wild geese.

The journey continued on towards the shore of Vättern, and in a while the geese came to the Sunna nursing home. Some of the patients had gone out on a veranda to enjoy the spring air and thus got to hear the geese cackling. 'Where are you going? Where are you going?' one of them asked in such a weak voice they could scarcely be heard.

'To the land where there is neither sorrow nor sickness!' the boy answered.

'Let us go with you!' the sick people said.

'Not this year!' the boy answered. 'Not this year!'

When they had gone yet another stretch, they came to Huskvarna. It was in a valley. The hills stood steep and beautifully formed around it. A river came rushing down the height in long, narrow falls. Large workshops and factories were under the rock walls, while over the valley bottom workers' homes were spread out, surrounded by garden plots, and in the middle of the valley were the schoolhouses. Just as the wild geese came along, a bell rang and a lot of children marched out, row by row. There were so many that the schoolyard was filled with them. 'Where are you going? Where are you going?' the children called when they heard the wild geese.

'To where there are neither books nor lessons!' the boy answered.

'Take us with you!' the children shouted. 'Take us with you!'

'Not this year, but next year!' the boy shouted. 'Not this year, but next year!'

NINETEEN

The Great Bird Lake

JARRO THE MALLARD

On the eastern shore of Vättern is Omberg. East of Omberg is Dagsmosse, and east of Dagsmosse is the Lake Tåkern. Around Tåkern the large, level Östgöta plain spreads out.

Tåkern is a rather large lake, and it seems to have been even bigger in the past. But then the humans thought it covered much too large a portion of the fruitful plain and they tried to drain the water from it to be able to sow and harvest on the lakebed. They were not successful, however, in draining the whole lake, which was probably their intention, because it still covers a lot of ground. But after draining the lake, it became so shallow that almost nowhere is it more than a few metres deep. The beaches have become marshy, muddy meadows and all over the lake small islands of sludge stick up above the surface of the water.

Now there is one thing that likes to stand with its feet in the water, as long as it gets its body and head up in the air, and that is the reed. It cannot find a better place to grow than along the shallow shores of Tåkern and around the small sludge islands. It thrives so well that it gets to more than a man's height and so dense that it is almost impossible to push a boat through it. It forms a broad, green enclosure around the whole lake, so that it is only accessible in a few places where people have removed the reeds.

But if the reeds keep out the humans, they also give shelter and protection to a lot of other things. Inside the reeds there are numerous small ponds and canals with green, still water, where duckweed and pondweed flourish, and where mosquito larvae, fry and warty newts are hatched in countless swarms. And by the shores of these small ponds and canals there are a number of concealed places where seabirds can hatch their eggs and raise their chicks without being disturbed either by enemies or by food concerns.

An incredible number of birds also live in the Tåkern reeds, and more gather there year by year, as it becomes known what a fine habitat it is. The first to settle down there were the mallards, and they still live there by the thousands. But they no longer own the whole lake, instead they have to share the space with swans, grebes, coots, divers, shovelers and a whole host of others.

Tåkern is certainly the largest and finest bird lake to be found in the whole country, and the birds must count themselves fortunate as long as they have such a refuge. But it is uncertain how long they will maintain dominion over clumps of reeds and muddy shores, because the humans have not forgotten that the lake extends over a great amount of good, fertile land, and time and again proposals come up among them that they should drain it. And if these proposals were carried out, the many thousands of water birds would be forced to move from the area.

At the time when Nils Holgersson was travelling around with the wild geese, at Tåkern there was a mallard whose name was Jarro. This was a young bird who had lived only one summer, one autumn and one winter. Now it was his first spring. He had just come home from East Africa and reached Tåkern in such good time that there was still ice on the lake.

One evening when he and the other young drakes were amusing themselves by shuttling back and forth across the lake, a hunter fired a couple of shots at them and Jarro was struck in the chest. He thought he was going to die, but to prevent the man who had shot him from getting him in his power, he continued to fly as long as he possibly could. He did not think about where he was heading, he simply strove to get far away. When his strength failed him, so that he could fly no further, he was no longer over the lake. He had flown some distance over land and now sank down in front of the entrance to one of the big farms that rise up on the shores of Tåkern.

Shortly after that a young farmhand walked across the yard. He caught sight of Jarro and came and picked him up. But Jarro, who wanted nothing more than to die in peace, summoned the last of his strength and nipped the farmhand hard on the finger so that he would let him go.

Jarro did not succeed in getting free, but the good thing about that attack anyway was that the farmhand noticed that the bird was alive. He carried him into the cottage very carefully and showed him to the mistress, a young woman with a gentle face. She immediately took Jarro from the farmhand, petted him on the back and wiped away the blood that was trickling through the down on his neck. She inspected him very carefully, and when she saw how beautiful he was with his dark green, shining head, his white neckband, his brownish-red back and his blue speculum, she thought it was a shame that he should die. She quickly arranged a basket where she bedded down the bird.

Jarro had been flapping and struggling to get loose the whole time, but when he understood that the humans did not intend to kill him, he settled into the basket with a sense of satisfaction. Only now did he notice how exhausted he was from pain and loss of blood. The mistress carried the basket across the floor to place it in the corner by the stove, but even before she set it down Jarro had closed his eyes and fallen asleep.

In a while Jarro woke up, because someone was gently prodding him. When he opened his eyes he was in such great terror that he almost lost consciousness. Now he was doomed, because here stood the one who was more dangerous than humans and birds of prey. It was no less than Caesar himself, the long-haired gun dog, who was nosing him with curiosity.

How pitifully scared Jarro had been last summer, when he was still a little yellow fledgling, every time it sounded over the clumps of reeds, 'Caesar is coming! Caesar is coming!' When he had seen the brown-and-white-spotted dog with a mouth full of teeth come wading through the reeds, he thought he had seen Death itself. He had always hoped that he would never have to meet Caesar eye to eye.

But to his misfortune he had chanced to fall on to the very farm where Caesar lived, for now the dog was standing over him. 'What sort of thing are you?' he growled. 'How did you get into the cottage? Don't you belong down in the clumps of reeds?'

Jarro was barely able to work up the courage to answer. 'Don't be angry at me, Caesar, because I've come into the cottage!' he said. 'It's not my fault. I've been shot. It's the humans who put me in this basket.'

'I see, it's the humans who have placed you here,' said Caesar. 'Then it's surely their intention to heal you, although for my part I think they would be wiser to eat you up, since you're in their power. But in any event you are protected in the cottage. You don't need to look so scared. We're not at Tåkern now.'

With that, Caesar went and lay down to sleep in front of the roaring stove fire. As soon as Jarro understood that this frightful danger was past, a great fatigue came over him and he fell asleep again.

The next time Jarro woke up, he saw that a bowl of grain and water was in front of him. He was still rather sick, but he felt hungry anyway and started to eat. When the mistress saw that he was eating, she came up and petted him and looked happy. After that Jarro fell asleep again. For several days he did nothing but eat and sleep.

One morning Jarro felt so healthy that he got up out of the basket and walked along the floor. But he had not gone far before he fell over and remained lying there. Then Caesar came, opened his large mouth and took hold of him. Jarro thought naturally that the dog intended to kill him, but Caesar carried him back to the basket without injuring him. In this way Jarro gained such trust in Caesar that at the next outing in the cottage he went up to the dog and lay down beside him. After this he and Caesar became good friends, and every day Jarro lay down and slept for several hours between Caesar's paws.

Jarro felt even greater devotion for the mistress than for Caesar. For her he did not feel the slightest fear, instead he stroked his head against her hand when she came and gave him food. When she went out of the cottage, he sighed from sorrow, and when she returned, he welcomed her back in his own language.

Jarro completely forgot how afraid he had been earlier of both dogs and humans. He thought that they were gentle and good and he loved them. He wished that he was healthy, so that he could fly down to Tåkern and tell the mallards that their old enemies were not dangerous and that they did not need to fear them at all.

He had noticed that the humans as well as Caesar had calm eyes and that it did you good to look into them. The only one in the cottage whose eyes he did not like to meet was Klorina, the cat. She did not do him any harm either, but he could not gain any confidence in her. Besides, she constantly teased him, because he loved humans. 'You think they are caring for you because they like you,' said Klorina. 'Just wait until you get fat enough! Then they'll wring your neck. I know them, I do.'

Jarro had a tender, loving heart like all birds and was unspeakably distressed when he heard this. He could not imagine that the mistress would want to wring his neck, nor could he believe any such thing about her son, the little boy who would sit for hours beside his basket and babble and chatter. He thought he understood that they both felt the same love for him as he did for them.

One day, when Jarro and Caesar were in their usual place in front of the stove, Klorina sat up on the top of the stove and started teasing the mallard.

'I wonder, Jarro, what you mallards will do next year, when Tåkern is drained and turned into fields,' Klorina said.

'What is that you're saying, Klorina?' Jarro called and leaped up, quite terrified.

'I always forget, Jarro, that you, unlike Caesar and me, don't understand the humans' language,' the cat answered. 'Otherwise you probably would have heard that the men who were in the cottage yesterday were saying that all the water would be drained out of Tåkern and that next year the lakebed would be as dry as a cottage floor. And now I'm wondering where you mallards will go.'

When Jarro heard this speech, he became so angry that he hissed like a snake. 'You are as mean as a coot!' he screamed at Klorina. 'You just want to get me worked up against the humans! I don't think they want to do any such thing. They must know that Tåkern is the mallards' property. Why would they make so many birds homeless and unhappy? You must have made this up to frighten me. You should be torn apart by Gorgo, the eagle. The mistress should cut off your whiskers.'

But Jarro could not silence Klorina with this outburst. 'I see, you think I'm lying,' she said. 'So ask Caesar! He was also in the cottage last evening. Caesar never lies.'

'Caesar,' said Jarro, 'you understand the humans' language much better than Klorina. Say that she didn't hear right! Think how it would be if the humans drained Tåkern and transformed the lakebed to fields! Then there would no longer be pondweed or duckweed for the grown ducks and no fry or tadpoles or mosquito larvae for the ducklings. Then the clumps of reeds would vanish too, where the ducklings can now stay hidden until they can fly. All ducks would be forced to move away from here and search for another place to live. But where will they find a refuge like Tåkern? Caesar, say that Klorina didn't hear right!'

It was strange to observe Caesar's behaviour during this conversation. He had been wide awake the whole time before, but now, when Jarro turned to him, he yawned, put his long nose on his front paws and was sound asleep within a moment.

The cat looked down at Caesar with a knowing smile. 'I think that Caesar does not care to answer you,' she said to Jarro. 'He is just like all other dogs; they never want to admit that humans can do anything unjust. But you can count on my word in any event. I will tell you why they want to drain the lake right now. As long as you mallards still have possession of Tåkern they did not want to empty it, because they still had some benefit from you. But now divers and coots and other inedible birds have encroached on just about all the clumps of reeds, and the humans don't think they need to maintain the lake for their sake.'

Jarro did not bother to answer Klorina, but he raised his head and shouted in Caesar's ear, 'Caesar! You know that on Tåkern there are still so many ducks that they fill the air like clouds. Say it isn't true that the humans intend to make all of them homeless!'

With this, Caesar got up and made such a violent attack on Klorina that she had to escape up to a shelf. 'I'll teach you to keep quiet when I want to sleep!' Caesar roared. 'Of course, I know that there is talk about draining the water out of the lake this year. But this has been talked about many times before, without anything coming of it. And this draining is a thing I don't like. For what would happen to the hunting if Tåkern is drained? You are an ass to be happy about such a thing. What are you and I going to amuse ourselves with when there are no longer any birds on Tåkern?'

The Decoy

SUNDAY, 17 APRIL

A few days later Jarro was so healthy that he could fly through the whole cottage. Then he was petted a lot by the mistress, and the little boy ran out on the yard and picked for him the first blades of grass that had come up. When the mistress petted him, Jarro thought that although he was now so strong that he could fly down to Tåkern at any time, he did not want to be separated from the humans. He had nothing against staying with them for his whole life.

But early one morning the mistress placed a halter or trap over Jarro that prevented him from using his wings, and then turned him over to the same farmhand who had found him out in the yard. The farmhand stuck him under his arm and went to Tåkern with him.

The ice had melted away while Jarro had been sick. Last year's old, dry reeds were still standing along the shores and islands, but the water plants had started to put out shoots down in the depths, and the green tops had reached up to the surface of the water. And now almost all of the migratory birds had come home. The crooked beaks of the curlews peeked out of the reeds. The grebes glided around with a new feather collar around their necks and the snipes were busy gathering straw for their nests.

The farmhand went down in a rowboat, set Jarro inside it and started punting along out on the lake. Jarro, who had now become accustomed to expect only good from humans, said to Caesar, who was also with them, that he was very grateful to the farmhand, because he was taking him out on the lake. But the farmhand did not need to keep him so tightly imprisoned, because he did not intend to fly away. Caesar did not respond to that. He was very taciturn this morning.

The only thing that seemed a trifle strange to Jarro was that the farmhand had brought his shotgun along. He could not believe that any of the good folks at the farm would want to shoot birds. Besides, Caesar had told him that the humans did not hunt at this time of year. 'It's closed season,' he said, 'although, of course, that doesn't apply to me.'

The farmhand, however, rowed out to one of the small, reed-encircled mud islets. There he got out of the boat, dragged old reeds together into a large pile and sat down behind it. Jarro, with the halter over his wings and tethered to the boat, could wander around on the bank.

Suddenly Jarro caught sight of some of the young drakes in whose company he had shuttled back and forth across the lake before. They were far away, but Jarro called them to him with a couple of loud shouts. They answered them and a large, beautiful flock approached. Even before they reached him, Jarro started to tell them about his marvellous rescue and about the goodness of the humans. At that moment two shots went off behind him. Three ducks sank dead down into the reeds and Caesar splashed out and picked them up.

Then Jarro understood. The humans had rescued him to be able to use him as a decoy. And they had succeeded too. Three ducks had died for his sake. He thought he wanted to die of shame. He thought that even his friend Caesar looked at him contemptuously, and when they came home to the cottage he did not dare lie down to sleep beside the dog.

The next morning Jarro was once again carried out on the shallows. This time, too, he caught sight of some ducks. But when he noticed that they were flying towards him, he shouted to them, 'Away, away! Watch out! Go a different direction! There's a hunter hidden behind the pile of reeds! I'm just a decoy!' And he managed to prevent them from coming within firing range.

Jarro hardly had time to taste a blade of grass, he was so occupied by keeping watch. He called out his warning as soon as a bird approached. He even warned the grebes, although he despised them because they force the ducks out from their best hiding places. But he did not want any bird to meet with misfortune for his sake. And thanks to Jarro's watchfulness the farmhand had to go home without having fired a single shot.

This notwithstanding, Caesar looked less dissatisfied than the day before, and when evening came he took Jarro in his mouth, carried him over to the stove and let him sleep between his front paws.

But Jarro was no longer content in the cottage; on the contrary, he was very unhappy. His heart suffered from the thought that the humans had never loved him. When the mistress or the little boy came up to pet him, he stuck his beak in under his wing and pretended to be asleep.

For several days Jarro continued his miserable guard duty, and he was already known all over Tåkern. Then it happened one morning, while as usual he was calling, 'Be on your guard, birds! Don't come near me! I'm just a decoy!' that a grebe nest came floating along towards the shallows where he stood tied up. This was not particularly remarkable. It was a nest from last year, and because the grebe nests are built so that they can float on the water like boats, it often happens that they drift along the lake. But Jarro still stood there looking at the nest, because it was coming so directly towards the islet that it appeared as if someone were guiding its journey across the water.

When the nest came closer, Jarro saw that a little human, the smallest he had ever seen, was sitting in the nest, rowing it ahead with a couple of pegs. And this little human called to him, 'Get as close to the water as you can, Jarro, and get ready to fly! You will soon be free!'

A few moments later the grebe nest was on the land, but the little rower did not leave it. Instead he sat quietly, curled up between the twigs and straw. Jarro also kept himself almost motionless. He was completely paralysed by anxiety that his liberator would be discovered.

The next thing that happened was a flock of wild geese came flying. Jarro then became alert and warned them with loud cries, but despite this they flew back and forth over the shallows several times. They stayed high enough up that they were out of firing range, but the farmhand let himself be enticed into firing off a couple of shots at them anyway. These shots were scarcely fired when the little imp jumped on to land, pulled a little knife out of its sheath and hacked Jarro's halter apart with a few quick cuts. 'Fly away now, Jarro, before the fellow has time to reload!' he called, as he himself leaped down into the grebe nest and pushed off from the land.

The hunter had his gaze directed at the geese and had not noticed that Jarro had been freed, but Caesar had followed what happened better, and just as Jarro raised his wings, he rushed forwards and seized him by the neck.

Jarro screamed pitifully, but the imp who had released him said very calmly to Caesar, 'If you are as honourable as you appear, you can't very well want to force a good bird to sit here and lure others into misfortune.'

When Caesar heard these words, he sneered nastily with his upper lip, but in a moment he released Jarro. 'Fly, Jarro!' he said. 'You are truly too good to be a decoy. That wasn't why I wanted to keep you back, but because it will be empty in the cottage without you.'

Draining the Lake

WEDNESDAY, 20 APRIL

It was truly very empty in the farm cottage without Jarro. The dog and the cat found the days long when they did not have him to argue about, and the mistress missed the happy quacking that he made every time she came into the cottage. But the one who missed Jarro the most was the little boy, Per Ola. He was just three and an only child, and in his entire life he had never had a playmate like Jarro. When he heard that Jarro had returned to Tåkern and the ducks, he refused to accept it, and thought constantly about how he could get him back.

Per Ola had talked a lot with Jarro while the duck lay quietly in his basket, and he was sure that the duck understood him. He asked his mother to take him down to the lake, because he wanted to see Jarro and convince him to come back to them. Mother did not listen, but the little one did not abandon his plan just because of that.

The day after Jarro disappeared, Per Ola ran out on to the farmyard. He played alone as usual, but Caesar was lying on the steps, and when Mother let the boy out, she said, 'Keep an eye on Per Ola, Caesar!'

If now everything had been as usual, Caesar also would have obeyed this order, and the boy would have been so well guarded that he would not have been in the slightest danger. But Caesar was not himself these days. He knew that the farmers who lived along Tåkern had frequent discussions about lowering the lake level and that they had pretty much decided

on it. The ducks would be gone and Caesar would never again
have an honourable hunt. He was so preoccupied by thinking
about this misfortune that he forgot to watch over Per Ola.

And the little one was hardly left alone in the yard before he
realized that now the right moment had come to go down to
Tåkern and speak with Jarro. He opened a gate and wandered
down towards the lake on the narrow path that ran across the
marshy meadows. As long as he could be seen from home, he
walked slowly, but then he picked up speed. He was very afraid
that Mother or someone else would call to him and tell him
that he was not allowed to go. He did not want to do anything
bad, just convince Jarro to come back, but he sensed that those
at home would not have approved of the enterprise.

When Per Ola came down to the lakeshore, he called several
times for Jarro. After that he stood for a long time waiting, but
no Jarro appeared. He saw several birds that resembled the
mallard, but they flew past and paid him no notice, and so he
realized that none of them was the right one.

When Jarro did not come to him, the little boy thought that
he would surely find him more easily if he went out on the lake.
There were several good boats by the shore, but they were tied
up. The only one that was not tied up was an old, leaky rowboat that was in such poor shape that no one thought about
using it. But Per Ola wriggled up into it without caring that
there was standing water in the bottom. He was unable to use
the oars, but instead he sat down to rock and bob in the rowboat. Surely no big person would have succeeded in guiding a
rowboat out on Tåkern in that way, but when the water level is
high and misfortune is at hand, small children have a strange
capacity to put out to sea. Per Ola was soon drifting on Tåkern
and calling to Jarro.

As the old rowboat bobbed out on to the lake like that, its
cracks opened up all the wider, and the water really streamed
into it. Per Ola did not question this in the least. He sat on the
little bench in the stem, calling to every bird he saw and wondering that Jarro did not appear.

At last Jarro really did catch sight of Per Ola. He heard that
someone was calling to him by the name he had among the

humans, and he understood that the boy had gone out on Tåkern to search for him. Jarro became unspeakably happy to find that one of the humans truly loved him. He shot down towards Per Ola like an arrow, sat down beside him and let him pet him. They were both very happy to see each other again.

But suddenly Jarro noticed what was going on with the boat. It was half full of water and very close to sinking. Jarro tried to tell Per Ola that he, who could neither fly nor swim, must try to get on land, but Per Ola did not understand him. Then Jarro did not hesitate a moment, but instead hurried away to get help.

Jarro came back in a little while, carrying on his back a little imp who was much smaller than Per Ola. If the imp had not been able to both talk and move, the boy would have believed it was a doll. And the little imp ordered Per Ola to immediately pick up a long, narrow pole that was at the bottom of the boat and try to punt it along towards one of the small reed islands. Per Ola obeyed him, and he and the imp helped each other drive the boat along. With a couple of strokes they were up by a little reed-encircled island and now Per Ola was told that he should go on land. And just as Per Ola set foot on land, the boat was filled with water and sank to the bottom.

When the boy saw this, he sensed that Father and Mother would be very angry at him. He would have started crying, if he had not immediately had something else to think about. You see, a flock of large, grey birds came and landed on the island, and the little imp took him up to them and told him what their names were, and what they said. And this was so funny that Per Ola forgot everything else.

However, the people on the farm noticed that the boy was missing, and had started searching for him. They searched through the outbuildings, looked in the well and peered around in the cellar. Then they went out on roads and paths, walking to the neighbouring farm to hear if he had gone astray there and also looked for him down by Tåkern. But however much they searched, they could not find him.

Caesar, the dog, understood very well that the farm folk were searching for Per Ola, but he did not do anything to lead them on the right trail. Instead he lay quietly, as if the whole thing did not concern him.

Later in the day Per Ola's footprints were discovered down by the boat landing. And then they happened to think that the old rotten rowboat was no longer on the shore. Then they started to understand how it all happened.

The farmer and his hands immediately pushed out boats and went to search for the boy. They rowed around on Tåkern until late in the evening without seeing the slightest trace of him. They could only believe that the old boat had sunk and the little boy lay dead on the lakebed.

In the evening Per Ola's mother went around on the shore. All the others were convinced that the boy had drowned, but she could not bring herself to believe it, so she was still searching for him. She looked among reeds and rushes, walked and walked on the marshy shore without thinking about how deep her foot was sinking and how wet she was getting. She was unspeakably desperate. Her heart ached in her chest. She was not crying, but she twisted her hands and called for her child in a high, plaintive voice.

All around her she heard the shrieking of swans and ducks and curlews. She thought that they were following her and that they, too, were complaining and wailing. 'They must be in sorrow, because they are wailing so,' she thought. But then she came to her senses. It was just birds she heard complaining. They probably had no worries.

It was strange that they did not fall silent after sundown. But she heard all the innumerable bands of birds that were around Tåkern letting out shriek after shriek. Several of them followed her wherever she went, others came sweeping past on rapid wings. The whole air was full of complaint and wailing.

But the anxiety that she felt opened her heart. She did not think she was so far removed from all other living creatures, as humans otherwise do. She understood much better than ever before what it was like for the birds. They had their constant worries about home and children, just like her. There was probably not such a great difference between them and herself as she had previously thought.

Then she happened to think that it was as good as decided that all these thousands of swans and ducks and divers would lose their homes here by Tåkern. 'It will probably be a great worry for them,' she thought. 'Where will they raise their young then?'

She stood and pondered this. It seemed to be a good and agreeable labour to transform a lake into fields and meadows, but there must be a lake other than Tåkern, another lake that was not home to so many thousands of animals.

She thought it was tomorrow that the decision about draining the lake would be made, and she wondered whether it was for that reason that her little boy had got lost today. Was it God's intention that sorrow should come and open her heart to mercy, before it was too late to avert the cruel action?

She quickly went up to the farm and started talking with her husband about all of this. She talked about the lake and about the birds and told him that she thought Per Ola's death was God's punishment for them both. And she soon noticed that he was of the same opinion as her.

They already owned a large farm, but if the lake level were lowered, such an extensive part of the lake bed would fall to them that their property would be almost doubled. For that reason they had been more eager for the enterprise than any of the other shore owners. The others had been anxious about the expense and that the draining would not be any more successful than the last time. Per Ola's father was aware that he was the one who had prevailed upon them to agree to the undertaking. He had used all of his persuasive powers to be able to leave his son a farm twice as big as the one his father had left him.

He wondered now if there was some meaning from God in this, that Tåkern had taken his son from him the day before he was to sign a contract for its draining. His wife did not need to say much to him before he answered, 'It may be that God does not want us to disturb his order. I will speak with the others about this tomorrow, and I think we will decide that everything should be left as it is.'

While the farm folk talked about this, Caesar was lying in front of the stove. He raised his head and listened very carefully. When he thought he was sure of his case, he went up to the mistress, took hold of her skirt and led her towards the door. 'But Caesar!' she said, trying to get loose. 'Do you know where Per Ola is?' she exclaimed after that. Caesar barked happily and threw himself towards the door. She opened it and Caesar rushed off down towards Tåkern. The mistress was so certain that he knew where Per Ola was that she simply ran after him. And no sooner had they come down to the shore than they heard a child crying out on the lake.

Per Ola had had the best day of his life together with Thumbkin and the birds, but now he had started to cry, because he was hungry and afraid of the dark. And he was happy when Father and Mother and Caesar came and got him.

TWENTY

The Prophecy

The boy was sleeping one night on an islet in Tåkern when he was awoken by the strokes of oars. As he opened his eyes, such a strong light shone into them that it made him blink.

At first he could not comprehend what was shining so brightly out here on the lake, but soon he saw a rowboat at the edge of the reeds, which had a large, burning tar torch set up on an iron rod in the stern. The red flame of the torch was clearly reflected in the night-black lake, and the dazzling glow must have lured the fish, because around the flame in the depths a number of dark streaks were seen, constantly moving and changing places.

Two old men were in the rowboat. One sat at the oars, the other stood on the bench in the stern, holding a short spear in his hands, which was furnished with rough barbs. The one who was rowing appeared to be a poor fisherman. He was

little, dried up and weather beaten and wore a thin, worn coat.
You could see that he was so used to being out in all kinds of
weather that he did not think about the cold. The other was
well fed and well dressed and looked like an authoritative,
self-confident farmer.

'Hold still now!' the farmer said when they were right in
front of the islet where the boy was. At that moment he thrust
the spear down into the water. When he raised it, a long, splendid eel followed along out of the depths.

'See there!' he said, while he released the eel from the fishing
spear. 'That one's not bad at all. Now I think we've got enough
that we can return home.'

His comrade did not raise the oars, but instead sat looking
around. 'It's beautiful out here on the lake in the evening,' he
said. And it was, too. It was completely calm, so that the whole
surface of the water was undisturbed and at rest, with the
exception of the streak where the boat had passed through,
which shone like a road of gold in the torchlight. The sky was
clear and deep blue and densely pierced by stars. The shores
were hidden by the islands of reeds, except to the west. There,
Omberg shot up high and dark, seeming much more massive
than usual, and cut off a large, triangular piece of the canopy
of the sky.

The other one turned his head to get the torchlight out of his
eyes, and looked around. 'Yes, it's beautiful here in Östergötland,' he said. 'But the best thing about the province is still not
its beauty.'

'So what's the best thing about it?' the rower asked.

'Well, that it has always been a respected and honoured
province.'

'That may be true, of course.'

'And then this, that you know that it will always remain so.'

'How in the world can you know that?' the one sitting by
the oars asked.

The farmer straightened up, supporting himself against the
spear. 'There is an old story that has passed from father to son
in my family, and in it you find out what the fate of Östergötland will be.'

'Then why don't you tell it to me?' said the rower.

'We don't usually tell it to just anyone, but I don't want to keep it secret from an old friend, either.

'On Ulvåsa, here in Östergötland,' he continued, and now you could hear by his tone of voice that he was relating something that he had heard from others and knew by heart, 'many years ago there lived a woman who had the gift that she could see into the future and tell folk what was going to happen to them, just as surely and precisely as if it had already happened. For this she became widely renowned and it is easy to understand that people would come from near and far to visit her in order to find out what they would have to look forward to, whether good or bad.

'One day, when the Ulvåsa woman was sitting in her room spinning, as was customary in the past, a poor farmer came in and sat on the bench far down by the door. "I wonder what you're sitting there thinking about, dear lady?" the farmer said after a while.

' "I'm thinking about high and holy things," she answered.

' "Then it probably wouldn't do for me to ask about something that's on my mind," said the farmer.

' "There's probably nothing on your mind other than harvesting a lot of grain on your fields. But I often get questions from the Emperor about the fate of his crown and from the Pope about the fate of his keys."

' "Yes, that sort of thing must not be easy to answer," the farmer said. "I've also heard that no one usually leaves here without being dissatisfied with what he has heard."

'When the farmer said this, he saw that the Ulvåsa woman bit her lip and moved higher up on the bench. "I see. So that's what you've heard about me," she said. "Then you can try asking me about what you want to know, then you'll see if I can give you an answer that satisfies you."

'After this the farmer did not hesitate to state his business. He said that he had come to ask about the fate of Östergötland in the future. There was nothing he held so dear as his home region, and he thought that he would feel happy even to his final hour if he could get a good answer to that question.

' "If there isn't anything else you want to know," the wise woman said, "then I think you'll be pleased. Because here, where I am sitting, I can tell you that the fate of Östergötland is that it will always have something to pride itself on ahead of all other provinces."

' "Yes, that was a good answer, dear lady," the farmer said, "and now I would be completely satisfied if I could just understand how such a thing is possible."

' "Why shouldn't it be possible?" the Ulvåsa woman said. "Don't you know that Östergötland is widely renowned already? Or do you think that there is any province in Sweden that can pride itself on having two such convents at the same time as the ones in Alvastra and Vreta and such a beautiful cathedral as the one in Linköping?"

' "That may be so," said the farmer, "but I'm an old man and I know that human nature is fickle. I fear that there will come a time when they will not want to give us any honour, either for Alvastra or Vreta or for our cathedral."

' "You may be right in that," the Ulvåsa woman said, "but you don't need to doubt my prophecy on that account. I will now have a new convent built on the Vadstena estate and it will become the most famous in the north. Both high and low will make pilgrimage there, and everyone will praise this province, because it has such a holy place within its boundaries."

'The farmer replied that he was quite happy to find this out. But he knew that everything was perishable and he really wondered what could give the country esteem, if the Vadstena convent ever came into disrepute.

' "You are not easy to please," the Ulvåsa woman said, "but I can see so far ahead that I can tell you that before the Vadstena convent has lost its sheen, next to it a castle will be erected that will be the most magnificent of its time. Kings and princes will visit it and it will bring honour to the whole province that it has such a jewel."

' "I am also very happy to hear this," the farmer said. "But I'm an old man and I know how things go with all the wonders of this world. And if the castle falls into decay, I really wonder what could draw people's attention to this province."

' "You want to know a lot," said the Ulvåsa woman, "but I can see so far into time that I can observe how there will be life and activity up in the forests around Finspång. I see how foundries and smithies are erected there, and I think that the whole province will be honoured because iron will now be produced within its limits."

'The farmer did not deny that he was incredibly happy to hear this. But if it were to turn out so bad that the Finspång mill also sank in regard, then it would probably not be possible that anything new might arise on which Östergötland could pride itself.

' "You are not easy to satisfy," the Ulvåsa woman said, "but I can see so far ahead that I observe how farms as big as castles are built up along the lakeshores by lords who have waged war in foreign lands. I think that those estates will bring the province as much honour as anything else I have spoken of."

' "But if there comes a time when no one praises the big estates any longer?" the farmer persisted.

' "You don't need to be anxious anyway," said the Ulvåsa woman. "I see now how mineral springs ripple on Medevi meadows near the shore of Vättern. I think that the wells at Medevi will bring the country as much renown as it can want."

' "That was a big thing to learn," the farmer said. "But if there comes a time when people look for their health at other springs?"

' "You should not worry yourself for that reason," the Ulvåsa woman answered. "I see how people swarm and labour from Motala to Mem. They are digging a waterway right through the country, and then the praise of Östergötland will again be on everyone's lips."

'But the farmer looked worried anyway.

' "I see that the rapids in Motala River are starting to drive wheels," the Ulvåsa woman said, and now a couple of red patches appeared on her cheeks, because she was starting to get impatient. "I hear hammer mills booming in Motala and weaving machines clattering in Norrköping."

' "Yes, that's good to know," said the farmer, "but everything is changeable, and I'm afraid that this too can be neglected and forgotten."

'Now, when the farmer was still not satisfied, the woman's patience ran out. "You say that everything is changeable," she said, "but now I'm going to mention something that will always be the same. And that is, that there will always be arrogant and stubborn farmers like yourself here in the province until the end of the world!"

'The Ulvåsa woman had barely said this before the farmer stood up, happy and satisfied, and thanked her for this good news. Now he was finally satisfied, he said.

' "Truly, now I understand what you mean," the Ulvåsa woman said then.

' "Yes, dear lady," said the farmer, "I mean that everything that kings and convent folk and gentlemen and townspeople build and establish is only in existence for a few years. But when you tell me that in Östergötland there will always be farmers who love honour and are persistent, then I know too that it will maintain its old honour. Because only those who go bowed under endless labour with the earth can keep this country in well-being and reputation from age to age." '

TWENTY-ONE

Homespun Cloth

SATURDAY, 23 APRIL

The boy was moving along high up in the air. He had the big Östgöta plain below him and he was counting the many white churches that rose up out of small clumps of trees. It did not take long before he made it to fifty. Then he got confused and lost count.

The vast majority of the farms were built with large, white-painted two-storey houses, which looked so stately that the boy could not help marvelling at them. 'No peasants must live in this country,' he said to himself, 'because I don't see any farmsteads.'

Then all the wild geese shrieked at once, 'Here the farmers live like gentry! Here the farmers live like gentry!'

Ice and snow had vanished on the plain and the spring work had started. 'What kind of long crayfish are those creeping along across the fields?' the boy asked after a while.

'Ploughs and oxen! Ploughs and oxen!' all the wild geese answered.

The oxen moved so slowly on the fields that you could hardly tell they were moving, and the geese called to them, 'You won't get there till next year! You won't get there till next year!' But the oxen did not owe them a response. They raised their muzzles in the air and bellowed, 'We get more done in an hour than the likes of you do your whole life!'

In some places the ploughs were drawn by horses. They moved along with much greater eagerness and speed than the oxen, but the geese could not refrain from teasing them as well. 'Aren't you ashamed to do ox work?' they called to the horses. 'Aren't you ashamed to do ox work?'

'Aren't you ashamed to be so lazy?' the horses whinnied back.

While horses and oxen were out at work, the stable ram walked around at home on the farmyard. He was newly clipped and volatile, knocking down the little boys, driving the watchdog into his kennel and then going around boasting as if he were the sole master of the yard.

'Ram, ram, what have you done with your wool?' the wild geese asked as they flew past up in the air.

'I've sent it to Drag's factories in Norrköping,' the ram answered with a long bleat.

'Ram, ram, what have you done with your horns?' the geese asked. But to his great sorrow the ram had never had any horns, and you could not annoy him more than by asking about them. He ran around a long time, butting in the air, he was so angry.

On the road came a man who was driving ahead of him a herd of Skåne hogs that were no more than a few weeks old and would be sold in this part of the country. They plodded along so pluckily, as little as they were, and kept close by each other as if to get protection. 'Oink, oink, oink! We have left our mother and father too soon! Oink, oink, oink! What will be the fate of us poor children?' said the little pigs. Not even the wild geese had the heart to make fun of such small wretches. 'It will be better for you than you can ever believe!' they called as they flew past.

The wild geese were never in such a good mood as when they got to travel over flat country. Then they were in no hurry, but instead they flew from farm to farm and joked with the domestic animals.

While the boy was riding along over the plain, he happened to think of a fairy tale he had heard some time long ago. He did not really remember it, but there was something about a kirtle that was half sewn of gold-woven velvet and half of grey homespun. But the owner of the kirtle adorned the homespun cloth with so many pearls and precious stones that it glistened more lovely and more costly than the golden cloth.

He remembered that part about the homespun cloth when he looked down at Östergötland, because it consisted of one large plain that was squeezed in between two hilly forested sections, one to the north and one to the south. Both of the forest heights were a beautiful blue and shimmered in the morning light, as if they were covered with gold veils, and the plain, which simply spread out in one bare winter field after another, was in itself no more beautiful to look at than grey homespun.

But the people must have been contented on the plain, because it was generous and good, and they had tried to adorn it in the best way. Where the boy was moving along high up, he thought that cities and farms, churches and factories, castles and railway stations were strewn out over it like small and large pieces of jewellery. The tile roofs glistened and the windowpanes shone like jewels. Yellow highways, shiny railway tracks and blue canals ran between the towns like silk-sewn coils. Linköping sat around its cathedral like a pearl setting around a precious stone, and the farms in the country were like small breastpins and buttons. There was not much order in the pattern, but it was a magnificence that you never tired of looking at.

The geese had left the Omberg area and flew towards the east along the Göta Canal. It was also in the process of getting ready for the summer. Workers were repairing the banks of the canal and coating the sluice gates with tar.

Yes, work was going on everywhere to welcome spring in the cities too. Painters and masons stood on scaffolding outside the buildings and made them nice, while servant girls climbed up in the open windows and washed the panes. Down by the harbour, sailboats and steamers were being cleaned.

At Norrköping the wild geese left the flat country and flew up towards Kolmården. For a while they had followed an old, hilly country road which wound along ravines and continued under wild rock walls, when the boy suddenly let out a cry. He had been swinging his foot back and forth and one wooden shoe had slipped off him.

'Gander, gander! I've lost my shoe!' the boy screamed.

The gander turned and descended towards the ground, but then the boy saw that two children, who had been walking along the road, had picked up his shoe.

'Gander, gander,' the boy shouted quickly, 'go up again! It's too late! I can't get my shoe back!'

But down on the road stood Åsa the Goose-girl and her brother, Little Mats, observing the little wooden shoe that had fallen from the sky.

'It was the wild geese who lost it,' Little Mats said.

Åsa the Goose-girl stood silent a long time and thought about their find. At last she said, slowly and thoughtfully, 'Do you remember, Little Mats, that when we went past Övedskloster, we heard them saying that on a farm they had seen a gnome who was dressed in leather breeches and had wooden shoes on his feet like any labourer? And do you remember that when we came to Vittskövle, a girl told us that she had seen a farm gnome with wooden shoes who flew away on the back of a goose? And when we came home to our cottage, Little Mats, we saw a gnome dressed the same way, and who also climbed up on a goose and flew away? Maybe it was the same one who is riding along up here in the sky and lost the wooden shoe.'

'Yes, that must be it,' said Little Mats.

They turned over the wooden shoe and observed it carefully, because it's not every day you find the farm gnome's wooden shoe on the road.

'Wait, wait, Little Mats!' said Åsa the Goose-girl. 'There's something written on one side.'

'Yes, there is. But the letters are so small.'

'Let me see! Yes, it says . . . It says "Nils Holgersson from V. Vemmenhög".'

'That's the strangest thing I've ever heard!' said Little Mats.